UNTOUCHABLE DARKNESS

#1 New York Times and USA Today Bestselling Author

Rachel Van Dyken

Untouchable Darkness
The Dark Ones Saga Book 2
by Rachel Van Dyken

UNTOUCHABLE DARKNESS

ISBN-13: 9781530774685
ISBN-10: 1530774683
Cover Art by P.S. Cover Design

To people looking for second chances
and redmption...
where there is DARKNESS, there is LIGHT.

I STOOD NEAR THE edge of the building where darkness met light. It was the perfect spot for me to be standing, all things considered.

That *was* my life.

The perfect rapture of darkness—light flirted on the outskirts, trying to seep through, but I knew better than anyone its chances of succeeding were slim. I held out my hand, and my fingertips kissed the sunlight peeking through the clouds. I twirled my hand around and let out a defeated sigh.

"Cassius." Sariel, my father and one of the head Archangels—the same Angels that hadn't appeared to the immortals for over three hundred years—spoke my name with such authority and finality that it was impossible not to feel the effects of the words as he released them into the universe. They slammed against my chest, stealing every ounce of oxygen I'd just greedily sucked in. "You have failed."

"Yes." I swallowed the lie, felt it burn all the way down my throat into my lungs. My cold, rotten heart picked up speed, maybe I really was dead inside like she said, maybe it was hopeless, all of it.

"I taste the lie on your lips, half breed."

"So taste," I fired back, as my eyes strained to focus

on the light. The yearning to *be* light, to fully allow it to consume me, was like a fire burning in my soul. "I have nothing more to say to you."

"You realize what this means?" The once purple feathers surrounding his bulky body illuminated red. My heartbeat slowed to a gentle rhythm as droplets of blood cascaded from his feathers in perfect cadence with my breathing.

"I do."

"Yet you do not fight?"

Finally, I lifted my gaze to his. His strong jaw ticked as his black hair blew in the wind. I knew I was the only one who could see him, compliments of my ancestors… my angelic blood.

"When one has lost everything worth fighting for…" I swallowed. "Tell me, what is the point?"

"You've never given up before," he said quietly, his voice filled with disbelief.

"I've never been in love like this before!" I yelled, slamming my hand against the brick wall. If anyone passed by they'd simply think I'd gone insane, and maybe I had.

Because of her.

Everything was because of her.

"It's best that I die. Best that I leave her."

Sariel's face broke out into a bright smile. The blood from his feathers pooled at his feet forming the shape of a heart. "Very well."

I prepared myself for the pain, for the sheer agony of ceasing to exist. I knew from stories that when a Dark One died, it was horrific, terrifying, for we never knew if we would rejoin light or the darkness.

I assumed I would go dark.

I assumed I would be consumed with evil.

I assumed wrong.

Because the minute Sariel touched my skin.

I felt nothing but empty.

"A gift." Sariel whispered into the air. "For my only remaining son."

CHAPTER 1

Thirty Days Previous

Stephanie

THE AIR CRACKLED WITH excitement. I watched as the couple sitting a few tables away from me grabbed each other's hands and leaned in for a kiss. I tried to turn away, but it was impossible. I was always drawn to affection, drawn to emotion like it was a homing beacon. Sometimes it really sucked being immortal.
I couldn't help but feel what others felt.

And I couldn't help but want that feeling for myself.

It would be too ridiculously easy to steal the emotional charge in the air or change it with a snap of my fingers. Heck, I could have that guy salivating over me in seconds. But it would be wrong.

And for the past week I'd been trying to do things right.

Ever since I'd unknowingly betrayed my only human friend, I had turned over a new leaf. I was a council member for crying out loud! An immortal Siren or a Dark One; whatever, I was too many things.

A few days ago I'd given the only Dark One I knew, our King, my essence thinking I'd die, willing to make that sacrifice. Instead, I'd woken up the next day completely the same as before, as if my immortality had been restored.

Only, I *was* different.

Before I even opened my eyes, I felt the power of death surge through me, the deepest sort of cold took root from my fingertips all the way down to my toes. And an eerie sort of darkness became a part of me, like a shadow I couldn't get rid of. Dread trickled down my spine.

To make matters worse.

I woke up to my entire room frozen like the arctic.

Which, for an immortal who'd spent the last few hundred years assuming she was nothing more than a Siren? Terrifying.

Besides, Sirens hated the cold; it was the exact opposite of what we represented, warmth, human emotions, heat, lust, fire.

Blah!

I shivered.

Would I ever be warm again? It wasn't the type of cold you could escape, it was a part of me, just like my heart, the very heart I'd given to Cassius, the only man I'd ever loved.

If you could truly call him that.

Half human, half Angel, he was the king of the immortals and not just completely off limits, but dangerous. A Dark One's touch was powerful enough to force humans into a cheerful slavery for a millennia.

To me, he'd simply always felt... *good.*

Until I discovered that he'd put a very powerful glamour on me when I was a child, hiding me away from the Archangels who swore to kill more Dark

Ones if they were ever created.

I sighed.

What was the point anymore?

Cassius was gone.

He'd disappeared the minute I'd opened my eyes that fateful morning two days ago to find my brand new Nike running shoes covered in snow.

The couple in front of me laughed again. It grated my nerves because I was jealous of them.

Of them! It was laughable. Or it should have been. A week ago I *would* have laughed. Now it was just bordering on pathetic.

As an elder among the immortals, it was my job to keep the peace and run interference between our kind and the humans.

Not sit at a Starbucks and watch a newly engaged couple with silent longing.

Cassius, our leader, the only King the immortals have ever known, had been missing for a few days, and it killed me to think it was because he was ashamed of me, ashamed of what I'd done to Genesis.

Not that it was my fault an Archangel had bitten me, seduced me and basically entranced me into doing something. Granted, the whole jealousy part was my fault, making the spell he put me under that much stronger.

I took a long sip of my latte and pouted.

I hadn't done that in ages.

It didn't help.

"You look like hell." Mason plopped down at the table. His shaggy brown hair was pulled back underneath a Seahawks hat. Black aviators hung loosely across his strong nose, framing his very deadly, yet undeniably sexy five o'clock shadow.

Stupid Werewolf. An underlying earthy scent like that of burned wood and pinecones floated between us with each casual movement he made. And believe me, he needed to look as casual as possible considering he just naturally attracted any cat within a ten mile radius.

"Yeah, well." I pointed at his hat. "You look like a tourist."

"Please." He snorted then grabbed my coffee and took a sip.

"Since when do you drink coffee?"

"I don't know." He pushed the coffee back and made a face. "Since when do you leave the house, pout for a whole damn day, and then stare longingly at a human couple like you're about to eat them?"

"I wasn't staring longingly," I grumbled, suddenly finding my hands fascinating as I wrung them together.

"You were. Saw the whole thing. Disgusting really."

"Do you have a reason for stalking me?"

"If I was stalking you, you'd already be dead." He smirked, "And yeah... I was out grocery shopping."

"So many things wrong with a Wolf grocery shopping."

"Orders from Genesis... she wants me to start eating again."

I squirmed in my seat.

"Everything's fine," he said in a gruff voice. "Water under the bridge, you've been redeemed, blah, blah, blah, come home."

"Really?" I chuckled and toyed with my straw. "That's the speech?"

"Ethan wouldn't write one out for me so take what you can get."

"A regular lady killer."

Mason groaned into his hands. "No idea why they sent me."

"You have the manners of a beast," I agreed.

"But you know I'm right. You belong with us at home, not out here at Starbucks of all places."

"He left," I whispered. Admitting it out loud was harder than I thought it would be. The only man I'd ever loved and tried to die saving.

Had *left.*

Like we'd had some sort of one-night stand he was ashamed of.

Ugh, my head hurt.

"He'll be back. He just needed…" Mason swore under his breath. "God save me from these types of conversations. Cassius needed time, and regardless of his feelings and your odd connection, he's still king so I don't give a flying rat's ass if he killed himself so you could live then professed undying love on Dr. Phil." He offered a dismissive shrug. "He's our king. What he says goes. He left, so let him leave. It's not your place to question him."

"Someone has to!" I pushed back my chair and stood.

Mason followed suit and pulled me into his embrace. I tried to fight him but it was impossible. The man was so strong he could break me in half, and that was saying a lot since I could seriously hold my own.

"Steph," Mason sighed into my hair. "Just… leave it. Ever thought of simply telling him thank you and moving on with your life?"

I sighed against him, inhaling his woodsy scent. "No."

"Try it."

"No."

"Steph…"

"I'll come back." My shoulders slumped as I gave in. "But what do I do if he comes to the house? What if he does come back?" That thought was almost as depressing and confusing as him staying away forever, or me being the reason behind his absence.

"Well I may have this ass backward all things considered—I mean, I eat pinecones—but you could always say hi."

THE RIDE BACK TO Ethan's house was almost unbearable. For one thing, Mason drove like a maniac. I'm pretty sure he's actually never passed a driver's test. When I asked to see his license he laughed and pushed down on the accelerator, shooting Ethan's brand new Lexus forward like a pinball out of the slot along busy city streets. You'd think he had a death wish, then again it would take more than a car accident to kill us.

By the time we pulled up to Ethan's mansion on

Lake Washington I was ready to kiss the ground and cuss Mason out.

The chance to get in the Wolf's face was taken from me the minute the car shut off.

"Stephanie." Ethan had already opened my door and was holding his hand out like a damn peace offering. My heart stopped beating so heavily in my chest. I glared up at him. Stupid Vampires and their ability to control things like hearts.

Why did I need mine anyway? Especially if it was going to constantly get broken by Cassius.

I swallowed the emotion tightening in my throat and placed my hand in Ethan's.

"Ethan." I challenged him with a glare and stood to my full height.

"You should always take someone with you when you go out." Ethan's eyebrows knit together as if he was actually concerned for my safety. "It isn't proper for you to be—"

"—drinking coffee by myself?" I finished.

He rolled his emerald green eyes. "Yes, well, try to be more careful. We can't simply snap our fingers and replace council members."

"Ah, so it's about the council."

"It's about you," Ethan half growled in my ear and shoved me toward the door where both Genesis and my brother were waiting.

I was half tempted to throw my hands in the air and blurt out, "I'm fine! I'm really fine! I promise!"

Genesis had a look of pity on her face.

And my brother looked like he was relieved I was still alive and well.

"Hey, guys." I managed a weak wave.

"You found her." Genesis winked at Mason.

"Wolves have amazing tracking abilities." He puffed out his chest then received a punch from Ethan.

"Please." I rolled my eyes. "You probably used the find a friend app on your phone."

"Still counts." Mason nodded and then tapped his head. "Tracker."

Genesis laughed softly then looped her arm in mine. "Don't run away. Next time just talk to us."

"Talk," I mimicked. "About Cassius? About the fact that my entire existence up until now has been a lie?"

The only thing that had changed in the past few days was that my hunger for Cassius had grown to epic proportions.

He'd rejected me all over again.

After kissing me, mind you.

And the place where my heart was supposed to be felt like it was slowly being ripped from my body.

I didn't just desire Cassius.

I needed him. Because I still didn't understand what I was or what I was capable of, and he was the only Dark One remaining who could actually tell me.

We were the last.

And it kind of sucked.

Dark Ones were typically male. I knew how they worked. But a woman? Who had Siren tendencies?

Ugh. I got a headache just thinking about it.

"You need him," Genesis whispered next to me. "He'll come, he just needed some time."

"Needed some time?" I snorted. "People who need time calmly tell their family where the hell they're going. They don't sneak off in the middle of the night without a trace! It's like he fled the freaking country!"

"To be fair he left his passport here," Mason joked.

Genesis glared. "Not the time."

He held up his hands and let out a little bark at my expense.

"He fled the country," I repeated. "To get away from me, from the awkward situation…" I pointed at myself and looked down. "From this."

"There's nothing wrong with you." Genesis squeezed my shoulder. I'd always pitied humans like Genesis, breeders, ones who were brought into the immortal fold in order to produce children with the immortals.

Then again she'd been the game changer. She'd brought balance to our world. Now she was like a goddess to our people and to her Vampire husband.

While I felt more human by the day.

I couldn't help but think that one day I'd wake up and simply… not exist anymore… or not care to. And that thought terrified me.

I could feel the darkness inside, swirling, trying to grab ahold. The bond between me and the darkness was building, strengthening, and I was so afraid I wasn't going to make it.

When I'd saved his life.

Because he'd saved mine.

I had no idea what I was doing other than I couldn't stand the thought of existing in a world without him.

Now I knew.

Every second I knew.

Because every second I existed, my heart yearned for his presence.

Alex, my brother, though we weren't actually related—something I still was having a hard time swallowing—slapped me hard on the back. "Think of it this way sis—you have to have had a huge effect on him for him to flee to China or wherever the hell he went in the dead of night."

"Wow... brothers." I nodded. "So helpful. Tell me where's the razor blades for my wrists again?"

"Please." Alex snorted, "You'd simply attract Vampires... not to mention send Ethan into a frenzy."

"Ethan doesn't want my blood... too strong."

"That's true." Ethan pushed past us. "Okay, family meeting."

"Cute." Mason stomped into the kitchen and put his feet on the table. "We're having family meetings now?"

"Cassius isn't here... but he isn't gone either." Ethan avoided looking at me which only meant one thing.

He still sensed him.

Embarrassment washed over me anew.

"So until we know where he is and how to proceed... we'll simply go about business as usual. Agreed? We have three weeks until the next council meeting, and now that the Archangels are talking to us again, we need to make sure we have complete order within all the species. Agreed?"

I hated to admit he was right.

The Archangels were terrifying.

And now we were on their radar again—thanks to the Genesis, Ethan, and Cassius love triangle.

My heart clenched again.

"He's right." Mason leaned back in his chair. "I'll check in with the wolves while Alex checks in with the Sirens and Demon."

"Hey!" Alex sat down and frowned. "Why do I have to check in with the Demon? Last time they tried to eat my hand."

"You have lovely hands." Mason nodded.

"Could it be because someone told them they tasted like ambrosia?" Alex kicked Mason's chair almost sending him toppling toward the ground.

"Easy mistake." Mason yawned.

"I'll check in with them," I found myself offering, and all eyes turned in my direction. I shrugged. "What? How hard can it be? Make sure they don't kill any humans… get a head count…" I shrugged again. Wow, I was doing that a lot. "No big."

"No big?" Alex grumbled. "Until they eat you."

"I'm a Dark One," I half whispered. "They could only try."

The room fell silent.

Because I'd just brought in the giant elephant and asked everyone if they wanted to go for a ride.

Well done.

"Great." Ethan broke the silence. "So, Steph will check on the Demon… tonight?"

"Yup." I nodded, feeling less enthusiastic than I looked. "They'll be on the prowl so it should be easy."

"It's not… dangerous is it?" Genesis asked.

Hell yes, it was dangerous. But maybe that's what I needed. A bit of danger. I shrugged, a third time, great, and made eye contact with Ethan. "We're immortal, what's the worst that can happen?"

Chapter 2

Stephanie

Going out and hunting for Demon ended up being a bigger pain in my ass than I realized. First of all, the leader—if you could even call him that—wasn't at his normal hang out meaning I had to basically bar hop all the way through Belltown asking Demon if they'd seen him.

Most of the Demons shied away from me.

Most of them were too smart to do anything like piss me off.

But there was always that outlier, the one individual who didn't play by the rules and thought his own crap didn't stink.

Meet, Jefferson.

"Go away." I shooed him with my hand and turned my back to him, ordering another glass of white wine.

"You smell like…." His voice was raspy and suggestive as he leaned close, inhaling from my airspace. "…sin."

"Wow." I took two large unlady like gulps of the wine and turned to face him for the third time.

He wasn't awful looking, if you favored blond curly hair and chocolate eyes. But I knew deep down what he was, a social climbing idiot who'd most likely try to kill me in my sleep just so he could steal some of the angel blood for himself and hope to gain more power.

"Ah, you're warming to me." He winked.

I nodded then placed both hands on his shoulders raising my knee to his balls in an effortless strike that had him collapsing to the floor in agony.

"If that's what you want to call it, sure."

"You bitch!" He wailed from the ground. "What the hell did you do that for?"

"You were pissing me off." I kneeled down next to him and tugged his black shirt so it almost ripped in my hands. "Now, where's your boss?"

"Busy." He spat in my face.

I punched him in the jaw.

"Damn it." Black blood oozed from his nose. "Would it kill you to give a guy a shot?"

"Yes. Yes it would." I released him, "Now stop wasting my time. My feet hurt. I've been out all night tracking…" I waved my hand into the air. "…smelly little street rats."

He let out a low hiss.

"Just tell me where he is."

Jeffrey paled and gulped all at once while a voice said near my ear in a harsh whisper.

"Behind you."

Every hair on my body stood on edge. Yes. Their leader was about an inch from my neck. Demon bites hurt like hell, and if I moved any more his teeth would graze my soft skin. Though, in the back of my head I remembered I was a Dark One right? So maybe I had more power in this situation than I thought.

Quickly, I turned.

"Timber." I put my hands on my hips. "About time you showed up."

"Well..." He rocked back on his heels and lifted his hand in the air. A beer made its way across the bar. He picked it up and took a long swig, the muscles in his neck constricting as he swallowed. Most humans would find him gorgeous. I just found him irritating and an abomination, but who was I to talk? "When a beautiful woman seeks me out..." He set the beer down and winked one of his baby blues.

I rolled my eyes. "Numbers, what are they?"

"Straight to business? No pleasure?" He eyed me up and down his blue eyes flashing red before going back to normal.

"No."

"You..." His eyebrows knit together as he leaned forward. "You smell... strange."

I backed up. "New perfume."

His eyes flashed even redder than before. "No, no, I don't think that's it."

It was like his body grew before my very eyes. He was transitioning into what a Demon really looked like—which was something out of a first grader's nightmare. Horns would pop up on his head, his teeth would elongate to fangs, and his face would hollow out revealing nothing but skull.

"Jeffrey," he barked. "Tell me, what do you smell?"

Not good. Definitely not good and as a council member it wasn't like I had backup or some sort of immortal mojo that would keep me from getting myself into trouble. I was a peacekeeper, I didn't fight. Not that I didn't know how, but now that the glamour of being a Siren was all but worn off, all I could do was feed off of others emotions. And since Cassius had abandoned me I wasn't sure what else I could do.

A syrupy sweet scent started filling the air.

Arousal.

I clenched my fists as I felt my body temperature drop. It wasn't on purpose—or controllable. It was like my body was getting ready to defend its angel blood if that was the last thing I did.

"Angel," Jeffrey whispered in a gleeful voice, his eyes rolling to the back of his head as he licked his lips and adjusted himself.

Gross.

"A baby one…" Timber tilted his head taking a predatory stance in front of me, his body continuing to grow. "Maybe we should continue this in one of the back rooms."

"Actually…" I stepped to the side. "If you just give me your numbers, I'll get going. It's late and you know how the council is…"

"Our numbers are growing… to epic proportions. That is all you need to know." Timber reached out to grab me. I jerked away so fast I lost my footing.

And fell directly against a muscled chest.

Strong hands wrapped around my shoulders. "Is this… thing, bothering you?"

The voice sounded familiar yet vaguely different. As if someone had… added warmth to it. My body responded to the warmth with an uncontrollable shiver.

"Yes." I leaned back into the warm body like it was my lifeline. Whoever the human was—he was ridiculously built. The warmth of his body gave new life to mine—making the cold not feel so cold, so… lonely.

"Pitiful human," Timber hissed under his breath.

But he knew he was stuck. Immortal rule number one was never to reveal yourself to humans.

And Timber knew if he did, Cassius would rain hell on the entire Demon population, wiping out every last one.

"Jeffrey," Timber snapped his fingers. "We should be going."

"Sure thing..." Jeffrey sniffed again in my direction and grinned.

I flipped him off.

He tried to charge toward me but Timber held him back. "Till we meet again... Angel."

"Not your Angel."

"Tell that to your blood." He licked his lips and pushed Jeffrey through the crowds. The scent of cinder stayed with me for a few minutes. I'd almost forgotten I was still in my rescuer's arms—until he gave them a squeeze.

"Oh." I stumbled forward then turned around, embarrassed that I'd been hanging all over him like a lovesick human. "I'm so sorry, thanks for the save though you really—"

My voice left me.

"I really... what?" He asked folding his arms across his broad chest. I followed the motion with greedy eyes. He was huge, built, tall, and gorgeous. Slowly I raised my eyes to meet his and nearly passed out.

"Cassius?"

"Sort of."

"But you're—"

"Human."

Chapter 3

Cassius

Ten hours. It had taken me ten hours since my damning meeting with Sariel to get used to my body.

A human.

My Archangel father had made me a human.

I briefly wondered if I'd get struck by lightning if I called him a bastard and had my answer when the sound of feathers ruffling together in protest floated through the air.

Ten hours after he'd condemned me, I'd gained several bruises, a cut across my hand, and sore joints—reminding me yet again that I was old and I was breakable.

I hated it.

Every damn second.

Until it rained.

And then I felt—*everything.*

I lifted my eyes to the sky and gasped as the rain drops splattered across my face rolling down my lips. It tasted pure. It tasted real, like life was getting poured on my body over and over again.

When you spend your existence focusing on the immortal parts of yourself—you lose that shred of humanity. It's a slow drain until you forget all the different components that made you human and simply embrace the supernatural.

And when you embrace the supernatural, or rather embrace your immortality, you forget the simple things.

Like rain.

And the way it feels.

I never had time to stop and let rain pour over my head. If the rain irritated me I simply waved it away. If the sun was too hot, I closed my white eyes and allowed the ice to spread through my veins—compliments of being part Angel, part human.

For the last thousand years I'd simply ignored one part of myself—one part that made me whole—and existed without it.

I roamed the streets for a day. Watching people, not because I was lost or bored, but because everything was so new to me, so exciting. So raw.

I felt everything all at once.

It was overwhelming, and for the first time in my existence—life was exciting again.

And then I saw *her.*

At Starbucks.

By herself.

And my world simply stopped, my breathing never returned to normal, and I was reminded yet again that I had thirty days.

And I was on day twenty-nine.

I'd lost one day.

Irritated that I'd let myself get so distracted, I followed her to the house, and followed her again when she left.

Each time a stupid human hit on her I laughed—until a little voice inside my head reminded me that I was just as bad, just as low on the totem pole.

I wasn't sure who the hell had sent Steph out to speak to the Demons, but they were going to have to answer to me. She was as defenseless as a weak little lamb out in a thunderstorm.

She had no idea what she was capable of and was oblivious to the scent she gave off to every male and female she walked by.

I *still* smelled it.

Maybe that was Sariel's cruelty coming to the forefront. He would turn me to a human, allow me to win the woman I loved, only to remind me yet again that I wasn't on an even playing field.

I was not her equal.

Maybe I'd never been.

"Cassius?" Stephanie reached up and cupped my face. It felt nice. It felt… warm. "What happened to you?"

"You wouldn't believe me if I told you." At least that was the truth.

Her eyes narrowed. "Were you punished? For what happened?"

"No."

"Then…" She shook her head. "Care to explain why your eyes aren't white but blue, why you smell like… rain—weird, you smell like rain? And, and—"

I gripped her hands in mine. "Later… for now we should return to the house before the Demons bring back friends to take you down."

"Well, I have you…" She shrugged. "They couldn't touch me."

As if realizing what she'd just said her face fell.

"I'm human." I said it again; it felt funny on my lips. As if my eyes had ideas of their own, I focused in on her mouth. Damn, it was pretty. I wondered if I'd ever really taken the time to appreciate her beauty.

Or maybe I knew that the minute I did—I'd be lost.

"Cassius?" She gripped my arm. I stared at that hand far longer than was necessary. "You're right... we should go."

I followed her out of the bar, pulling my hands into tight fists to keep from reaching for her body.

It was hard to focus on anything except for the outline of her hips. Damn, being human was sending me into madness fast. I was hypnotized by her every movement, following her like she was my reason for existing.

We weaved in and out of the crowd and finally made it outside. The silence wasn't awkward, but her stares were.

I'd never been insecure about anything.

But I came to realize that being human meant I was feeling emotions I wasn't used to feeling. Like insecurity.

Why the hell was she staring at me so hard?

And why did my body respond in such a heated way that I was consciously looking for a place to push her against so I could trap that soft body and capture those lips? Was it this hard for all humans? My thoughts went into dangerous territory as she nervously licked her lips over and over again. Body dizzy with want, it was getting hard to walk in a straight line.

"My car's over here." Stephanie pointed to Ethan's newest Lexus.

"Don't you mean Ethan's car?" I smirked, quite cheered at the fact that she'd most likely scratch the piece of machinery before the week's end. Ethan and I had always been at odds, now even more so.

He was arrogant.

And ever since our falling out over his first mate's death—it had been easy to let him hate me, to blame me for her death and everything since, when none of it was really my fault. Rules were not meant to be broken.

Yet as I thought those very words, I had to wonder, what part of me being fully human fit into the strict set of rules and guidelines given to the immortals since the beginning of time.

"We're sharing." She shrugged.

"I bet." I chuckled.

It sounded funny.

Stephanie let out a little gasp.

I shrugged because, really, what else could I do? Laugh more?

Once we were on the freeway heading back toward Ethan's, Stephanie finally started talking. Maybe she needed those minutes to process. Hell, I'd taken a whole day, and I still wasn't sure what my plan was.

Touching her would do nothing—I was without any of my angelic power. She wouldn't be seduced by it, and even if I was still a Dark One, so was she, which meant… what? Would our powers equalize? Or destroy us both? Was I playing at heartache even now?

"You even sound different," Stephanie muttered under her breath. "Your voice is gruffer."

"Yes." The word caught at the back of my throat making me sound like an idiot.

"Do you bruise?" She pulled to a stop at the next light and stared at me.

I licked my lips and ran my fingers through my dark hair. "I guess so—"

The punch was so hard I was pretty confident one of my ribs simply broke in half.

"What the HELL?" I roared rubbing my left side while trying to suck in enough air so I didn't pass out. It hurt to breathe.

"How dare you leave me!" She hit the accelerator causing me to slam back against the seat.

"Stephanie." I held out my shaking hands. "Damn it, calm down."

The car picked up speed. Shit.

Fear wasn't something I was accustomed to but there it was slamming against my chest as she weaved in and out of traffic gaining speed.

I gripped my seatbelt. "Steph, just calm down for a minute. If you listen I think you'll understand and—"

"Understand?" She laughed. "You left me! Alone! I don't even know what I am! And you left me!"

"I had no choice!" I roared as the car damn near collided with a semi.

The atmosphere in the car turned to ice. I knew the look in her eyes well. It was the same as I'd seen reflected on my face a few thousand times.

Her eyes turned a stormy white.

Icicles formed around the steering wheel.

If she didn't calm down the entire car was going to freeze and explode into pieces of icy dust.

"Stephanie, listen to me." I touched her icy arm. "Can you at least do that? I'm here now, does that tell you nothing?"

Her breath froze in front of her face.

My teeth clattered together. This wasn't going to end well for me if she didn't relax. She'd be just fine.

I'd be worse off than the car.

"Pull over," I barked.

She shook her head.

"Pull the car over. NOW!" I jerked the steering wheel.

She didn't fight me.

Instead the car rocked to the side and screeched to a halt right at our exit.

Out of control. She was out of control. She needed to get warm before the cold took over, before the darkness consumed her. She had no idea what powers she was playing with, how losing control of your emotions could destroy you, put you in a catatonic state for weeks.

She still wasn't responding to my voice.

So I did what any human would do.

I kissed her.

Stephanie

His lips felt hot—not cold like before. They were warm, inviting, but the touch of his mouth just reminded me—he didn't want me.

Reluctantly, I pushed against his chest.

He slammed back against the seat—hard, like I'd just punched him with every ounce of strength I had.

With a gasp I covered my mouth with my hands and whispered. "I'm so sorry."

Cassius winced, bringing his hand to rub the back of his head. "I may not be able to taste your lies anymore—but I'm not stupid, the last thing you are is sorry."

"But I am!"

"Lie." Cassius's face broke out into a mocking grin. "Though I'll go as far as to believe you didn't mean to kill me." He alternated between rubbing his stomach and checking the back of his head for blood.

"Of course not!" The thought made me sick to my stomach. "Are you hurt?"

He didn't answer, but his face was paler than before, and I noticed his breathing was a bit uneven. Was it from the violence or the kiss?

"If you don't learn to control your emotions we'll both be dead by the time we reach Ethan's. If we make it that far." Another wince. "Now, I know everything is very new to you, but if you could try not to kill one or both of us within the next ten minutes, I'd be eternally grateful. I'm still not used to being fully human."

I swallowed and looked away in shame. "I don't really know how to control certain things—where you're concerned."

"Wouldn't have guessed that," he said dryly, his eyes narrowing in on me with the precision of a sharp knife.

"What?" I licked my lips nervously and stared ahead out the window.

"Nothing, it's just I'm trying to decide if that's a compliment or not."

I stole another glance at him. How was he so calm? And why didn't he lose all of his good looks the minute he turned human? How was that fair? His blue eyes were electric in the night sky. His skin still so smooth and flawless that I wanted to reach out and touch it.

Thank God he couldn't still read my thoughts.

"Don't look at me like that if you don't plan on following through," he snapped, his white teeth flashing against the blanket of darkness in the car.

"Fine." I put the car back in drive. "So, I just have to keep myself from losing control emotionally—for the next what? Ten miles?"

He sighed. "Yes."

"And then once we're safely within the walls of Ethan's little compound?"

Cassius shook his head, an amused grin spread across his face. "Well then, I'll allow you to try to kill me if that's what you really wish."

"I don't want you dead."

"Things would be easier if I were," he whispered.

"Since when have you ever taken the easy way out?"

He broke eye contact and looked down. I'd never seen Cassius do that in all the time I'd known him. His confidence never wavered.

Yet as a human I could see chinks in his armor as if he was falling apart before my very eyes.

"Hey." I grabbed his arm, and immediately I regretted it as tiny ice crystals formed around my fingertips and imprinted themselves against his smooth skin.

He hissed and pulled back. "Huh, never thought I'd be on the receiving end of that."

"What?" I clenched my hand into a tiny fist, flexing my fingers.

Cassius caressed the spot on his arm that I'd just touched or marked was more like it. You could still see the indentation where my hand had just been. "Pity… and…" He let out a long exhale like it was getting harder to breathe. "It's not easy to combat, is it?"

"What? Pity?" Was he losing it? Was being a human finally taking a toll on his once immortal brain? Was that part of his punishment from Sariel?

"The pull… the flavor…" He licked his lips as if he could taste me. "The promise of a Dark One's touch."

"But I just touched you. I didn't…"

"You tried to mark me." He exhaled again and rubbed his arm vigorously. "We should go, before you kill me."

"I would never—"

"Just drive the car, get me to Ethan's in one piece,

and then I promise we'll talk more."

"No more running away?"

"Where could I possibly go where you wouldn't find me?"

I wasn't sure if that was a compliment or just a jab at my stalker tendencies considering he knew how I felt about him, so I left it alone and pulled back onto the freeway.

The car ride was as silent as death the entire way to Ethan's.

And I couldn't help but wonder if Cassius being turned human, was the final nail in the coffin.

Hope died in my chest as I realized—I would never be his equal even as a Dark One. He would always be on step ahead of me. He would always be—Cassius. And I? I would always be the little girl he saved.

Never the woman he loved.

Cassius

My body was hot and cold all at once. It was an odd feeling, like my face was burning up, but the rest of my body had a chill. Maybe I was dying. Hah, wouldn't that be part of Sariel's cruel trick? Give me thirty days but kill me before I can even attempt to do anything.

I was doing a hell of a job—of pushing her away, that was.

Every single time I opened my mouth it was like I lost complete control over what I should say and just blurted out things that I knew caused pain. My thoughts were jumbled—when I'd been immortal I was able to compartmentalize, to attack each problem, find a solution, and then deal with the next. Being overwhelmed was never an issue because it never occurred.

But in that car, driving toward Ethan's, I was so overcome with—life that it was hard to breathe, hard to keep my thoughts straight. It didn't help that I was ninety-nine percent sure I had internal bleeding and would have trouble getting out of bed in the morning.

I wanted to claim her.

Yet I worried she'd resent me.

I wanted to help her.

And at the same time a part of me was fearful of what she was capable of, even as I was fully aware of how weak I was.

And then her scent would suddenly invade the car and I was lost again to a wave of lust for her—something I'd never in my life experienced until now—because I had no power to push it away.

When I had been a Dark One, I was able to recognize the lust for what it was and shove it away to the furthest recess of my mind. But ignoring the Siren's call had been manageable, never easy. And now? I shook my head. Impossible. The air was filled with her scent; my arm still tingled where she'd left her fingerprints. Damn it, she could have easily marked me; she was the equivalent of a superhero who'd just discovered they had supernatural powers.

She sighed.

I held my breath. Afraid I'd do something stupid.

As a human it was damn near impossible to ignore anything—hell, even her breathing had me leaning toward her, just wishing she'd turn her head so I could kiss her.

That wasn't the way to win her over—a sneak attack.

At this rate I was going to die before anything even started.

"Home sweet home." Stephanie said it like a curse as she pulled the car to a stop in front of Ethan's compound and turned off the car. "This should be… interesting."

The ice that had formed across her beautiful skin was receding—good, at least she'd calmed down enough not to kill both of us.

"And here they come," Stephanie muttered, then pushed open the car door leaving me in silence as I watched Ethan, Mason, and Genesis approach, followed at a distance by Alex, Stephanie's brother, who I assumed was still pissed off at me on account that I told Stephanie the truth about her heritage.

Slowly, I unbuckled my seatbelt, opened the car door, and stood.

The talking that had been animated only seconds before I stood ceased altogether.

I didn't lift my head.

Didn't acknowledge anyone at all, simply stared at the ground and walked, only stopping when I saw a pair of black boots step in my way. Slowly, I looked up and into Ethan's flashing green eyes.

"You smell..." He blinked, sniffing the air around us, then eyes wide, took a big step backward. "Hell, that's not good."

"Baths." Mason growled and walked toward me. "You should try one Dark—" His face paled as he joined Ethan.

I turned to Alex, waiting for his reaction to be the same. It was normal—typical, for an immortal to give a human, at least a male human, a wide berth. They had no use for male humans, and our history wasn't necessarily a pleasant one all things considered.

My scent reminded them of the wars fought.

The wars lost.

The wars yet to come.

The kings that had sworn fealty to us only to hunt us later.

It would be hardest for them since they were the oldest, old enough to have been involved in many of the great battles that nearly wiped out both the humans and immortals.

Alex tilted his head, his eyes held mild amusement. "My, my, how the mighty have fallen."

In response, I had such a strong desire to run my fist through his mouth, that my hands shook. It would only end in blood—my blood—being spilled. Therefore, I chose not to do anything. A complete first for me, I'd always been a man of action.

"Get it?" He walked closer and elbowed me. "Because technically you were like a Fallen Angel with your half blood, only now you're just…" He shrugged. "Human." He wrapped his arm around me, pulling me tight against him, not enough to hurt me but enough to remind me that I was yet again on the low end of the food chain. His ability to snap me in half wasn't lost on me at all—it was humbling, and irritating as hell. "I imagine there's a story here, care to tell it?"

"Care to go to hell?" I countered.

"Super." He nodded. "You've been cursed to humanity, and yet you still have that chipper attitude…"

"Cassius?" Genesis interrupted. "You look…"

"Rough." Mason coughed. "He looks rough."

I sighed, "As much as I love family reunions, can we please take this inside? I'm cold."

The minute the words left my mouth I felt weak.

And ashamed of my weakness, so much so that I felt my cheeks heat again. Shit, I didn't like this, not one bit. How the hell was I supposed to win over Stephanie when I had nothing to offer her?

No protection.

Only weakness.

I was beginning to realize I hadn't made a deal with

an Angel, but the Devil, and I was going to end up paying with my life.

Stephanie

"Did he just say he was cold?" Alex repeated after Cassius's disappearing form.

"Yeah." The words felt hollow coming out of my mouth. "He did."

Alex tapped his chin then looked at the doorway Cassius had just walked through. "Interesting."

Interesting? Try terrifying.

I rubbed my arms, I wasn't cold, just uncomfortable… It almost felt like we'd switched places, though I had never been human to begin with, so I couldn't even imagine what Cassius was going through—or what desperation had taken place in his mind to get him to a place where turning into a human was even a bargaining chip.

It was a punishment. It had to be.

Ethan put his muscled arm around my shoulder and kissed my temple. "So it seems you have a lot of explaining to do… or maybe just Cassius?"

I shrugged. "I know just about as much as you guys."

"Well." Mason rubbed his hands together and cackled. "This should be fun."

"Play nice," Ethan snapped. Then, as if realizing what he was saying, he chuckled. "I should probably remind myself of that."

Genesis nodded. "You did try to kill him a few days ago."

"He wanted what was mine," Ethan fired back, his eyes blazing green as he hissed out a curse.

I stepped away from his embrace and made my way slowly into the house. Cassius was sitting in the kitchen staring out the window like it was going to suddenly turn into a TV and show him his destiny if he stared hard enough.

"Penny for your thoughts?" I joked.

He was silent.

The room was strung with tension.

I gulped.

"Weak." Cassius whispered the word. "I had forgotten how weak humans were."

"Are," I interjected without thinking.

His nostrils flared, "My apologies. Are. Present tense."

"Grammar lessons?" Mason waltzed into the kitchen and pulled out a chair; it scratched across the floor loud enough to make my ears hurt. "So Cassius, feeling… all right?"

Cassius rolled his eyes. "Just come out and ask it, Wolf."

"You look funny."

Cassius snorted out a laugh. "That all you got?"

"Smells funny too." Ethan joined in from behind me.

"And let's not forget." Alex patted Cassius on the shoulder. "Your eyes aren't freaky anymore."

"I was never freaky," Cassius defended looking completely insulted as he crossed his bulky arms over his chest. Pieces of his dark hair fell to his sharp chin.

"You were," everyone except me said in unison.

Cassius briefly glanced down at the table then back out the window. I sat next to him, not really knowing if it was my place to offer him comfort or just wait for everyone to finally pry out of him what the heck had happened.

"So." Ethan spoke after a few minutes. "Now that we're in the safety of the house, mind filling us in?"

Cassius gazed at me out of the corner of his eye, his jaw was set in a firm line almost like he didn't want me to be there.

"It's a… test of sorts," he finally said. "From Sariel."

Mason grumbled "bastard" under his breath as he walked over to the island and started pulling out pots and pans. He'd turned into one of those people who stress cooked even if he didn't eat what he cooked—which was fine considering Genesis was still human and now that she was pregnant really needed food. The guy could probably compete on MasterChef and win by a landslide. Ever since Genesis had moved in, it seemed all he did was watch the cooking channel and go grocery shopping.

Odd behavior for a species known for ripping humans' throats out.

"A test," Ethan repeated. "Care to elaborate or is that all we're going to get?"

Cassius was silent.

Of course.

No emotion. It pissed me off. At least being human I expected him to do something, react somehow, at least the way he had in the car, but now it was like staring at a stone wall.

"It involves Stephanie." He said my name like a curse. I recoiled slightly into myself, nobody seemed to notice how his words affected me, how they made me want to flinch and scream all at the same time. Instead, I plastered an indifferent look on my face and waited. "I'm to… help her."

"Help her what?" Ethan's voice was laced with dread.

"Find herself?" Cassius said it as more of a question.

"Is she lost?" Alex piped up.

"She was at Starbucks staring at couples, let's not forget that," Mason called out from the kitchen, while my face flushed with heat. "And she's been moody."

"She's right here," I hissed.

"Her powers…" Cassius shrugged. "She's unstable, dangerous. I'm here to help her but I need to be human in order to do that."

"Why?" I blurted out.

He shrugged.

I rolled my eyes in response.

"Seems odd…" Ethan put his hands on his hips, his muscles were tight like he was ready to pounce on something—maybe Cassius.

"What's odd?" Cassius folded his muscled arms across his chest. Damn, did he have to still be so built? I scolded myself for my fleeting thoughts and quickly looked away.

"Well," Ethan's voice was doubtful. "Why would Sariel need you to be human in order to do that?"

"I don't make a habit of questioning Archangels,"

Cassius said in a hollow voice. "Do you?"

"Man has a point," Alex piped up. "So what, you're human, you help her, she kicks ass, and then you go back to normal?"

I stole a peak out of the corner of my eye to gauge his reaction. Cassius's mouth turned down into a scowl. "Yes. Something like that. But I'll need to be with her twenty-four seven, and I can't very well do that if I'm not living… near her."

Was it my imagination or did he just blush?

I blinked.

The pink tinge was gone.

Right, my imagination.

"House party," Alex sang, "Does that mean we get to finish watching all the Disney movies Genesis set us up with?"

"No," Cassius barked out while everyone else said yes.

"Outvoted." Mason pointed with his spatula. "Trust me, Cassius, it will do you some good. After all, it's good to remember what humans are like, think of your time here as a… learning experience."

Cassius growled low in his throat. "I'd rather not learn from movies."

"Don't worry…" Alex swatted his back. "We won't make you watch the romantic ones about kissing and falling in love and sweeping women off their feet and—"

"What?" Cassius blurted. "What did you say?"

"Uh, romantic movies, sweeping women off their feet?"

Cassius fidgeted in his seat. "It may help… learning how to deal with women, since I'll be dealing with a prickly one for the next few weeks."

Right. Now I was prickly. Had he been immortal I would have knifed him in the chest.

"Great!" Alex clapped his hands. "So that's settled. Cassius stays here until Stephanie learns how to control herself... considering we don't really know what she is..." All eyes turned to me with pity. "And since technically she gave her immortality to you..." Alex's eyes narrowed. "Yet, now she has it back and you're... human."

"No." Cassius cleared his throat. "For the time being no... but all will be well soon..."

"Not immortal," I repeated out loud. I'd forgotten about that... barricaded the damn memory so far into my mind that I wouldn't recall what it was like uniting myself with Cassius...

Because it was the only time in my entire existence that I'd belonged.

And it had been ripped from me the minute he chose to walk away. Granted he returned but I imagined there was more to the story, like if he didn't help me the big bad Archangel was going to stab Cassius in the throat.

So really he had no choice.

My heart plummeted to my stomach.

"I think I'll go lay down for a while." My voice was weak. I didn't look back, not even Alex called after me or even when I felt the ice start to tickle down my fingertips and lightly frost the air next to me.

Cassius

My eyes weren't used to the dull colors around me. Gray used to be my favorite color—it masqueraded as something trivial and boring when really it consisted of a million different speckles of blues, greens, blacks, and even some white, constantly changing, shifting in its color—evolving.

Now, I glanced around at the gray countertop, the gray or what some would call silver appliances.

And I was bored to tears.

And irritated that something as simple as enjoying the visions in front of me, was suddenly gone—taken from me. Humans really had no understanding of the depth of color, and now I was realizing that first hand.

Particles of dust used to float in front of my face, pieces of moisture collected into the air, ready for me to use had I needed it.

Now, I sucked in air through lungs that by my calculations would stop working around the age of seventy-eight, possibly seventy-nine; it would be something simple that would take this body.

Morose thoughts clouded my vision—making it impossible for me to really see anything but my own demise, and the very simple fact that last week I had been different, I had been better.

This week… I was facing the greatest challenge of my existence, getting Stephanie to see me as someone other than her protector, her King, a monster.

I wasn't sure what was typical. Did I wait an hour to go fetch her? Two? Maybe three? So I sat, my ass pressed against an extremely uncomfortable chair, and imagined a simpler time when I was able to simply force my will on anyone and be done with it.

The coffee Mason had given me was cold.

The ceramic cup cheap, breakable.

I think he meant it as a joke when he gave it to me. After all, it had some silly Vampire looking character on the front of it, blood dripping from his fangs. I scowled and turned the cup to face the other direction.

"She's upstairs," Alex grumbled from the corner. "You know, just in case you haven't turned into a statue. Then again with a heart that cold…"

I rolled my eyes and stood. "I'll see to her."

Alex moved in front of me, his cat like eyes narrowing in suspicion, his fingertips pressed against my chest, it hurt like hell, not that I was going to actually admit to the Siren that he was stronger.

Because the very thought—the idea that he could end my life, when I'd spent the better part of mine protecting his kind—it didn't rub well. It felt all too humbling.

Damn, I hated that word.

"She's… fragile." He retracted his hand. "Remember."

"She could break my finger with a flick of her wrist." I shoved past him, ignoring the already bruising skin on my chest. "Think of it this way, if I make her angry you'll simply have to burn my body to finish me off."

"Ah, fire." Alex snapped his fingers. "I always forget about the fire."

I didn't. I hated fire. Fire represented my future—if I couldn't get her to fall for me, to love me, just as I was—I wouldn't just die.

I'd be burned alive.

While Sariel most likely watched.

With a bowl of damn popcorn. Buttered.

"Just—" Alex's sigh grated my nerves. "Be careful."

"I'll do that." I had no idea how I was going to manage being careful, that word hadn't ever really been in my vocabulary. Being careful meant I actually cared.

In all my existence I'd only cared about one person.

Her.

And now the game was twisted, altered, some of my chess pieces missing, the board falling sideways off the table.

"You're stalling," Alex called from behind me.

I grunted and made my way slowly up the stairs. I couldn't smell her—there had once been a time when I'd been able to pick out her scent from across the room in a crowd. It had been all I could do to keep myself from pulling her close, from breathing deep, from kissing her deeper.

My footsteps were loud, awkward, as I made my way down the hallway to her room. I knocked.

She didn't answer.

I didn't expect her to.

I nudged the door open. Stephanie was sitting in front of the window, her hands placed demurely in her lap, her head cocked to the side as if she was watching something very carefully.

The beauty of Stephanie wasn't in just her form, but the way she made you feel by simply glancing in your direction. Weakness made me crave it; my humanity demanded I stay in her presence forever, convincing me that walking away would only result in such physical and emotional pain that I wouldn't survive it.

Her hair was like warm caramel chocolate, her eyes, an icy blue. She was tall—most immortal woman were—but she wasn't thin, not by any stretch of the imagination. Calling her thin would be an insult.

She had curves.

The kind that made any man, mortal or not, stop and take notice. I imagined she was the epitome of the perfect woman.

I coughed behind my hand.

She ducked her head, but didn't turn around. "So you've come to… train me? Is that it, Cassius?"

I moved toward her, slowly, carefully, because even though I knew she wouldn't hurt me physically—my weak body was completely aware she could.

And that was enough.

"In a manner of speaking." I pulled a chair next to hers and glanced out the window. "What are you looking at?"

"Birds."

"Birds?" I repeated.

"Do you need me to speak slower? Ears aren't what they used to be, huh Cassius?"

I scowled. "My ears are just fine."

She smirked.

I wanted to kiss that smirk right off her face about as much as I wanted to snap my fingers and freeze her ass for defying me so blatantly.

"Birds have it easy. They build nests, find worms, eat, sing, reproduce, they get to fly…"

I held my sigh in. "Stephanie, if you want to be a bird I'm sure Sariel can arrange it."

She laughed out loud. "Sariel can turn me into an animal? I'd believe that when I saw it."

I chose not to comment. "This is why you need me."

She turned her icy glare in my direction. "Because I'm bird watching?"

"Because you don't realize…" I leaned in and tilted her chin toward me, my fingers nearly fell away from the electrical shock her skin gave me. "You don't even know where you come from, where I come from, what our real purpose is, why they call us Dark Ones, why we're feared, revered, why according to any human gifted with good sight—we're considered gods. You know nothing of our secrets, of our lies, of our struggle against humanity, of our struggle to save it. You. Know. Nothing."

Stephanie hung her head, a tear slid down her cheek, freezing as it met her lip and the cool breath ignited between the two of us. "Then teach me and be done with it."

"I'll teach you."

She stiffened.

"But I won't ever be done with you." I placed my hands on either side of her chair and jerked it forward until we were nose to nose. "I will never be done with you. Not now. Not tomorrow. Not a year from now. Understood?"

"Don't make promises you can't keep."

"It's not a promise. It's simply truth in its finest

form. You and I will never be separate, hate me all you want, but our lives are intertwined now."

She broke eye contact, and her breathing became erratic.

"Do you regret saving me?" I whispered.

"I did." She cleared her throat. "I regretted it every day you were gone."

"And now?"

"Now…" The air turned icy. "I guess we'll see."

Chapter 8

Stephanie

He was too close, but he would notice if I shifted away, and I didn't want to appear weak, not when I'd already done so over and over again.

If he wanted to train me, fine.

I imagined it was a forced punishment, but my pride wouldn't let me go there. Somehow imagining it was way better than him actually admitting it.

"You must have done something very, very bad," I said under my breath, stealthily moving my chair away and standing, so much for not going there. "After all, when was the last time a Dark One was given mortality? Made human?"

"Never," he said in a clipped tone. "I would know considering my age."

"Yes let's rehash your age, that always goes over well. You're how much older than me?"

His blue eyes narrowed into tiny slits. "We'll have to do something about that attitude of yours."

"Oh, I'd love to see you try," I challenged.

He grinned.

I didn't like that grin.

It was beautiful.

It was also terrifying.

I backed away farther, even though I knew I had the upper hand, I still couldn't forget, maybe my mind wouldn't let me—he was a Dark One, or he had been. He could own my ass with a simple snap of his fingers.

Granted he was human now.

But for how long?

What if I pissed him off, and he was changed back tomorrow?

Right. I wasn't taking any chances.

Regardless of my feelings for him—or the way he kissed me—he was a cold, heartless bastard.

Imagining anything else just made my heart sick.

Cassius stalked toward me, his steps purposeful, I walked backward until my body collided with the wall.

He tilted his head, his black hair falling across his strong angular jaw. "A Dark One never cowers."

I arched my eyebrows and opened my mouth but he clamped his hand over it.

"And Dark Ones always respect their elders."

I rolled my eyes, still unable to talk.

Slowly, he removed his hand.

"You know," I whispered. "You could try to at least be nice to me while we're training."

He frowned. "Am I not being nice?"

"Are you insane?"

"Is that sarcasm?"

Cassius looked genuinely confused, like I'd just shouted that I wanted to ride a zebra in for dinner.

"You aren't smiling at me, you haven't even asked what I want in this whole scenario, and you touch me like I'm diseased!" I shouted. "Is that your definition of nice?"

His nostrils flared as he pounded a hand next to my head, a mirror crashed to the floor. "Smiling takes an effort I'm not willing to extend lest it become a habit, especially in your presence! I'm not asking your opinion because frankly I don't give a shit what you think. And I don't touch you because the very idea of your skin coming into contact with mine sends this ridiculously human body into flight. And I refuse to run away—from a woman."

Forget about not wanting to kill him.

I slammed my hands against his chest, his body went flying across the room, landing on my bed, hammering the posts into the wall and creating giant holes I knew Mason was going to be pissed about fixing and hiding from Ethan.

The air in the room fell below zero as ice trickled along my veins. My skin turned a vivid white as my eyes took in every bit of moisture in the air, freezing it to my advantage so I could create an icy stake to plunge through Cassius's cold, heartless chest.

My hands snapped forward, the ice joined together in front of my eyes. I gripped the makeshift weapon and launched myself into the air, arm raised.

When I landed on the bed, straddling Cassius.

It wasn't terror, or fear, I found.

But elation.

His smile was huge, beautiful.

I dropped the ice stake and fell backward, my body turning warm again. "What the hell was that?"

"That—" His grin widened. "—is what happens when you piss off a Dark One. Good to know you aren't defective."

"I could have killed you."

"I'm human. Therefore, every second I suck in air, I'm dying. It would have been worth it to see you what you're capable of."

"But!" I covered my face with my hands. "I'm dangerous, you said so yourself, in the car, you said to control my emotions, you said—"

"I said a lot of things," he interrupted. "Listen to what I'm saying now. I'm truly here to help you. Not because I was punished."

My heart sped up automatically as my head snapped to attention and I sought his gaze. "Really?"

He nodded, his eyes drinking me in. "I'm here out of an intense desire to help you—and to make sure you don't kill the rest of your family in one of your adolescent mood swings."

"I'm not a child."

"Says the little girl who created a spike out of ice with the intent of stabbing me in the chest, all because her feelings were hurt."

"You were *mean*."

"It was necessary."

"How do you figure?"

"How else am I supposed to help you?" Cassius leaned up on his elbows. "If I don't allow you to see the darkest parts of yourself?"

"That's what you want? To see my darkness?"

"No." His eyes flashed. "I teach you how to fight the darkness—so you can recognize the light."

My breath hitched.

Warmth trickled throughout my chest as I stared at his mouth. His eyes gave nothing away—and everything at the same time. He kept his expression indifferent, yet I could hear his heart race.

It sounded like mine felt.

I pressed a hand to his chest.

He covered the hand with his.

With a sigh I leaned down and pressed a kiss to his cheek, then brushed my lips against his mouth.

He didn't kiss me back.

Rejection washed over me. Obviously I'd read the situation completely wrong. His heart was racing but not for me.

"Don't." His hoarse voice rattled my confidence even more. "Don't kiss me—not unless you mean it."

"What?"

"Kiss me when you're calm… not when you've just come down from what any human would consider the ultimate adrenaline high. Then you'll mean it. But don't kiss me out of curiosity, out of thankfulness, or even out of attraction. It doesn't work that way."

Ashamed, I looked down, unable to keep eye contact because I hated that he was right. I loved the man.

But he was right.

"And anytime you'd like to get off of me that would be great," he finished, grinning. "Because as much as I'd like to compliment you on your lithe body—you're about two minutes away from crushing my liver."

With a scowl I jumped off him, but when he tried to follow, I pushed him back onto the bed.

He grunted and tumbled over the other side.

I smiled to myself and started walking toward the door. "Hurry up, human. We don't have all day."

"You forget," he said from the floor. "You may be a Dark One, but you gave up your immortality the day you saved my life."

"I'd conveniently forgotten that part, since it was

magically given back to me when you disappeared."

"I haven't... forgotten." Cassius reached for my arm and led me out of the room. "Now, I think I need to eat before we begin."

"How do you think you need to eat? You're either hungry or you're not."

"I think this pain is hunger." Cassius rubbed his stomach with one hand and frowned. "And that bird looked delicious."

"Okay..." I patted him on the back, "Humans these days don't have to shoot their own birds, let's just ask Mason to cook something, he's probably bored to tears anyway."

We walked by the window.

The bird chose to land on the tree closest to us.

Cassius tensed.

"When was the last time you ate?" I asked.

"Ate?"

"Food."

He licked his lips. "Dark Ones don't need food we eat because food tastes delicious."

"As a human," I clarified.

He shrugged. "I haven't."

"No wonder you want to go all Elmer Fudd on his ass."

"Elmer Fudd?" Cassius shook his head in confusion. "Is that a figure of speech for eating birds?"

"No." I patted his shoulder. "It's Bugs Bunny."

"Bugs or bunny? They can't be one in the same."

"Maybe you do need to watch some TV with everyone—"

I managed to lead him away from the window, though he turned around twice. I may be stronger, but it was still awkward trying to push him down the stairway when he kept trying to turn around and make creepy eye contact with the feathered creature.

"Someone say TV?" Alex was leaning against the bottom part of the stairway, his naturally bright smile even more amused than normal. "And Bugs Bunny is a rabbit."

Cassius shrugged. "Of course the bunny is a rabbit. I was confused about the bugs part."

"It's his name."

"But he's a rabbit—bunny." Cassius argued.

"Humans name pets."

"Funny." Cassius smirked. "They name pets, I keep them as pets…"

"Still talking a big game for being one of them." Alex grinned. "And sister." He peered up at me with loving eyes. "I think the best thing for you right now would be to get Cassius caught up on pop culture."

Cassius groaned. "I'm not stupid. I know about the Backstreet Boys."

Alex burst out laughing. "Oh this may be my favorite moment—of my entire existence. Right up there with the time I watched Ethan take his first bite of pizza thinking the sauce was blood."

A giant scowl formed on Ethan's face, and he gripped the edge of the table where he was seated. "Well, if you hadn't *lied* about it…"

"Best. Day. Ever." Alex winked.

Genesis finished setting the table by folding white napkins beneath the forks; it was cute that she did it, even though the only people who ate were her and sometimes Mason.

At least now Cassius could join the ranks.

"Sorry, Cassius." Mason tossed a plate at Genesis, she caught it midair and placed it at the head of the table. "Backstreet Boys aren't really the in thing anymore."

"Fine." Cassius rolled his eyes. "I'll just go to the store and grab a few CD's and why is everyone looking at me like I've lost my mind?"

Ethan shook his head. "You've been that busy? Unable to even turn on a TV? Do an Internet search? You have more money than the very country you live in, and you can't afford cable?"

Cassius walked away from me and sat at the head of the table. Funny that he'd take his usual seat. I guessed he was still our King even if he was a bit under the weather. "When would I have time? With the Vampires fighting, the Werewolves hiding, the Demons whining..."

"I'd like to know who's doing your job while you're..." Mason tilted his head, and his lips pulled into a sneer. "Indisposed."

Cassius flashed his teeth.

I'm not sure what he was trying to accomplish considering the minute he poked the bear—or in this case Werewolf—Mason flashed his fangs. Then Ethan felt the need to flash his, followed by my brother nearly glowing. Was it wrong that their reactions at least made things feel more normal?

I sat down and crossed my arms. "Let's all just agree that Cassius needs this much-needed break to train me and learn the wonder that is the internet... and iTunes."

"Yes he needs this much-needed break because he needs to fulfill his basic human needs." Alex said in a smug tone.

"I know what iTunes is." Cassius glowered in my direction, immediately changing the subject.

I tilted my head. "Oh, yeah?"

"Songs."

"You'll have to do better than that."

"Songs that people…" He gulped. "Sing."

Alex burst out laughing.

Cassius rolled his eyes and glanced out the window. The bird, the same damn bird appeared.

"Food!" He jumped out of his seat.

I quickly got to my feet and pushed him back down. "Sit."

"But—"

"Uh…?" Alex raised his hand. "Why is Cassius bird watching?"

"He's watching because he wants to eat it," I explained.

Mason placed a salad in front of Cassius.

You'd think he'd just asked Cassius to tend to the garden and eat raw tomatoes. "What's this?"

"Salad." I scooted the dressing toward him.

"It's green."

"Hey, at least you've got your eyesight," Ethan remarked.

"But the bird?" Cassius pointed behind him, "Why aren't we eating meat?"

Mason looked heavenward. "I must have done something seriously awful to be cursed with a Dark One who suddenly wants food. He'll eat everything!"

"He's starving!" I pointed at Cassius. "Come on, fix him something good Mason. Salads are for girls."

Genesis laughed and reached across the table to

grab Cassius's plate, but he was busy poking the tomato with a fork or trying to.

"It's like watching a baby learn how to walk. Come on Cassius, you can do it!" Alex clapped behind him.

And earned a fork in the thigh.

"Shit!" Alex collapsed to the ground. "What the hell, I thought you weren't a Dark One anymore."

"So, I've lost my aim?" Cassius snorted. "Hardly. And next time you make fun of me I'm grabbing a knife."

"Ethan has a gun case, the code is 1492." Mason said in a cheerful voice.

Alex glared. "Thanks, Mason. Real helpful."

"Please, it wouldn't kill you."

"It damn well wouldn't tickle either, you bastard!" Alex shouted.

"Guys!" I held up my hands. "Do I need to order take-out, or do we have enough meat to feed…" I pointed to Cassius. "…this?"

"Not even a person anymore." Alex cackled behind him. "How's it feel?"

"About as good as a bullet between the eyes, Alex, care to experience it?"

Alex jerked the fork out of his thigh and tossed it in the sink. "Wash the blood off why don't you, Mason?"

"I can't concentrate with all the yelling." Mason reached for his cell. "I say we go out to eat."

"Yes!" Genesis stood. "We haven't done a date night in weeks!"

Ethan reached for her hand and kissed it.

"Date night?" Cassius frowned. "A night with dates?"

I leaned forward and rested my forehead on the table. "It's romantic."

"Date night," he repeated again.

I stood. "Whatever, let's go somewhere close because Cassius is about five minutes away from molesting that bird."

"I would never!" Cassius stood, outrage pouring over his face.

"Sarcasm." Alex slapped him on the back. "You should try it, Dark One."

Cassius jerked away from Alex. "I know what it is."

"Clearly." Alex nodded in mock understanding.

"The Lodge." Mason grabbed his keys. "They always make room for us. Let's go, kids… before Dad eats the family pet."

"The bird is your pet?" Cassius looked horrified.

Alex sighed and whispered again, "Sarcasm."

Cassius shoved past him then stopped in his tracks and turned. "Stephanie, will we be riding together?"

His eyes were hopeful.

What game was he playing?

He held out his hand.

I took it, still frowning.

"Uh, sure. We'll drive separate since we can't all fit in Ethan's car."

"They're all my cars," Ethan said under his breath then sped past us with Genesis in tow.

I nodded toward the garage. Cassius followed, our hands still linked.

"Well, which one of Ethan's toys do you want to take?" The lights flickered on as Ethan and the rest of the crew piled into his white Mercedes.

"That." Cassius pointed at the red Hummer.

I sighed. "Of course. Big bad Dark One wants a big

bad car."

"It's tall. I'm tall..." He shrugged, his smile flirtatious.

My heart skipped in my chest. "Fine, but you do realize we're in Seattle, right? People are going to flip you off for just driving something that gets only eight miles per gallon."

"Does it matter?" He was giddy. "When we can run them over anyway?"

"Good point."

"I'd like to think so."

"I'll grab the keys." I still hadn't moved.

His eyes were penetrating as he held my gaze. "All right."

"Keys," I repeated.

"To drive the monstrosity."

Slowly, I shook my head as I left his side and grabbed the keys then met him back at the car. He was already inside, strapped in and looking about as pumped as a ten-year-old at a carnival.

"Fast," he commanded, and then cleared his throat. "I mean... please?"

I smiled and started the car. "Only because you said please."

His eyes met mine. "I'll have to remember that for future reference. Say please, and... she says yes."

My body hummed with anticipation.

Or maybe it was irritation...

...that as a human he was completely wreaking havoc on my emotions—even more so than when he was immortal.

Cassius

Pompeii 79 AD

"Secrets are the real war," I whispered into the darkness as Sariel made his way toward me through the mist, purple and blue feathers expanded separately from his body testing the purity of the air. He was searching for lies, yet again testing me—testing us.

"They are," Ethan agreed, standing to my right while Alex held the sword against the King's throat.

"Why do you disturb me?" Sariel asked calmly. With a tilt of his fingers Alex's sword was pulled back and the human king was thrust to his knees in a bowing position. "I have more important things to focus on than the measly war between humans and immortals."

"We've been at peace for the last hundred years," I said through clenched teeth. "And we disturb you because there has been a... situation."

Sariel's eyes went white as ice as his wings spread out across the large room, the span of them reached fifty feet. The blue and purple feathers fluttered and then stuck straight out. The air shifted and the feathers turned black as Sariel sucked in a gasp. "You dare defy me!"

King Ebal began to weep. "I was told immortality was obtainable. And they were right!"

"Demons use your greatest desires against you, weaving small truths into great lies. They will justify anything."

King Ebal moaned out a curse. "I'm sorry! I didn't know!"

"How much did he have?" Sariel asked aloud.

I sighed. "The Demon showed him how to put each of us in an immortal sleep. There's no way to tell how much he took unless we spill his blood. Ethan has already tried tasting."

Sariel's wings suddenly wrapped around his body and then disappeared. Damn, that meant he was staying a while. He towered over the King. "You may look at me now, human."

King Ebal lifted his head, his eyes wide with fear. No human could be in an Archangel's presence and not fear the end of his own life. I knew firsthand that Sariel was the cruelest of the Angels, sometimes choosing to show humans a reflection of their own demise the minute they locked eyes with him.

"You have consumed immortal blood—it is their essence. You know this."

"My girl!" the King sobbed. "She is sick! And they refused to heal her!"

"Are they God?" Sariel asked with exaggerated wonder. "Do you truly think they have the power to snap their fingers and make someone well?"

"Angel blood." The King ignored the question. "Mixed with the other immortals' blood heals all! She was well this morning!"

"Word spread," I interrupted dread filling my stomach. "And his wife started handing out small vials of the concoc-

tion to friends and family."

"How many people?" Sariel's voice shook the room.

"By now?" I sighed. "A hundred, maybe."

"Shall I destroy one city for your sin?" Sariel addressed the king again.

"You don't want us to be healthy! You want us to rely on you for everything! Have I not served you well?" The King challenged. "And yet you refuse to heal my little girl! But the Demon said he could!"

"Of course the Demon said he could!" Sariel yelled back at him. "Because the only way to save a life that's already been claimed for death is to die you fool!"

"But—" The King sputtered. "She's alive!"

"Is she?" Sariel shook his head slowly. "Do realize you could have simply called for a miracle? Do you realize that you could have called upon the One who holds the key to life? Instead, you have damned her to hell."

"No!" The king shook his hands in front of his face, tears streamed down his cheeks. "She is alive! Just this morning I—"

"Bring the girl," Sariel stormed in an icy whisper. "Show her in."

The door opened. Eva, held the tiny six-year-old in her strong embrace. Already the girl's eyes were turning black, her body trembling as Darkness took hold.

"She was meant to die." Sariel pointed at the girl. "In two days she would have been taken to paradise. On this day. She will lose her soul, along with every person who consumed the blood."

The King sobbed, falling to his hands and knees. "Take me! Don't take my little girl. Take me!"

"I take no one. These lives are no longer mine to take, that choice was pulled out of my hands the minute you de-

cided to play at Creator." Sariel glanced out the window. "If a hundred have the blood—within twenty-four hours the city will fall to sickness, they will need blood, they will have no choice but to feed from one another."

Humanity had no place in this decision. I looked at the immortals I'd sworn to protect and then glanced out amongst the thousands of humans that would die for one man's stupidity.

Sariel tilted his head in my direction. "This is your realm. What will you do?"

The human screamed at the unfairness of the situation, it begged, it pleaded, it bled.

It had no place in this decision.

"I will destroy them all." I ignored every shred of human emotion. One day, I feared, I wouldn't feel them at all, they'd simply disappear. "I will destroy the city, and every Demon in it."

Cassius

"SLOW DOWN," ETHAN HISSED out of the corner of his mouth as I tore off another hunk of warm bread and shoved it into my mouth. "You look like a damn animal."

"Mason." Alex nodded thoughtfully. "I imagine he looks like Mason does when he feeds."

Mason let out a low growl and clutched his beer tightly with his hand—though that same hand was shaking, his nails elongating. Alex better watch it lest he get his throat slit before dessert.

Ah, dessert.

I patted my stomach.

Why hadn't the hunger subsided?

I reached for the bread basket. Empty. Damn. "Who ate all the bread?"

"You." Genesis smothered a laugh. "What? You blacked out during the last of the loaf?"

"I uh…" My cheeks heated. "Sorry."

"Gasp." Alex said in a monotone voice. "I wasn't aware that word was in your vocabulary."

I ignored his jab. "Alex, make yourself useful, seduce the waitress and get more bread."

"You know, that technically breaks council rules." Alex grinned. "Seducing a human woman for a Dark One's benefit."

Ethan groaned and pinched his nose. "For the love of God, Alex, just do it, Genesis is starving, I can hear her hunger, which in turn makes me hungry, and nobody wants to see me bite."

Mason shrugged. "I don't know. It would be kinda nice, dinner and a show..."

Stephanie stifled a laugh. "Maybe Alex doesn't think he can do it anymore... lost your touch, brother?"

His eyes narrowed just as the waitress came by again. I think his hesitation had more to do with the fact that she was in her late seventies, and looked like someone's nice old grandma—the grandma who knits sweaters for Christmas and crafts homemade cards for every special occasion.

"Are you ready to order?" She tilted her head. The nametag flashed Fran. Threads of silver hair wove around dark hair, all pulled tightly into a bun. "I see you've finished your bread."

"One of us has," Genesis grumbled in my direction.

I gave her an apologetic smile and received a kick from Ethan that hurt like hell, did the man forget I was breakable? He's lucky he didn't break my leg in half!

"Fran," Alex said in a smooth voice, his blue eyes brightened, his skin took on a flawless appearance, his words were spoken slowly in a lazy drawl that had Fran leaning forward, eyes heavy. "I know we're only now ordering but is there any way we can get our food... say, in a few minutes? We're positively..." he licked his lips. "Starved."

"Too far." Mason coughed under his breath.

Fran blinked. "Yes well, yes that… that would be nice."

"Two orders of the filet mignon." Alex grinned. "Six orders of the New York Strip, six Caesar salads, and I think we'll also take some more bread."

Fran wrote everything down and then glanced up. "I'll be sure to get this to you as soon as possible."

She didn't move.

Alex yawned.

Stephanie smacked him across the chest.

His smile was anything but guilty. "Oh thanks Fran, you're dismissed."

"But…" Her eyebrows pinched together, like she was trying to solve a puzzle. This was the problem with Sirens. They flirted, they gave off such an intense emotional charge that if they didn't follow through, usually, the spell was broken within minutes. He had to touch her to solidify it—kissing her would be better. I'd known Alex for a long time—I imagined he was too lazy to do either.

With a sigh he slowly rose from his seat and reached for her hand, bringing it to his lips with a quick kiss.

Fran flashed a toothy smile and walked off.

I gave one solitary clap. "Could you have gone any slower?"

"Could you be any more jealous?" he countered.

"Of your love affair with the elderly?" I tilted my head. "Jealousy wasn't really the word I was thinking."

"You're welcome." He leaned back in his chair, placing his hands behind his head. "At least now you won't have to resort to eating the table cloth."

"You can eat the table cloth?"

"Sarcasm!" Alex said in an exasperated tone. "Learn it!"

I smirked. "I was kidding."

You'd think I'd just announced I was going to go on a killing spree. All eyes fell to me, movement ceased.

"What?" I reached for my water and took a tentative sip.

"Dark Ones don't joke." Mason said seriously. "Did this whole humanity thing also replace your personality?"

I glowered. "Really, it's like you're begging me to kill you once this is finished."

"And what *is* this?" Ethan's eye narrowed. "You haven't really said. And I can't imagine you taking this type of… *test* sitting down."

"Standing." I licked my lips. "I was standing actually."

"Sariel said nothing else?" Stephanie asked, her voice dripping with doubt. "Nothing about his reasoning?"

My mind flashed back to a few days earlier, when I offered up everything for a chance at—everything. A chance to fix an error.

A lapse in judgment.

The council members, the individuals sitting at that very table, knew me the best.

They'd seen me raze cities. Save lives. And do my fair share of destroying.

Yet even they didn't believe me capable of having a shred of humanity. Which in turn made me question everything I'd come to know about myself. Was I their leader because they respected me?

No.

I was their leader.

Because they feared me.

Because they had no choice.

They weren't my friends, hardly even colleagues. It had never been so painfully apparent as it was in that moment.

I truly had nothing in this world.

And maybe that was Sariel's plan all along, his last cruel trick. Make the Dark One—who has no feelings—feel.

Because I felt a hell of a lot while I sat there.

Shame, disappointment, rage, embarrassment.

I felt it all.

And I had nobody to blame but myself.

Chapter 11

Stephanie

"I WANT TO SHOW you something." Cassius's deep voice caused my body to shiver in anticipation, delight, lust—take your pick.

I lifted a shoulder. "Oh?"

"I doubt Ethan would mind if we borrowed his car for the evening."

"Evening?" My entire mouth went dry. Hadn't we just spent the evening together? At least dinner? I watched helplessly as the rest of the crew piled into Ethan's car and drove off, leaving me alone with Cassius, so very much alone. "The whole evening?"

Cassius grinned. "You look scared."

"Tired," I blurted. "This is the look of exhaustion."

"Pity." He pulled the keys from my hand and opened the passenger door, ushering me in. "I guess I'll have to do my best to keep you from over exerting yourself, then."

I gulped. "Guess so."

Cassius didn't respond, but he did seem amused at my expense as he started the car and weaved through traffic, nearly clipping two cars in the process.

"Thought you didn't know how to drive." I said

through clenched teeth.

"Fast learner." He flashed another smile and kept driving at breakneck speed until we took the next exit.

I frowned as he went toward Lake Stevens.

The sun was setting, the sky was growing dark. Demons would soon be out and about, seducing humans, biting them, drinking their blood just because they could. Vampires would be sleeping because as much as people liked to believe they only came out at night, they could do whatever the hell they wanted—within reason.

"What will you do?" I cleared my throat at an attempt to rid my mind of what dangers prowled at night. "If you haven't finished this little test before the next council meeting?"

Cassius stared blankly at the road ahead, giving nothing away. But the dim light from the dash revealed that he was gripping the steering wheel so tight his knuckles were turning white. "That won't happen."

"But it could." I frowned. "And if the Vampires, Demons, heck if anyone sees you like this—"

"They won't!" He yelled.

I held up my hands. "Okay, sensitive subject, but I'm glad you're that confident in this whole testing thing."

He scowled. "Confidence has nothing to do with it."

"Oh?"

As the car rolled to a stop at the light, he turned toward me, his face void of emotion. "If I fail, I die, case closed."

What? Panic rose in my chest. "If you fail as a human you die? If you fail with me?"

Color tinged his cheeks as he slammed down on the accelerator. "Right, something like that."

"How many days did he give you?"

"Thirty."

"As of today?"

"As of two days ago."

"You have twenty-eight days!" I shouted, frosting the windows with ice.

He muttered a curse and quickly turned on the defrost. "Careful, you're going to make me think you actually like me."

I crossed my arms and gazed out my window. "You know I like you."

He was quiet for a minute then cleared his throat. "Do you like me enough to trust me? Do you like me enough not to kill me?"

"What is this? First grade?" I laughed, his teasing eased my fear. "Cassius, I like you, I'm circling yes on the note you just passed me, what's your deal?"

"I'm not familiar with that expression."

I pinched the bridge of my nose. "You aren't familiar with anything."

"That's not true." He steered the car down a winding road near the lake.

"Yes it is! What have you been doing, you know other than watching over me making sure I don't know my full potential, keeping your dirty secrets and making sure immortals don't go to war?"

"You want to know what I've been DOING?" he yelled as he stomped on the brake and the car jerked to a stop.

"YES!" I matched his voice. "Where do you go when shit gets real, Cassius? When life gets too hard.

When you're forced to face your demons."

"We're here."

"We aren't done discussing this!"

Cassius sighed and pulled the keys from the ignition. "I meant we're here, here is the place I go to. My home."

I jerked back and fumbled with the handle to the car door and jumped out of the car.

We were in front of a house.

A giant modern white house, with large bay windows, nestled between at least a dozen or so trees, just feet from the lake.

It was beautiful.

Not what I'd imagine a Dark One living in. "This doesn't look like you at all."

"Oh?" Cassius chuckled. "And what did you expect?"

"A cave." I nodded as the white pristine house caused unwelcome sensations to bubble up within me. This part of Cassius just made me more curious. "Possibly hell."

"Great," he said in a low voice. "You think I spend my time in the fiery pits of hell until I'm ordered to go eat small children, is that it?"

I shrugged, technically the shoe fit, not that I'd say it out loud.

He cursed.

As if things had been going well up until this point?

The sound of crunching gravel as he walked away was really the only indicator that Cassius wanted me to follow. I moved slowly behind him as we neared the house. He pulled a key out from under the mat and slid it in the door.

"Clever, nobody would ever look there." I nodded my head.

Cassius stopped and turned, his blue eyes menacing. "Do you truly think I care if someone steals from me? Or tries to break in? Believe me, it would be more of a nightmare for them, than for me. I'd simply... make sure they ceased to exist." He snapped his fingers into the air.

"Done it before, have you?" I arched my eyebrows up.

"Once." Cassius shrugged and moved in through the doorway. "He was at least eighty, I thought it a kindness to further things along, his memory wasn't well, had no family. I touched him and—"

"—he died?"

"Quickly," Cassius said smoothly.

"That's horrible!"

"As opposed to him dying alone in his home? He died with me—an honor I don't bestow on just anyone."

I frowned. Is that what was going to happen to me? I'd touch nice old men and decide to steal their lives? As if on cue, a Darkness started spreading throughout my stomach, like a warmth I couldn't control, and then as soon as it appeared it dissipated like it was never there in the first place.

Unsettling.

I hated feeling out of control.

"You forget." He turned to face me, his face dazzling beneath the moonlight and stars. "We are better than them. We always will be. That's not me being cruel or arrogant, it's a simple fact. The blood that runs through your veins..." His fingertips danced across the pulse point on my wrist. "It's holy."

I licked my lips in irritation. The last thing I felt was special—and definitely not holy. "Doesn't feel that way."

"You're part Angel," he said slowly. "It will never feel the way it's supposed to simply because you are missing half of the whole. Being a Dark One means being in a constant state of loneliness without any way to alleviate the pain."

I flinched. Was that what this feeling was? This hollowness in my chest that made me stare like a lunatic at every single human relationship like I was starved for attention? For physical touch?

"Ah..." Cassius nodded knowingly. "You've been wondering if something's wrong with you, am I right?"

I swallowed and broke eye contact unable to bear his scrutiny; he saw too much, even as a human it was like he saw beneath the surface of everything.

"So, you really were at a coffee shop..." He reached out and touched my face. His fingertips were warm. "Watching humans hold hands, laugh, love..." His head tilted to the side, not in a mocking way, almost like he was puzzled. Or maybe I was the puzzle. "Tell me, did it burn?"

"What?" I croaked, how did he know?

"After the hollowness slices open your chest." He moved closer to me, dropping his hand so that his body was almost pressed against mine. "I used to call it the burn of wanting what I knew I could never have. Humans were created for partnership, companionship. Angels, as you know, are the exact opposite. Thus, the burn, the feeling of being ripped in half. Your Angel blood tells you it's ridiculous, stupid even, to want what you can't have, and why it says, why want something so weak when you are who you are, what you are?" His voice broke. "But the human side of you… it longs. It desires." His forehead touched mine. "Oh… it burns all right. It burns you from the inside out. And the darkness beckons during the burn, it calls."

"Does it ever go away?" I whispered, completely unnerved by our conversation. I had a sudden urge to itch my chest, to make the burn go away because even then my body was remembering it, like a thirst I couldn't quench.

He let out a long sigh then backed away from me, away from whatever private moment we were sharing. "It can."

"Did it for you?"

He froze, his hand midair as he was reaching for a light switch. "Once."

"When?" The air stilled around us. "When did it stop?"

Cassius hung his head. "The minute our lips touched, those brief seconds you saved me, touched me, joined with me. For those measly seconds—seconds of living a lifetime of a million lonely seconds—I was complete."

I covered my face with my hands.

"Let's go," he said gruffly. "There's more to show you."

He left the room.

But I was glued to the spot, unable to do anything except focus on breathing in and out. I wanted to ask so many more questions, was he angry at me because the only moment of peace he'd had was in my arms? Was that it? My heart clenched as rejection washed over me.

Of course.

That's why he'd run off—hidden.

Maybe that was why he was being punished, because he did hide, he did run. And it was my fault.

I'd made him want.

And now… he was forced to spend the next twenty-eight days with me. I guess the only positive out of the situation was that he was human. I had no effect on him.

Because if I did, he'd have already fallen.

Humans were weak.

Slaves to their emotions.

Dark One or not, in an entirely human state, Cassius wouldn't have stood a chance against me.

But he continued to do so.

Which made the rejection sting all that much more—as a Dark One, I couldn't even entice him.

"Stephanie," Cassius barked from somewhere deeper in the house. "We don't have all night."

Scowling, I stomped after him. I could last the next three and a half weeks with him. I just needed to keep my heart on lockdown—just like he was doing.

If a measly human could do it.

There was no reason I couldn't.

Chapter 12

Cassius

Pompeii 79AD

"You can't do this!" Eva screamed at me as I moved farther up the mountain. "Cassius, STOP!"

The ice in my veins rose to the surface as a flash of lightning lit up the sky. "And what would you have me do? Save them all? Only to have them turn on us? Destroy us? They are an abomination, Eva! They. Must. Die." White filled my vision as the screams of people in the city started to multiply.

"Earthquake." I spoke the word in ancient Aramaic, the tongue of Angels.

The ground shook beneath my feet.

I kept walking.

Eva followed.

Finally, I turned on my heel. "Do not make me destroy you, Vampire!"

Her eyes closed, and then she held out her hands, palms facing toward me. "Cassius, most of them are innocent. Will you destroy them? The children? The mothers? The grandmothers?"

"If I let one go free, one who is infected…"

"Then choose, Cassius," Eva said in a challenging voice.

"Choose who goes free, save a few. All I ask is that you save some."

"You misjudge our relationship, Vampire." I hissed out the lie as the air took on a bitter taste from my own inability to admit the truth. "Only you would ask this of me. Notice how the rest of the council members have already fled the city, and yet here you stand."

She lifted her head. "Here I stand."

"Damn it, woman." I closed my eyes for a few brief seconds, allowing a sliver of humanity to slip through. God, it burned, nearly slicing me in half as my Angel blood roared with anger at the weakness. Strength and weakness, could not co-exist, not for long. Eventually my angelic blood would destroy what humanity I had left.

I'd felt it since the beginning of time.

I knew.

One day.

It would no longer be possible.

This was not that day.

"Twelve." I sighed. "I will save twelve."

Eva bowed her dark head. "Thank you, Cassius."

"Do not thank me."

"I will always—" She took a step forward and held out her hand. "—thank you, when you show the weak mercy."

I took Eva's hand without thinking and was nearly brought to my knees as the emotional connection she offered burned through our palms. She had no idea what her touch did to me—what it made me crave.

"Earthquake," I whispered again, this time the ground beneath us split down the middle. I pulled Eva into my arms and envisioned the docks. We landed with a thud against the wood.

People scrambled about mindlessly as the ground shook

and then the volcano erupted into the sky.

It would be the ash and the gas that would destroy the people… the heat alone… I refused to think about it.

"You promised," Eva reminded me as she stepped into the boat and waited.

I glanced at the pier.

"You." I pointed to a young boy. "Where is your family?"

"I—" The boy's face was spattered with dirt and blood. "They got trampled, sir."

"Then come," I instructed. He stepped into the boat. Eva embraced him and offered a warm smile.

"Eleven more to go, Cassius." Eva said.

"Irritating Vampire," I grumbled, as, with each life I saved, the darkness receded, restoring my humanity.

Within five minutes I had another eleven.

All children.

"Let's go." I waved my hand in the air as the water carried the ship to safety.

When I turned back to glance at the once Great City, it was to see Sariel hovering over the volcano, his eyes sad.

Clouds spread around his wings, and then a large being descended next to him.

"The Angel of Death," Eva whispered linking her hand with mine. We watched as his black feathers descended slowly covering the city until all was blackness.

And then…

It rained red.

Chapter 13

Cassius

THE SCREAMS OF PEOPLE I'D killed seemed to lessen the farther I walked into my house. It had always been a safe zone.

Quiet.

Where I conveniently forgot all the blood that was on my hands.

My heart, stupid muscle that it was, refused to stop slamming against my chest as perspiration collected around my temples. My knees buckled, my vision blurred. It wasn't a heart attack, I at least knew that much.

No, it was more like deep rooted fear.

Fear she would find out before I had my chance to convince her of… of what? That I wasn't as cruel of a bastard as she'd originally thought? That I loved her beyond what logic told me? That my entire being felt like it had been waiting—for her? So close to blurting out the truth—telling her everything.

And then what? She'd laugh in my face. The words about burst from my lips, but I knew no matter what I said, if my actions didn't match them, the outcome wouldn't be in my favor.

I was doing a damned horrible job of even getting her to see me as a friend—and as a lover? Something told me I was going backward when I should have been going forward.

Agitated, I clenched and unclenched my fists as I made my way through the dark house. I hadn't returned since that fateful night with Sariel, not sure why, maybe because this house, this haven reminded me of who I was, and I was trying desperately to be anyone but that person.

I flipped on the nearest switch. Light flooded into the large living room. A place I'd spent many years sitting in, reflecting, reading, shutting out the world because as much as everyone would love to believe that I adored passing judgment on immortal and human beings alike, it wore on me. Half Angel meant that although I was damn good at what I did, I still ached for something more.

"This is..." Stephanie did a circle of the room, her eyes most likely taking in the floor to ceiling book shelves filled with dusty reminders of just how old I really was—manuscripts flooded the large oak desk, ancient scrolls were tossed onto the floor beneath it. A coffee maker older than Genesis sat in the corner near two large purple-cushioned chairs. The bay windows overlooked the lake, and large black velvet curtains were pulled back with gold rope, revealing the beautiful view. "So not what I expected." She picked up a book and frowned. "You have an original copy of Pride and Prejudice?"

I shrugged. "Never read it."

She gasped and then closed her eyes, in horror? Disappointment? I wasn't sure, I wasn't near as good at reading anymore, but I felt embarrassment wash over me all the same. "You've never read one of the most classic love stories of all time?"

"Love story?" I parroted, feeling like an idiot. Why hadn't I thought of that? Books! I could read books about love! I could give her books.

Stephanie's smile widened as she opened the first page.

"It's yours," I blurted.

She glanced up, her lips curving up into a dazzling smile. "Why, thank you, Beast."

"Hardly the time to call me names," I grumbled.

"Um…" She placed the book back down on the table. "It was a joke. You know, Beauty and the Beast? He gives her a library."

Well damn, and here I just gave her one book.

Another fail.

"I don't have a library."

Stephanie pointed around the room. " Kinda seems like you do."

"I like to read."

"I can see that." Though clearly not romance.

Why was conversation so stilted? And why the hell was I tapping my foot like I was an impatient bastard? I'd never felt so uncomfortable in my life, confidence used to ooze from every cell in my body, I never worked for it, never had to, I knew what I was, and what I was capable of.

Now?

Uncertainty laced my every breath.

"So." I coughed into my hand and turned around so she wouldn't see the panic on my face. "I just wanted you to see."

I felt her come up behind me; the chill caused goose bumps to rise across my flesh. Ice crystals formed along the edges of the windows. "You wanted me to see, what exactly?"

I bit my lip in frustration. "Me." I hung my head. "I wanted you to see me. It may seem ridiculous, but when I'm not doing my actual job for the immortals or serving my sentence as I'd always put it mildly. I'm here. Reading. Relaxing." I spread my arms wide, rejuvenating, pushing out the negative swirl of emotions that grate on a person like me—for doing what I did on a daily basis.

"I like it." Stephanie finally said, her voice husky. "As far as lairs go yours is way better than Ethan's. Much more gothic."

I coughed out a laugh. "Yes well, we both know Vampires prefer light to dark."

Stephanie touched my arm.

I flinched.

"Do I hurt you?"

"No." I pulled away slowly. "I think it's instinctual. Every time you touch me I shy away, not because it hurts, maybe it's a deep rooted fear that all humans have, and now that I'm fully human..." I shrugged.

"Can I control you?" Stephanie's eyes narrowed. "Technically, a Dark One can't come into contact with an unmated human without them going insane with desire, lust— I mean, why aren't you...?" She blinked and then looked down. "I can't believe I just asked you that."

"Why am I not overcome with insanity in your presence?" I chuckled. It was nice to see her uncomfortable for a change.

"Yeah." Her chest rose and fell with even breaths, and I concentrated on her breathing; it made me calm, counting every inhale, every exhale.

"I imagine Sariel wouldn't think it fair."

"Fair?"

I clasped my hands behind my back. "But you're welcome to try."

Stephanie rolled her eyes. "How do you know I haven't been trying?"

"Because I'm alive."

Her eyes widened. "So if I try, I kill you?"

"Possibly, who really knows?"

"No thanks."

"Take a chance."

"No." She stepped farther away from me, her back colliding with one of the book shelves.

I pursued, nearly slamming my body against hers, not because I wanted to force her but because I couldn't help the aggression pounding through my veins. When she retreated I wanted to pursue. I couldn't help myself any more than I could stop myself from breathing.

"Where's your sense of danger and adventure?" I taunted, pressing my hands to her cold arms. "Try."

"I could kill you."

"I'll try not to die."

"Oh," she muttered and cursed under her breath. "How reassuring."

"Do it."

"No!"

"Oh, so you're afraid." I nodded mockingly, "Don't think I've ever met a Dark One who experienced fear."

Her nostrils flared. "Don't push me." The room temperature plummeted.

I arched an eyebrow then very slowly leaned forward and whispered in her ear. "Chicken."

It was immature.

I knew that.

She knew that.

But it didn't stop her reaction.

With catlike reflexes she pushed me across the room, I landed perfectly in the chair, she jumped into the air and pounced, straddling me with both legs. One tilt of her head and our eyes locked.

Hers turned white.

It was eerie, watching someone else do what I'd done thousands of times, this time with me being on the receiving end.

I was completely riveted by the way she looked at me—as if I was the only being in existence.

My breath came out in a gasp as the room dropped below zero. Ice crackled across the surface of the wood floor, moisture once clinging in the air frosted the windows.

"That all you got?" I licked my nearly frozen lips.

Stephanie leaned forward, her nails digging into my arm. "I'm not exactly practiced in the art of Dark One seduction."

"The next step..." Why was I teaching her this again? When I was so weak? Right, because if I died, it would all fall to her. If I failed she was the last.

"Yes?"

"The Marking."

Her eyes swirled back to blue then went white again. "Yes, that sounds like a good idea. How do I... what do I...?" Her focus wavered. She was unsteady, too new, too unpracticed. I imagined she wouldn't have the concentration to actually kill me.

"Two choices." The human side of me was ready to bolt out of the chair and find a weapon. I stayed put, even when her nails dug deeper. Warm blood started trickling from my arms. "You mark with your mouth or your hand."

Stephanie nodded, the room got colder. Damn, maybe I'd just freeze to death. Clearly, I hadn't thought through all the horrible scenarios.

"You take your palm and press it against the neck, cupping the human flesh, you simply force your will upon them, whatever it is. Do you need a slave? What about a task completed? How about undying love and devotion? What you need, you think, you force it upon them so heavily that it becomes the very air they breathe. Without you, they would die, you must believe it, so they will believe it."

Stephanie nodded and pressed her palm against my neck.

The stirring of ice flickered through my veins.

"Or..." It was freezing, yet I felt cold and clammy, like being hot and cold at the same time. "You mark with your mouth... more personal, no drawing of blood, think of it as a love bite. It's more personal because Angel blood is in every cell of your body, including your saliva, therefore, your blood comes into contact with the human. Regardless of how strong you are—it will work because human blood yearns for it."

"Why?" Her eyes darted back and forth, she was tiring. Good.

I slowly moved my arms, her nails released. "Because humans want power, they were born wanting more, and the minute they experience a fraction of what more feels like—they want it all."

My gut clenched as memories of the last time humans got ahold of immortal blood assaulted me. I'd destroyed them all—well almost all of them.

Demons were allowed to live. But at what cost?

There was no warning, no hesitation on her part.

One minute I was talking.

The next, her mouth was on my neck, her tongue swirling a devastating design across my skin, her breath freezing my veins in the most delicious way.

Visions of us together flashed through my brain. Kissing, making love, holding hands, laughing, and then the vision altered and I was on my knees in front of her.

Her… shaking as blood ran down her hands.

I was still as a statue.

And then she pulled the knife from my chest and tossed it on the ground, her eyes wide with fear as Darkness swirled around her like a smoke, invading her nostrils.

Sariel watched with sadness as I clutched my chest, but I wasn't recovering. I was not healing.

A tear slid down his cheek as Darkness consumed me.

I fought.

I lost.

And light flashed.

Stephanie jolted back from me, her eyes filled with horror. "What just happened?"

My heart splintered in two. Rage consumed me. "You will betray me."

"What? NO! I was trying to show you—"

"You were trying to impose your will…" I stood on

shaky legs. "Instead, you showed me my future."

Stephanie covered her mouth with her hands.

"I think we're done for the evening." Numb, I walked over to the light switch and flicked it off. "After all, Ethan will be expecting us."

"Cassius, I had no I idea. Futures can change, can't they?"

"I'm tired." I ignored her question. "And so are you."

Cassius

Greece 79 AD

WHAT DO WE DO with them?" I stared at the children completely dumbfounded, I possibly hadn't thought that through. They needed parents. They needed something.

"Well, we can't eat them," Mason grumbled crossing his arms. He'd been hungry for two days, but tough shit because we'd been at the docks for the past forty-eight hours to make sure nobody escaped. We couldn't take the chance that any of the infected humans made their way over land or sea—to the general population.

The screams of the dead caused my head to ache. It couldn't be avoided. Their souls were upset.

They had a reason to be upset.

It wasn't their time.

But it couldn't be avoided. I always dealt with a heavy hand. Not that I took it lightly. Humans needed to know there was a reason to fear the immortals.

To double cross us was to invite death.

"The princess." Eva sighed. "The Demon came for her when you started burning the city."

"And what did Timber have to say for himself?" I kept

my eyes focused on the horizon as smoke filled the air.

"He screamed at me, though he was able to take her as far as the door, Mason took care of the rest."

"You killed him?" My eyebrows shot up. He was a powerful Demon, just as old as us, he'd been alive since the fall of man.

"He ran." Mason sighed. "I got two bites in before he disappeared."

"Damn." The horizon wasn't changing. There were no boats. Only blackness.

"So..." Eva's scent was altogether too intoxicating. I moved away from her so I could think. "What are we going to do with the children?"

"Sariel can never know." I breathed out an irritated sigh and glanced at Eva out of the corner of my eye. "Understood?"

Blood must always be spilled. And once judgment was passed, mercy did not exist.

Because of my weakness for a woman I could never have—I allowed it.

Eva's green eyes blazed as she gave me a firm nod. A Vampire's word meant everything. I knew she would take it with her for eternity.

"And I imagine the children will do what children do..." One last look at the horizon, and I snapped my attention back to Mason and Eva. "It shouldn't be too hard to find them homes, but Eva?"

She was already hugging one of the boys who'd started to cry for his mother. "Yes?"

"They aren't your children." I said it slowly. "The minute they have homes, you are never to see them again. Children notice more than adults do, it would take them mere days to figure out something was different about you. And

I'm not sure how Sariel wants to proceed. I imagine we are going to need to be more careful regarding to whom we reveal our true selves."

"All right." Her eyes went back to their natural brown color as she started singing to the little boy.

My chest felt like someone had cracked it open, seeing a *small boy in her arms, that's what it would look like.*

If she were mine.

But that existence wasn't for me.

It would never be a part of my future.

CHAPTER 15

Stephanie

THE FRONT DOOR SLAMMED so hard I was afraid it was going to crack right down the middle. Cassius rushed past Ethan like I was chasing him with a gun, and he actually pushed Mason out of the way to reach the upstairs bedrooms.

Another door slammed.

I winced.

"Trouble in paradise?" Alex joked as he waltzed lazily out of the kitchen. His smirk was undeniably irritating. If he wasn't family I'd probably attack him or at least freeze his ass for being such a pain in mine.

"No," I lied. "He's human. They get grumpy when they don't sleep."

"Uh-huh." Ethan nodded. "You sure that's what you want to go with? He's tired?"

Genesis walked into the hallway and stifled a yawn. "Who's slamming doors?"

"Cassius," Alex said helpfully. "I'm just going to come out and say it, he was uncontrollable when he was actually able to control his emotions and could choose not to feel. Now that he's human? He's a danger not only to himself, but the rest of us."

"How cute." Mason chuckled. "The Siren's afraid." He winked. "Don't worry, the dog will protect you."

Alex flipped him off. "When has a Siren ever needed protection?"

I held up my hands. "Guys, like I said, he's fine, just tired. We were at his house and—"

"Whoa!" Mason froze in place, gaping at me. Then he shook his head as if coming to his senses. "Back up. He has a house?"

I swallowed. "Of course! Where else would he hang out?"

"Funerals, prisons, Antarctica." Alex sighed and examined his fingernails, "Take your pick."

"It was nice," I said defensively.

All movement in the hallway stopped.

Ethan was the first to speak. "Did you… hurt him?"

"Oh, good grief." I pressed my fingers against my temples. "No, I didn't hurt him, everything's fine. I'm fine, Cassius is fine, the whole world is fine."

"Fine." Alex grinned.

My temper surged as I thought of freezing one of his fingers off.

"Ouch!" Alex stumbled back against the wall then held up his hand. "What the hell was that? It felt like someone was sawing off my finger!"

I shrugged.

His eyes narrowed. "He's been teaching you tricks, damn him."

"Maybe." I pushed past him. "Maybe not."

"Stephanie," Ethan called out. "Wait."

I paused in the doorway. "What?"

There they went again with the shifty eyes and uncertain posture.

I growled. "Just tell me."

"The numbers don't match."

"What numbers?"

"Demon." Ethan shoved his hands in his pockets. "According to our reports from last month they've added another sixty to their ranks."

"Sixty!" I blurted. "But that's insane! They have to keep their numbers under three hundred! If they added sixty—"

Ethan held up his hand. "It makes no sense. I know. They're claiming that they've been the victims of a Vampire attack leaving them with no choice but to… create."

My blood chilled. "That's illegal not to mention stupid, they can't just create more of themselves. Not without the help of Angel blood."

I hadn't been alive back when Pompeii was destroyed but I knew the toll it took on all of them to this day. Ethan had said Cassius refused to talk to anyone for weeks. I knew there was more to the story. One of Cassius's closest friends had been killed soon after the city was destroyed, but nobody talked about it.

Immortal blood should never be in the hands of the Demons. Because to create a Demon—you had to give up your soul. And most souls didn't go willingly.

"Right." Ethan sighed. "But with this whole Cassius scenario we can't really send him in there to settle things down."

Guilt crept over Ethan's face. Cassius truly was the only one who could control the Demons, and if they went against him, he simply destroyed them with a snap of his fingers.

"Crap," I mumbled searching Ethan's eyes. "You

want to send me."

"But you aren't ready." Genesis said softly.

At least *she* was on my side.

"We discussed this." Mason crossed his arms. "I can take care of it."

"Like hell," Alex spat. "If any of us go we're just putting ourselves in a situation that we may not be able to get out of without Cassius's help."

I licked my lips. "Maybe I can talk to him..."

"Oh?" Alex's eyebrows shot up. "And how's that been going for you?"

Another door slammed upstairs. What the heck was he doing? Just opening and slamming doors because he could?

"Stephanie," Ethan reached for my hands. "We need you... and for some reason he still won't explain, Cassius needs you too."

I hung my head.

Shame filled me to the core.

I was going to kill him.

That was the future I had seen.

I just didn't understand it, no way was I naïve enough to believe that it was the only future ahead of us. Futures changed, just like the wind. I refused to concentrate on one so fleeting and meaningless. I loved Cassius, I would never hurt him—ever.

It would take ultimate betrayal.

And even then, I wouldn't be able to follow through with it.

Besides, love or not, he was my King.

"I'll try harder." I bit down on my lip, nearly drawing blood. "I'll have him teach me, and I'll try to be less argumentative."

Alex snorted.

I glared in his direction, and he held up his hands.

"I can do it." I took another deep breath. "This is my job, right? All of us have jobs on the council, mine's just shifted a bit."

"Right." Ethan's eyes narrowed. "I'll send a few of my men with you, just in case."

"And by men he means starving Vampire soldiers who would love—and I do mean love—to get a good meal in." Mason gave Ethan a fist bump and walked out of the room. Alex and Genesis followed.

Ethan didn't budge. His green eyes flared to life. Oh great, I'd somehow pissed him off. How, I wasn't sure.

He stalked toward me, picked me up off the floor and slammed my body against the wall as his fangs slowly slid out from his lips. "Tell me I can trust you."

In all the years I'd known Ethan, he'd never been violent toward me.

Ever.

I knew it was his love for Genesis that made him paranoid, but it stung that he thought so little of me.

"I swear." My voice trembled. "I would never betray any of you."

"Or Cassius." Ethan's grip tightened on my neck as he squeezed. Somewhere in the back of my mind I knew I could fight back—potentially kill him or hurt him, but I had no control over what I could and couldn't do. They were right, I needed Cassius. We all did.

"Never." I gasped.

Ethan released my body abruptly. I crumpled to the ground and rubbed my neck, I was going to have marks from his fingers.

"Betray us again—" Ethan shrugged, his fangs digging into his lower lip. "And I'll be forced to take you to Sariel."

My body chilled at the thought. "Ethan, you can trust me."

He nodded, his incisors retracted, and a friendly smile flashed across his face. "Good talk. Sleep tight."

I rolled my eyes and leaned my head back against the wall. "Damn Vamps."

"Heard that," he yelled from the other room.

I glanced down the hall and at the stairway. I could do this. I just needed Cassius's help.

The last thing we needed was the Demons gaining a foothold. The peace between immortals was only kept if each of the groups stayed within their boundaries, and if they kept to the council rules.

If you wanted to procreate, you needed an approved human from the list, just like Genesis had been brought to us. She'd brought balance back to a world full of chaos, meaning we were already going to be opening up the calling again.

Where we'd call numbers of humans who were, in our opinion, superior to others, and allowing them into our world.

An immortal needed a human in order to create more immortals, possibly the reason that we kept our numbers low was because for so long the humans had died at our hands. But now… now, things were working again.

Thanks to Genesis and Ethan's love fest.

I rubbed my neck again. If the Demons were already picking off humans we had a much bigger problem than Cassius trying to teach me millennia of self-control.

We'd be faced with war.

And possible annihilation.

The Archangels only let us exist if Cassius ruled with an iron fist, and Cassius was at this moment throwing a temper tantrum upstairs and his fists were anything but iron.

The last time Cassius had shown mercy—immortals had died.

I exhaled and rose to my feet. At least he only had twenty-eight more days—and we'd have good ol' grumpy Cassius back.

I'd miss the human one—he at least smiled—and in rare times, blushed.

Cassius

Greece 79 AD

"Eva!" I hissed out her name, she reeked of human. "Where have you been?"

"Out."

"Do not lie to me." I'd never been so angry before in my existence. "I trust you will tell the truth so I'll give you another chance. Where have you been?"

Her shoulders slumped. "I can't stay away!" She shook her head. "I know I'm supposed to wait for a mate, and I will, Cassius, you know I'm patient. I just, the children are so innocent, so different from us. The way their minds work…" Her smile was contagious. "Just this morning, John said an entire sentence and was able to spell his name and—"

"John?" I repeated. "You named them?"

"They had names!" she argued.

"If you want a pet. I'll buy you one." I stalked toward her as the air between us filled with an icy haze. "But you are NOT to visit the children anymore. If Sariel discovers my treachery, it will be my head!"

"He won't!" Eva argued. "I promise, just—at least let me say goodbye."

"No." Her entire face fell. "You've spent enough time there. Write a letter, but you are not to visit them again." Cursing, I pressed a fingertip against the inside of her wrist. "Already you smell of human, when was the last time you fed?"

She frowned. "I don't know, a few days…"

"So, not only have you been with humans you haven't been taking care of yourself? What if Timber returns, hmm? What if he tries to fight you? And because of your inability to follow the rules, he kills you?"

Eva hung her head. "I'm sorry, Cassius."

"Stop being sorry and simply be better, Eva."

"All right. I will Cassius. I swear it."

CHAPTER 17

Cassius

My body ached—what the hell had I done? I flexed my muscles and tried stretching my arms above my head, but nothing alleviated the pain. I slammed two doors trying to gain control of my anger at my crippled state. Did humans have to deal with this on a daily basis? Not only was my body failing me, but my emotions were swirling out of control.

I could taste fear on my tongue, it had a hollow, bitter flavor. And my brain wouldn't stop conjuring up images of Stephanie killing me.

Or my own father helping her do it.

I wiped my face with my hands and shuddered out a breath. Something wasn't right. Then again, how would I know? My IQ had dropped since the Angel blood was no longer coursing through my veins.

The only thing I could do was ask Stephanie for some of hers.

But I figured that was the stupidest idea I'd ever conjured up considering I had to win her affection by being human.

I groaned in frustration and lay back against the fluffy mattress, head pounding, I had twenty-eight days left and I was pretty sure I was actually getting worse as time progressed.

"Hey, there." Stephanie walked into the room. I didn't get up. Didn't look at her, just stared at the ceiling above and wondered for the tenth time that evening what the hell I'd been thinking, trying to save us both, trying to love her when I clearly didn't even understand how.

"Hi," I grumbled.

"Wow, someone's happy."

"It hurts." I rose up on my elbows and glared. "This ridiculous body hurts."

"You're human, aches and pains are part of it, I'm afraid." She offered a tentative smile. "You could always take a pain killer."

"Pills." I spat the word out. "I've never needed help!"

"Maybe that's why."

"Huh?"

Stephanie moved toward the bed and sat on the edge. "Maybe that's part of this test. Maybe Sariel did this so you'd learn to rely on others."

The idea had merit even if it was totally off base. "Maybe."

"So," Stephanie tapped her fingers against her thigh. "There's a slight problem with something."

My eyes narrowed. "You look nervous."

"How soon do you think you can get this training thing down with me? I mean, how much can we push the limits before you think I'll be ready to face things on my own?"

Face things? She wanted to do it without me? "I don't understand. What would you possibly have to face?"

"Demons." She swallowed. "Say an extra sixty shiny new ones with pointy horns and uncontrollable appetites."

Every muscle in my achy body tensed. "What the hell? Please tell me that's your idea of a joke."

"Afraid not." Stephanie pushed away from the bed and walked toward the window hugging her body. "According to Ethan, the numbers reported to us don't match. They've been creating."

"That's forbidden!" I yelled, jumping off the bed, ready to march down to their headquarters and light them all on fire. "They know this, they wouldn't dare. Ever since Pompeii the rules have been—"

"I know the rules." Stephanie arched an eyebrow. "They dared all right, they dared at least sixty times without calling a human number, meaning they're picking off randoms wherever they can find them."

My headache flared to life. "I can't do anything—not as a human."

"I can." Stephanie turned to face me. "Teach me what I need to know, and I can do it."

"But—"

"Please." Her blue eyes flashed a brilliant white then dimmed and saddened as she glanced away from me and back out the window. "I have to help. I mean you said you'd help me learn what I am, right? You said you were here to help train me. So, what's the problem?"

The problem? I forced my irritation inward. The damn problem was that if I spent all my days training her—and believe me it would take all day and all night—I wouldn't have time to romance her. To win her over, to prove my love. After tonight I'd already decided to switch tactics. I needed to do better. Dedicate my every waking moment to winning her the way she deserved.

How the hell was I supposed to do that while training her? I'd be helping her access the darkest parts of her soul. I'd be hurting her, she'd be hurting me. It was a nightmare.

"Sure." My humanity won out, blurting the answer before my brain could catch up. "Sure I can do that. But I refuse to let you go into any of their compounds by yourself. You take either Ethan or Mason with you."

"Not Alex?" she teased.

I rolled my eyes. "Sirens are all about love, not war. You know this."

She nodded. "I know it firsthand."

I had a hard time focusing on the words coming out of her mouth, especially when her eyes were so bright, so inviting. I looked away. "You'll always have that part of you, Stephanie."

"The Siren part?"

I smirked. "Don't all women?"

"Funny."

"I mean it." I frowned as a piece of her hair fell across her face, shielding those gorgeous eyes I was so obsessed with. Without thinking, I brushed her hair back with my fingertips, her mouth opened with a little gasp. "It was easy, casting a Siren's glamour, because you were so beautiful it wouldn't take much convincing for other immortals to buy into it."

Was it so wrong? To hide her away for hundreds of years? To keep the truth of her heritage hidden from her, until now? At the time I was protecting her.

Thinking Sariel would kill her. Dark Ones were still an abomination, regardless of our parentage.

She gulped and looked down, her chest rose and fell, though she didn't need oxygen, she was sucking it in like she was about to pass out.

"I'm sorry," I mumbled. "For suppressing your powers. I did it—" The words hung up in my throat. *Out of love. Out of devotion. Out of fear.* "I did it to protect you."

She glanced up. "I know, Cassius. I'm not upset, not anymore. I just wish..."

"What?" I stepped closer, our bodies nearly touched. "What do you wish?"

"Why did you always walk away from me?"

I licked my lips and leaned in until our mouths almost touched. "Walking away—when all I wanted to do was walk toward you—had to be the hardest thing I've ever done. But everything I did—every decision made—was in order for you to flourish, to survive, to become something great."

She let out a little laugh. "Wow, I must be such a disappointment then. I can't control any of my emotions, and I'm one hissy fit away from freezing your ass or killing people I love by simply willing it."

"You won't," I vowed. "I mean you won't kill your family. And you are the furthest thing from a disappointment."

She shrugged.

"Look at me."

Slowly, Stephanie lifted her head, her eyes filled with shame.

"You're perfect," I whispered reverently. "And I wouldn't want you any other way."

"So you want me now?" she asked with an intriguing lilt in her voice. A smile gently curved her lips. I could tell she said it in a lighthearted way, but it didn't matter. I knew that. My heart skipped a beat anyway.

"More than you'll ever know."

My answer surprised her. She took a step back, her eyebrows knit together like she was trying to figure out my answer.

Twenty-eight days. My mind reminded me. With a flourish I jerked her body against mine and kissed her.

She melted against my body.

And my body—loved it. Drank her in like she was my salvation. My only reason for existing. I moaned, unable to control the sounds coming from my mouth, the physical reaction from my body as she deepened the kiss, as I tasted every inch of her mouth.

"Ahem," someone said from the door.

Stephanie jerked away from me.

Was she ashamed? Or embarrassed?

Irritated, I barked out, "What?"

"Attack." Ethan moved into the room, followed by Mason. "At Belltown. We need to go investigate. It looks like a few Demons got into it with a few Vampires, though nobody's talking."

Stephanie placed her hand on my chest. "We go, he goes."

"Agreed," Ethan snapped. "We'll need his expertise, though if I tell you both to run, you run, got it?"

I rolled my eyes.

"Don't." Ethan hissed in my direction his eyes going green with fury. "You're both important, the last thing we need is one of you dying. A dead council member? A dead king? It would start an all-out war."

"We may already be there." My skin tingled with awareness, something wasn't right. I just didn't know what, and I wasn't sure how I could help other than appear to look in control.

Ethan cleared his throat and pointed at my body. "You'll need a glamour spell to hide your pasty human skin."

"My skin isn't pasty!" I said defensively while Stephanie placed a hand against my chest.

"I can do it." Mason stepped forward an excited grin on his face.

"Like hell you will!" I yelled. "The last time you performed a glamour, you turned Alex into a woman!"

"On purpose." Mason sniffled.

I rolled my eyes. "You were supposed to make him appear feminine, big difference."

"I'll do it." Ethan crossed the room at lightning speed then slammed me into the wall, his incisors nicked the inside of my right wrist. Eyes green, he murmured. "What I see others see. What I know. Others know." He reached behind him. "Stephanie, come here."

I doubted Stephanie had ever seen a glamour performed as it was usually male immortals who did it—and the only ones capable were Mason, myself, and Ethan—compliments of our age and the hierarchy of the council.

Eva had been the only woman capable of it.

But she was gone. Long gone.

Once Stephanie reached my side, Ethan leaned over and bit her finger then squeezed it over my wrist. Three drops of blue blood splashed into my cut and healed it immediately. The veins in my wrists turned an Angel blue as cold spread throughout my body.

It was a familiar feeling. One I missed.

I closed my eyes and leaned my head back against the wall as ice over took my entire body. I convulsed, once, twice, and then opened my eyes.

The room was brighter, the air sweeter. I was still human, but the Angel blood fused with my cells enough to make me see better, my sense of smell more acute. It also took away the aches and pains in my body.

"Well done, Ethan." Mason clapped twice. "He looks possessed again."

I glanced at my reflection in the mirror across the room. My eyes were white, my skin glowing, even my hair was shinier. Everything about me looked the same.

But I was different.

And I wondered in that moment, if this was the beginning of the end. If I would ever be a Dark One again, or if I'd die trying to give Stephanie back the precious gift she should have never given me in the first place.

Maybe she would be my downfall after all.

The words echoed in my head.

"Let her live and she will hurt you," Sariel warned.

"She's innocent!" I screamed. "She's done nothing wrong."

Sariel smiled sadly. "But she will. Believe me. She will. Remember what your love did to you last time."

"Time's wasting." Mason's eyes turned black. "We need to hunt."

Stephanie reached for my hand. I squeezed it once, intent on letting it go, but decided to hold it a bit longer, because she felt good and because I knew I needed to start appreciating every minute I had with her.

Because something told me—they would add up—

and my time wouldn't just be over—but nonexistent.

Cassius

Greece 79 AD

I followed her scent. I would stop her at all costs if things got out of hand. She'd promised.

She'd lied.

Again.

I wanted to turn a blind eye, mainly because whenever Eva was near, the world didn't feel as dark or desperate.

The way she laughed and smiled through her immortal life was a thing of beauty, and I hated being the one responsible for dampening that light.

"Shh, I'll return one day." She whispered to the little child. His face was wet with tears. "Just be good for your mama, alright?"

He wrapped his tiny arms around her neck then kissed her cheek. "I love you."

The air filled with sadness, drenched with such a hollow emptiness that I sucked in a breath.

Vampires weren't supposed to be so emotional.

Leave it to a child to bring out the worst of human weaknesses in all of us. God forbid I ever felt such weakness.

"I love you too, John."

Eva set the boy on his feet. He reached up and captured one of her dark curls between his fingers dropped it, and then turned on his heel and walked off.

"He's precious," she said aloud, already sensing my presence. "It was his birthday, I couldn't allow him to think I didn't care anymore."

I crossed my arms. "Eva, there will always be something. A birthday, a holiday… You must leave him for good."

"I want children." Eva hung her head as I approached her from behind. "I've always wanted children."

I could taste her desperation in the air as tension swirled between us. I'd known for a while Eva felt strongly for me, the way I felt for her.

But a union between a Dark One and a Vampire would do nothing but present us with hurt feelings when a bond failed to take place. We could not mate with one another.

And children were an impossibility.

"I can't give you that," I whispered, setting my hand on her shoulders. She gripped my fingertips. I shuddered from her warm touch.

Eva turned, her eyes green and beautiful as they gazed up into my cold depths. "We could adopt."

I smiled at that. "Humans adopt. And you and I… will never be."

"Immortality." She wrapped her arms around my neck. I never allowed such liberties. "Not for the faint of heart, hmm Cassius?"

"No." The temptation to kiss her was too strong to deny any longer, my mouth descended, fusing with hers, creating a hum of energy between us as her blood heated out of control, my touch cooled her as fangs descended past her top lips.

Our tongues twisted in a fight for dominance as I lifted

her into my arms. The last thing we needed was to be seen in a forbidden embrace, not only was she a council member, but she was a Vampire, not mine.

She would end up with a snotty-nosed human.

One who would get her pregnant.

One who would love her like I never could.

Slowly, I pulled away from her, my hands pressing against her wrists as I lowered her arms to her sides.

"One day..." Her voice was filled with sadness. "...I'll be mated to someone and you'll forget all about me."

"I highly doubt I'll ever forget your taste, Eva."

The air charged with a thick flowery scent. Eva's eyes widened just as a voice said from behind me. "What have you done?"

Slowly, I turned.

Sariel's eyes were white, his hair a blazing rainbow of blue and black streaks. His feathers protruded then shuddered as if they tasted the wrongness in the air. "Survivors?"

He shoved past me and Eva and pressed his fingertips against the door of the house.

"Two survivors. How many more? And why aren't they destroyed?"

I couldn't lie.

It wasn't in my makeup as a Dark One to want to lie to my creator—to my father.

"I saved them," I admitted while I grabbed Eva and shoved her behind me. "I saved twelve."

"Twelve!" Sariel roared as the ground shook beneath our feet. "You were to destroy them all! Every. Last. One."

"I did not."

Sariel's wings turned purple, the color of angelic royalty. He was about to pass judgment. "Then, you will die. Blood must always be spilled, you know this."

I nodded, unable to conjure up any guilt over doing something that gave Eva happiness no matter how temporary.

I took a step forward.

"No!" Eva shouted. "It was me!"

"Eva!" I hissed out her name and shoved her body into the nearest wall, she stumbled back and glared. "Stay out of this."

"You will not DIE because of me!" Her eyes glowed green as her fangs elongated past her bottom lip. Her gaze snapped to Sariel. "If you want a life. Take mine. I asked Cassius to save them. It is I who is at fault."

"Very well." Sariel nodded.

"You cannot be serious!" I charged Sariel fists clenched. "She's a council member! She's been around for centuries! You cannot simply eliminate her for one bad choice!"

"Oh?" Sariel's head tilted to the side as he pulled a purple feather from his wings and held it out in front of him, the edge was black. The color of the Angel of Death. He meant to truly kill her, to make her no more. "We live by the rules, we die by the rules, Cassius. She broke the rules. She dies."

"But—"

Head held high, Eva pushed past me and got down on her knees, her head bowed toward Sariel.

"Sariel, think about this." I knew reasoning with him would do nothing, but I couldn't stop myself, this was Eva, my Eva. I'd had her by my side since I was created. She was the reason the darkness wasn't so dark—the reason I was always pulled back into the light. Without her, what was I?

"And there it is..." Sariel nodded. "She makes you weak. She makes you second guess your decisions. Not that it matters, one of you must die for this serious lapse in judgment, and Eva is right. The fault lies with her, and I need you to

lead the immortals. Therefore…" He held out the feather to me. "Life is taken."

"Cassius." Eva whispered, tears filling her eyes. "I love you."

Sariel sucked in a breath.

Now he knew.

I'd failed him twice.

Because I loved her back.

"Eva, I will always love you," I whispered, taking the feather from Sariel and holding it over her head.

Sariel's anger was tangible. "Cassius, you are their king. She pays for your sin… kill her."

"I can't." My body was empty so empty.

Eva locked eyes with me. "Cassius, promise me you'll check in on John, promise!"

At death's grasp and still she was worried for the boy.

I didn't understand that type of love—so maybe I'd never really loved her after all. Had I?

"I promise." My voice shook as I pressed the tip of the feather to the base of her neck. It slid in through her skin, she slumped against my arms as immortality left her body.

Right before my very eyes, my dear friend, my love, aged. She aged so horribly, her tight skin became wrinkled and paper-thin. It lost all the glow of youth, her hair turned ten different shades of gray before finally falling out of her head, the bones in her body were brittle, the muscle detached from the correct positions, and as she took her last breath, I saw what it would be like to be human, to love a human and watch them die.

The pain was unimaginable.

Her frail hand reached up and caressed my face with the lightest of touches. "Cassius… you will always be more light than dark."

She died.

In my arms.

"For her sacrifice," Sariel whispered. "The twelve children will live."

I didn't see Sariel again for five hundred years.

Cassius

Demons didn't have the decency to hide in the shadows of rundown buildings and dark alleyways.

They thrived around the constant buzz of mortals.

It was impossible to survive as a Demon without others. And the easiest way to kill them off was to get them alone. They were interconnected like a complicated mass of webs. Where there was one Demon, there were always several others. It was an odd pack-like mentality that spread throughout every race of immortals.

All but Dark Ones.

Destined to walk the earth alone, seeking the light, cursed to the shadows. I shivered as we turned onto the street that would take us to Blu, a bar in downtown Seattle that doubled as a Demon Den.

It was the biggest web of all. Humans loved the dark atmosphere and promise of cheap drinks, having no clue that the minute they crossed the threshold they were taking their lives into their own hands. As the leader of the immortals, I kept the peace, but that also meant that I at times had needed to rule in favor of the Demons. Human lives were precious to us because we needed them to continue to thrive, but that didn't mean accidents never happened.

Stephanie stopped the SUV in front of the bar.

Marcus, a Demon I'd had the great displeasure of meeting upon a dozen occasions stood on the sidewalk, rain dripping down his blond head onto his chiseled jaw as he nodded discreetly toward our SUV and shoved his hands in his pockets.

At six-foot-four, people gave him a wide berth as they stepped around his bulky body. Men shied away, and women stared. Not like they could help it. Men were bred to fear the evil. And if Demons were spiders with webs—that made women the perfect fly.

"I'll go." I exhaled a loud breath, the air in front of my face crackled with the sound of ice breaking. I should feel like my old self. Instead, it felt foreign, and terrifying. Not something I wanted to admit to anyone, least of all Stephanie. That what used to feel so natural and right, now caused my human heart to skip a few beats and this ridiculously frail body to sweat as if I was over exerting myself by merely existing.

Stephanie turned to face me, her eyes already going white. "But... this is my job, right?"

"No," I said in a rough voice. "Believe me, if Marcus has called, then Marcus will need to be... disposed of."

"And you don't want me getting my hands dirty?" The temperature dropped in the vehicle.

"Temper, temper." I kept my voice teasing even though my body was screaming *Danger!* as loud as it could. Teaching Stephanie to control herself was going to take more patience than I possessed.

Never thought I'd see the day where I'd teach the

person I loved, how to kill me, and how to kill me well, because that's exactly what I would be doing.

"Just trust me," I barked out. "And let me speak to him first. If he tries to take off my head you have my permission to decapitate him without asking questions first."

"Permission?" Stephanie repeated, her eyes lit up like a flashlight. I quickly got out of the car and slammed the door.

"Stay," I mouthed.

Frost exploded in the inside of the car lining the windows.

Smirking, I turned on my heel and made my way slowly toward Marcus. The human inside was already telling me to run, my body trembling with the awareness that what I was approaching was pure evil, that I needed to run in the other direction.

Save yourself! my mind screamed.

Damn it. I was a Dark One.

I would not run!

My heel turned, as if my body was physically making the choice that mentally I hadn't the capacity to do.

"Marcus." His name slid from my lips like a slow dark curse. "Why don't you start at the beginning?"

"Cassius?" He frowned, his blue eyes narrowing into tiny yellow cat like slits before returning to their regular color. "You look… different."

"I smell different too. Must be new soap." I offered with a dark chuckle. "Now stop staring at me or I'm going to get the wrong idea."

Marcus didn't move, but his nails elongated into small spikes, ready to attack or slit my throat, whichever came first, I supposed. "Something is different."

I could feel the power surging through my veins but knew if I expended too much the glamour would dissipate into thin air, and he truly would take off my head in front of a handful of people.

With as much strength as I could muster, I allowed the angelic blood to float to the surface of my body and blew a harsh amount of cold air across his face, freezing his lips shut.

"There." I nodded. "Much better. Why don't I do the talking? And if you keep staring I will gladly freeze your eyes as well, though a bit of warning, you'll be blind once they melt." I motioned for Stephanie to get out of the SUV just as Mason, Ethan, and Alex pulled up in the second car. "Now, we can do this here, on the street, you can calmly explain what you saw and why you're willing to die for telling us, or we can all go into the bar. Your choice."

Marcus eyed the rest of the council as they walked up behind me, his lips were already starting to melt, with a quick nod he crooked his finger and we followed him into the abandoned bar.

Human bodies were scattered around the floor.

Drained of blood.

The bartender, half Demon half human, snarled in our direction as he stacked bodies to the side of the stage and lit a match.

Like dry firewood they went up in flames, sadly the families would never know what happened to their loved ones.

All could have been prevented if I wasn't a damn human. I would have seen this future.

Prevented it.

It was my own human fear that kept me from teaching Stephanie. She'd already seen one future, and the horror it would expose her to was damn near life ending.

"You froze his lips shut?" Ethan whispered out of the corner of his mouth. "Why have you never done that to Alex?"

"Because Alex has a nice voice," Alex piped up. "Smooth, sexy, just enough husky to get the ladies excited, but not so deep that he sounds like a lumberjack in need of a shave."

"Silence," I barked, elbowing Alex and bruising myself in the process. Must remember how weak I was, before I suffered internal bleeding.

Mason frowned as we neared a back door. "No." He shook his head. "No!"

"Mason?" I sniffed the air but even the Angel power couldn't help me. I tried again, all I picked up was the scent of… sulfur.

Sulfur.

And the high-pitched screams of lives lost, as if the person on the other side of the door was replaying the scene from Pompeii.

"Come." I motioned to the small boy. "We'll protect you."

"Will you be my papa?"

"No," I barked gruffly, Eva elbowed me in the ribs. "But we'll find you one."

"They're afraid," she murmured as the children huddled in the corner of the boat. "They think we mean them harm."

I sighed as the scent of sulfur filled the air and smoke crawled across the ocean toward us. Lifting my hand, I created a shield of water as the boat led us to safety. The little kids gasped in awe as droplets turned to ice crystals decorating the inside of the darkness with pure light, pure winter.

Giggling, one of them stood and started dancing in circles as the ice crystals formed under the dome, shimmering in the air, twinkling and then falling to the floor.

Soon, more children stood.

And Eva… began to sing. She'd always had the most beautiful clear voice, most Vampires did, unlike Sirens who could lull you into a slave-like state, but beautiful still, almost as much so.

"Thank you," Eva whispered, her hand reaching out to touch mine just as Mason turned and growled in our direction.

"We should not give them hope," he barked.

The Wolf was right. But I could not bring myself to tear the smiles from their faces. Nor to release Eva's warm hand.

Though I should.

I should have done all those things.

I fell to my knees as a whoosh of air left me.

"Cassius?" Stephanie was at my side. "Are you okay?"

Marcus turned. "A problem? It's just beyond this door."

"Death is beyond that door," I whispered, my voice shaking the foundation of the bar. I was expending energy fast. I needed more blood, I needed it immediately. Already Marcus looked suspicious, his hand pausing on the large metal black door, his fingernails elongating.

Ethan smoothly pushed Alex and Mason toward Marcus while he shielded me and Stephanie with his body, biting swiftly into Stephanie's wrist and swiping the blood across my mouth.

It was over in seconds.

And as if someone had just pumped my body full of adrenaline, so much power surged through me that I nearly blacked out.

Because it was enough to see.

It was enough to see with immortal eyes.

Something, I never wanted to see again.

"My, God." I shuddered pushing past the group and nearly impaling Marcus against the doorknob in an effort to break down the door. "What have you done?"

"Not me." Marcus's lips turned up in a smile. "This… is all on you, my King."

"Arrogant bastard." I shoved him aside and pulled open the door. .

"John?" I whispered.

John's eyes widened and then narrowed as he whispered in a low voice. "You."

"John." I shook my head, unable to process how he was standing in front of me. Had he been given immortality? Was this Sariel's doing? How was he alive? He should have died in Greece.

"You killed her!" John screamed. "And you will die for it. You will all die."

Stephanie stood in front of me just as John charged, with a flick of her wrist she slammed him against the wall and then covered her mouth as if shocked that she was able to do it in the first place.

John was knocked unconscious.

"Someone gave him immortality…" Marcus folded his arms as if he didn't have a care in the world for the angry Demon. "And someone… is helping him create more Demon… almost as if…" Marcus's grin was slow, as his teeth protruded into long yellow fangs. "…

as if history is repeating itself, hmm Cassius?"

Mason howled.

For it had been Mason who had checked in on the children when it was too painful for me.

And it had been Mason, who had lost track of them.

A Wolf lost track of their scent.

A year after we saved them.

A year after her death.

It was as if they no longer existed.

"We'll take him back," I said.

"We'll what?" Ethan repeated. "You're kidding right? No chance in hell am I putting a Demon in my guest room!"

"Don't be silly." Alex flicked his hand. "We'll put him in the dungeon. Been years since we've had a plaything in chains. Think of the Instagram posts we could have!"

Mason went over to John and leaned over his body. "It is him, it is his scent. Do we know who did this to him?"

Marcus sighed. "Your guess is as good as mine, but he knows how to create. And has been creating for the past three weeks. We've killed off the ones that were… created wrong."

"And when you say created… wrong?" Stephanie asked.

Marcus swallowed. "Immortality does not always take."

Stephanie shared a look with me, but I shook my head, it was for another time. After all, it was no fairy tale, the deformities that attacked a human body when it rejected immortality.

"Thank you." Offering thanks to the Demon was

the exact opposite of what I wanted to do, but he had helped us. "What is it you hope to gain from helping the council?"

Marcus licked his lips. "There is a human girl. She was created, she's… I feel for her. I do not wish to destroy her, nor do I wish for her death. If you could…" Marcus eyes were pleading. Oh hell, I knew what he was going to ask.

"Everyone leave but Stephanie," I whispered.

Ethan growled, "Like hell, Cassius."

"Am I not your king? Have I not spoken?" The air swirled around us in a shade of white hot icicles.

Hissing, Ethan took a step back. He could by all rights kick my ass and leave me for dead, but in front of Marcus he had to pretend that I held all the power. "Try not to die, *King*."

Alex chuckled while Mason shot a worried glance in my direction. A bunch of women! I was fine!

I didn't want to use Stephanie in that way, it would be grueling to try to protect my thoughts while she invaded me.

With both hands I clapped once and opened my palms together as moisture gathered between my fingers. Closing my eyes, I concentrated on sucking the moisture and then forced it around Marcus's head, first blinding him, and then causing him to be in an essential bubble so he could not hear, see, taste, feel, smell, he simply ceased to exist.

For ten minutes.

It took every ounce of power I had.

Leaning against Stephanie, I could barely lift my head as I whispered in her ear. "He wants his soul back."

Stephanie clung to my body, "Cassius, we don't do that. We're not the freaking Grim Reaper!"

"Who?" I repeated. "Is a Grim a type of Angel?"

"Never mind." She rolled her eyes. "And why did you do that? You just used all of the Angel blood you had!"

"Had to," I gasped. "You need to make him think we gave him his soul back... and you need to put a mark of protection over him."

"A what and a what?" Stephanie said, teeth clenched. "Cassius, I can barely get angry without killing things! You want me to concentrate hard enough to mark him and make him believe something took place that didn't actually take place?"

"To be fair..." Damn it, she smelled good, my hands just naturally went to her long dark hair, tangled in it, tugged. "I'll be doing it, but we'll be joined in body and soul, therefore you'll be watching."

"So..." Her breathing accelerated. "You'll be possessing me?"

"No." I chuckled. "You'll be possessing me, more like joining."

"How do we... um..." She shook her head. "Stop distracting me!" Taking a step back, so I stumbled toward her, she asked, "How do we join?"

"I need your hand, we need to be touching. We have around six minutes left. Better make it fast." I was enjoying her hesitation more than I thought I would. "Open your palm."

Stephanie chewed her bottom lip and stepped closer to me. Her right hand trembled violently as she held it out, palm up. "Now what?"

I pressed my palm flat against hers, my fingers

gripping into her wrist as I pulled her flush against me, our mouths fused in a frenzied kiss as light exploded between us.

Already I could sense her awe at the brilliant light, of the drunken power that surrounded us. But her wonder would be short—lived because where light existed, darkness always followed. It was the gamble we made, why we were called Dark Ones. We could not use one half of ourselves without leaving ourselves exposed to the other.

The light was swallowed up by a swirl of icy black as it wrapped around both of our arms linking them together.

Stephanie gasped as our minds linked.

It was dangerous.

As a human, I was Pandora without a box. With everything I had, I focused our attention on Marcus. Away from me, away from my thoughts, my desires, away from her.

Watch. I whispered into her head.

Her eyes widened.

Marcus. You have been restored. I mouthed the words.

Marcus's body relaxed as I lifted my free hand, the one not linked. Palm open the black from Marcus's body slowly twirled away from him like I was spinning wool, it wrapped around my free hand, leaving him bathed in light. He convulsed as his body fought to take demonic form.

Light and dark would always fight for dominance.

But light. Light was better at winning.

Finally, a cry broke free from his lips as the water evaporated around him, his blue eyes opened.

"He is free?" Stephanie's voice sounded in my head.

"He is has been given a second chance to get his soul back, since Marcus's was taken from him by another greedy Demon... it seems that he has been given a trial. If he proves faithful, he will be restored. There are always second chances."

"But what if he's a horrible human? What if"—

"That is not our decision to make. As Dark Ones, we do not pass judgment. We simply create the opportunity for judgment to be passed. Sariel will watch him. It is out of our hands now."

Marcus crumpled to the ground.

John was still out.

"I can't handle your power much longer."

Stephanie nodded.

"I will collapse from exhaustion after this. Have Ethan and Mason carry me to the car. Our link is still very active. Wait until the warmth is gone."

"Warmth?" Stephanie repeated and then laughed. *"You're right. I feel... so warm! Why do I feel warm"?*

"Linked. Dark Ones linked creates a firestorm of darkness."

"Why don't we do this all the time?"

"Because two Dark Ones cannot co-exist in this state very long without one killing the other. And because once we use the light—our darkness also links—it could easily overtake us both if we stay this way."

She recoiled.

"Thought you'd feel that way. Thank you for allowing me use of your powers."

I pulled my hand away and succumbed to the darkness that I knew my human body would not be able to process or handle.

And as my eyes closed, all I saw was black.

CHAPTER 20

Stephanie

CASSIUS HAD BEEN OUT for two hours. Ethan and Mason were hardly gentle with his human body as they carried him up the stairs, banging his head against the wall at least twice before finally managing to get him into my bed.

He seemed so foreign there.

So beautiful.

Dark and light mixed in one. Swirls of blue spread throughout his wrist and pushed against his fingertips as little icicles attached themselves to my bedspread. The Angel blood was leaving him.

I kind of hated it.

As a Dark One, I knew what to expect from him, complete indifference or on rare occasions pity, where he'd let me spend time in his arms for a brief second, only to push me away hours later in shame.

I swallowed my pride and moved to stand by the bed. He'd said not to touch him… but the temptation was too strong.

Ethan, Mason, and Alex were too busy going all medieval on John's ass, stuffing him in a dungeon I didn't even know existed until Alex skipped toward the kitchen pantry, pressed a button and gleefully clapped his hands chanting. "Dungeon, Dungeon, Dungeon."

Clearly my brother needed a hobby if this was the highlight of his week, which he repeated over and over again while he carried the body downstairs, and then again as he attached the metal chains.

I'd nearly puked when I saw a rat.

Working out of fear, I froze it and then nearly burst into tears while Mason groaned out, "We used to eat those in the old days."

"It amazes me you even remember eating meat," Alex pointed out. "Don't pinecones give you stomach troubles? How does one even process that?"

"Magic," Mason barked. "I'm magic."

"I had a girl tell me that once in bed..." Alex smirked off into the distance as if recalling the memory. "Rocked her world twice for the compliment then sadly had to wipe her memory so she wouldn't commit suicide after discovering no man would ever compare."

"As much as I love hearing you bicker like women," Ethan said, his dark hair falling around his chin, "I'd really love to get back to my wife. Mason, secure the last chain, and Alex find a mirror."

Alex flipped him off.

While I stared in horror. Is that really what our lives have come to? Chaining someone to a wall?

"You're young." Ethan was at my side instantly, his grip on my wrist was painful, but I think he meant it to be, to gain my attention. "You don't know how we used to do things because you never had to see the ugly... we've lived through so many wars, so much death, plague, destruction. Believe me when I say, this is Disneyland."

Alex moaned. "I would give at least six sexual favors for a turkey leg right now. After all those Disney movies Genesis made us watch I looked it up online." His blues eyes widened. "Tons of turkey legs."

"Just a guess." Mason shoved past Alex and adjusted the metal casings around John's legs. "But sex for turkey legs is probably frowned upon by King Disney."

"King Lion!" Ethan grumbled. "Disney is no King. He's a man."

"Genesis says so," Mason argued as if it was complete truth. That was just the type of relationship they had, and frankly I was getting a dizzying headache from all their arguing, not to mention I kept hearing screaming.

It was faint.

But it was there.

Gulping, I'd gone back upstairs to take a nap.

Only to find a giant of a man in my bed.

A perfect man.

The perfect blend of good and bad.

His lips twitched as he kicked his legs and then stilled again.

Just one touch. I promised myself before my fingertips grazed his strong jaw.

"Eva!" Cassius's voice was thick with emotion as he held nothing but dust in his hands. Like diamonds, the glittery dust spread in a perfect circle around his body, his head was hung, his shoulders tense.

Sariel was standing behind him, looking just as menacing as ever. Then he disappeared, leaving Cassius alone.

I'd never seen a Dark One cry, didn't know they

were capable of it. Ever since my change I'd had trouble even conjuring up watery eyes. Although I felt sadness, I couldn't express it.

Cassius, was wrapped in a red type of toga, a sword was laid at his side, he slowly pulled the sword from its silver casing and held it out in front of him.

"Don't." Ethan appeared in front of Cassius. "Put the sword down, brother."

"She's gone," Cassius whispered. "I have nothing left."

"You have Alex." Ethan joked. "He's like a two-year-old. He needs guidance, you know how new he is."

Cassius continued to stare at the long sword. "I want to forget the pain."

"You'll go dark if you do, Cassius. You know this. Forgetting emotions isn't human."

"I am no human!" Cassius spat. "I'm an Angel!" He stood to his full height, his body shimmering with iridescent whites and purples as he called upon his Angel blood, pushing the humanity so far away that my eyes hurt to look at him. Snow fell in the spot over his head. "I am to be worshipped!"

"Brother..." Ethan's voice was still calm. "You are fallen."

As if a reminder of what he would never be, wings appeared at Cassius sides, but they were completely black.

Dripping with blood.

As the storm increased what was once bright turned so dark I stumbled backward.

His eyes went black, his teeth elongated into fangs, and his body grew another foot.

"Evil and good always did have a problem co-existing," Ethan said in a bored tone. "Come back, brother.... killing yourself is not the answer, for you will lose your soul and turn into your greatest nightmare, meaning one of us will eventually have to kill you, and I've hunted enough friends, don't make me hunt my family."

Cassius fell to his knees as the diamonds of dust burst into the air. He lifted his hand and caught a few particles and pressed them to his heart. "So I never forget the pain of remembering."

"Pain..." Ethan answered just as Mason appeared, sword raised. "...isn't reserved for mere humans, but for everything in creation. It would not be fair that we never experience it."

"I don't want to feel." Cassius stood, sheathing his sword and facing both men. "I refuse it."

Mason looked uncertain at what to say, but Ethan nodded. "One day, you will regret that choice. And I do hope I'm still alive to see it."

The vision shattered in front of me into a million shards of glass. I gasped as I was transported to last year.

Genesis had just been brought to one of the immortal parties.

I hung on Cassius like a whore.

Ashamed, I looked away.

Minutes passed, maybe an hour.

And I was across the room, talking to a few friends. Cassius stared, his mouth ajar and then flexed like he was both in awe and irritated.

"Happened faster than you would have liked, I'm sure, even though it's been what? A few thousand years?"

"Go to hell," Cassius muttered.

"Interesting choice, however." Mason crossed his burly arms and chuckled. "I wonder what the council would think."

"The council needs to mind their own damn business."

"She is beautiful."

"She's mine!" Cassius roared slamming Mason into the nearest wall.

Mason brushed him off, smirking like he'd just won the lottery. "Is she? I haven't seen your mark."

Cassius recoiled. "I would only mark my true love and even then, we cannot be."

"But if you could?" Mason asked.

Cassius didn't answer. He simply watched me, and when my friends disappeared he held out his hand and whispered, "May I have this dance?"

I shivered remembering the way he'd touched me that night, so different than other nights, like he wanted me as a woman.

Saw me as his equal.

We danced for hours, and when it was time to leave, he tugged me against him and whispered against my mouth, "Come with me."

"Is that allowed?" I teased back.

"I make the rules." He tugged my body against his, he was so big… everywhere, that it was overwhelming to all my senses. Even then I'd been powerless, so powerless.

"Good." He chuckled wickedly. "You can try to fight me… but you'll give in… in the end, they always do."

The thought that he'd been with others pissed me off. I pushed him off and spat. "Don't you have a human to chase?"

"Why chase a human? When I've tasted you?"

"Why taste me when you can have her?" I countered.

His mouth snapped shut.

Fresh pain washed over me as the vision shattered again.

And I was back in my room.

And Cassius—was awake.

"What did I tell you?" He tried to get up, but was still too weak. After three tries he lay back down and cursed. "You cannot simply invade my thoughts while I sleep. It isn't fair." I invaded his sleep? "And before you try again, remember you can only do it once within a REM cycle, and I'm very much awake thanks to your erotic musings."

"Erotic musings?" I repeated, crossing my arms. "I wasn't the one going all Viking or caveman!"

Cassius frowned. "I am neither of those things and I don't appreciate being called a Neanderthal."

"It's a figure of speech! You know, cavemen, who pulled woman by the hair and had sex with them."

Cassius face blanched, and he looked absolutely appalled. "I'll have you know my favorite human was a man who lived in a cave!"

"Of course! Because you're older than dirt!"

"Another untruth!" Cassius fired back. "Dirt has been around for at least a millennium longer than I!"

I groaned. "You're giving me a headache."

"It's the Angel blood, not me." He sniffed the air. "Damn it, I cannot smell anymore, at least not how I could before. You're too new to dream walk. I'd suggest against it, but you're like a child with a new toy."

"Am not."

"Are too!" he argued.

I burst out laughing. "Now who's acting immature?"

He glared. "Still you."

Sighing, I sat down on the bed. "I'm sorry for…" I waved my hand over him. "That."

He looked down. "Oh, a simple chemical reaction to your kiss."

"Huh?" I looked where he was looking and then nearly burst into flames. "Um…."

He was still staring. "Though it's quite large? Is that normal for a human?"

Still blushing, I looked away. "How would I know?"

"You're a woman."

"So?"

"So you've lain with human men."

My eyebrows nearly met the sky. "Excuse me?"

"Siren." Cassius seemed confused. "It was your glamour. Therefore, you practiced seduction, mainly of humans, did you not?"

"Not! Most definitely not!" I yelled. "I never… slept with them!"

"Silly, who sleeps? You *fornicate*."

"Please don't say fornicate. In my bed."

"Would you rather I stand and say it?"

"Why? Are you so ancient that simple manners during conversation escape you?"

"Sorry… You fornicate in bed… please?" He looked even more confused.

Alex's laughter from down the hall didn't help. "Sirens love manners in bed!"

"Shut up!" I yelled slamming the door in his face and glaring back at Cassius. "Look, maybe we should talk about what I saw, and then you can start my training."

Cassius clenched his jaw. "You saw a memory, nothing more."

"But—"

"And you're training…" He heaved himself out of the bed and stood on wobbly feet. "…begins as soon as Mason cooks meat."

I rolled my eyes. "Fine, we feed you again and then lesson time?"

"Yes." Cassius leaned toward me and whispered, "Why do you smell so good?" His eyes dilated as he reached out to touch my skin.

"I'm a Dark One. I think that's part of the attraction, right?"

"Right." He stumbled over his words. "Yes, that's it, of course. We should… eat."

Chapter 21

Cassius

"SLOW DOWN, TIGER." ALEX LAUGHED at my expense, but I was too hungry to care. Why was I always so hungry? As if my stomach was in constant anger at its emptiness?

I chewed then swallowed. "I am not a tiger."

"Sar—"

"—casm," I finished for him. "I'm not an idiot, but name calling is lost on me. I'll slow down when this—" I patted my stomach. "—is full."

"You've had three steaks." Mason spooned more steaming green beans onto my plate. "You're going to put us in the poor house with the way you're putting away food."

"Impossible. Immortals have endless amounts of resources and money."

Alex reached for one of my green beans. "Not with the way you're eating."

I stabbed at him with my fork and growled, "Get your own."

"I don't need food. I just find great satisfaction in trying to steal yours. What are you going to do about it?" His smile deepened. Damn I wanted to punch him.

"Fight me?"

"Poke the bear, and when he wakes up from his hibernation he may just remove your intestines with a fork." I lifted my fork in the air and matched his smile. "And it pleases me that the only time you could ever beat me in a fight would be when I'm this weakened. Sirens aren't known for their muscle."

"No." Alex's lips twitched. "But we are known for our prowess in bed. Try not to be jealous, Dark One."

I snorted. "The last thing I'd be jealous of is the poor humans that stumble into your bed while you promise eternity only to fan your own narcissism."

"My touch saves lives." Alex chuckled. "Or so I've been told."

Mason plopped down between us and snarled as he started slowly, methodically, slicing his meat into tiny pieces.

Pieces fit for a mouse.

Mason had always been more sensitive than the others, so I kept my mouth shut… or tried, that is, until he started lifting the fork to his lips.

Alex's eyes went so wide I thought he was going to explode on the spot.

We both watched. Waited.

But the minute the meat was brought to Mason's lips, he frowned and set the fork back down.

Alex let out a defeated sigh and looked away.

"Mason." I licked my lips and pushed my plate away so I could lean across the large wooden table. "You honor her by trying."

Mason had once been mated. But the curse of the humans had taken his mate's life during the night. He'd woken up to her cold in his arms.

I had seen it coming.

But I was never allowed to alter those types of futures, the ones that dealt with life or death.

That was above even the Archangels.

We were not allowed to play Creator. It was not our place, would never be our place. It was why, saving Genesis a few weeks ago had gone against everything I'd been taught.

Thankfully, Sariel had agreed with our decision as had the Creator, or we would have all been… nothing but dust.

"The scent of meat reminds me of her," Mason finally said, his voice gruff. "She loved steak."

"Most Werewolves love steak," Alex mused while slowly bringing a glass of wine to his lips.

I shook my head at him. He was so callous at times that he was truly lucky he had the ability to seduce women with his looks. It sure as hell wasn't his warm personality.

Alex glared. "Like you should talk."

I'd forgotten he could hear people's thoughts, though usually only when very close and typically only of the female variety.

"Chill." Alex rolled his eyes. "You're a dude. Promise."

"Er, thanks." I scooted my chair back and stood. "It's time to train Stephanie." Yawning, I covered my face with my hands and was half tempted to steal some coffee, so I had energy enough to stay awake.

"You know you could always spike yourself with a bit of vamp blood." Alex shrugged. "Just saying…"

"No." I shuddered. "Never again."

"I wasn't that bad…" Ethan stumbled into the room

and retrieved two bottles of water from the fridge, while memories of drinking from Eva ran rampant through my brain.

Alex's eyes narrowed in on mine. "Yeah, I don't think he was talking about you."

The room fell silent.

I let out an irritated sigh. "Must you muddle through my thoughts, Siren?"

"Must you think so loud?" he fired back.

"It was only a dozen or so times," I said defensively. And then, "Because we were in battle."

A vision of Eva and me locked in a heated embrace flashed to the forefront of my mind. Nothing had happened, but we were in a cave for two days. She shared her blood and I shared mine, with no other choice but to strengthen one another before facing the fighting again.

"So if I had a bite of Dark One..." Alex's lips twisted into a thin line as he rubbed them together. "I'd basically be a ninja."

"Eva knew how to fight without my blood. It just enhanced her regular abilities. You're too sedentary. I imagine a Dark One's blood would just turn you into a comatose state."

Ethan smirked. "So he'd be the same then?"

Alex scowled his eyes narrowing into tiny slits as he glanced in my direction, his face impassive. The bastard was picking away at my thoughts. Self-preservation told me to back away and go upstairs, but my feet felt sluggish, my body, exhausted and sore as if I'd taken on an entire army by myself.

"Sleep." Alex said helpfully. "You're a human now, you need actual rest."

"I just woke up!"

"Good, then you'll remember how to go back to sleep," Stephanie said walking into the room. "You've spent no time sleeping, most of your time trying to do everything you used to be able to do sans power. Sleep and then we can train."

A scream erupted from downstairs.

John.

"No." I shook my head vigorously. "Absolutely not."

"Yes." Stephanie held out her hand. "For me."

Her voice was so enticing, before I knew it, I was grasping her hand and following her up the stairs as Alex parroted, "for me," in a high pitched voice.

I chose to ignore him.

Because she'd be upset if I tried to kill him and I was the one that ended up dead. At least I hoped she would be.

If I ever had my powers returned, if the future ever changed and Stephanie didn't kill me, I was going to have a serious talk with that Siren.

He mimicked her voice again and burst into a laughter.

A very serious and damning talk.

The thought cheered me the entire achy way up the stairs.

Stephanie

Nothing about Cassius was frail. His physical body was in peak condition, but his eyes? Mannerisms? The way he carried himself? It was like was dying before my very eyes, which seemed silly, but there it was, his blood, not pumping as fast through his system.

If I closed my eyes when I pressed a fingertip to his arms, it was as if I could feel the cells dying, his body aging, but I didn't have any proof of it just this insane natural ability to be able to read his body chemistry. As if his physical body was already mourning the loss of years it would never see.

Once we reached the room Cassius was staying in, he frowned, and then moved back down the hall and walked into my room.

"Sure, let yourself right in," I mumbled while Cassius's exhausted body weaved its way toward the bed.

"This body exhausts me." His mouth formed a curse against the large white pillow as his hands clenched the blanket around him. "I'm constantly at war with myself, hot, cold, hungry, full, angry, happy, sad." He yawned.

I sat down next to him, reaching out to comfort

him, laying my hand across his back. "You're useless tonight, we'll start training first thing in the morning."

He groaned. "We can train… just…" Another yawn. "A few hours, in our dreams."

"You want to train me in your… mind?" The thought was extremely unsettling. I'd been in his head; it was a dark place, a dark and lonely reminder of my future.

"I'll go to sleep." He flipped onto his back. "You did it by accident the first time. There are two ways to enter someone's dreams, one has to be taught, the other is quite simple."

"I'm listening." Was I ready for this? For more of the dark? My body shivered uncontrollably with the possibilities.

"The strength of every human lies… within their heart." Cassius grabbed my hand and pressed it on the pulse in his wrist. "Follow the pulse."

I frowned. "I'm sorry I don't understand, what do you mean follow the pulse?"

"Follow it." He yawned again, and his words became slurred. "I'll see you in my dreams, Stephanie."

Something about the way he lifted my fingertips to his mouth as a curved smile spread across his face. The way he tenderly held my hand.

It wasn't just confusing. It was hurtful, because I knew, that when he was given his powers back, the darkness I saw in his eyes, in his dreams, would consume him once again, and he'd block me away from his life.

He had no room for love.

I waited a few minutes as his breathing became heavy and then another five minutes after that just to be sure.

"Here goes nothing." I pressed my fingertips to his pulse and closed my eyes. How the heck was I supposed to follow the pulse?

And just as I thought it, the pulse started to call to me, as if a single thread was placed from my conscious into his subconscious.

Thump, thump, thump. The thread tugged me with each heartbeat until blackness burst forth into a beautiful night sky.

A campfire was set up with fur coats laid across the log nearest the crackling fire. A small cabin was in the distance, smoke billowing out of the chimney.

"You made it," Cassius whispered from behind me, as a fur coat was spread across my shoulders.

Turning, I gasped when I noticed his eyes. They were white, powerful, he looked like he used to. "How did you—"

"My dream," he answered quickly. "In my dream I imagine myself to be whatever I want to be, in my dream I am still me… and in order to train you, I figured this may aid in getting you there faster."

Nodding, I followed him over to the fire and held out my hands. "It's not warm."

"Nothing, in our dreams will ever be warm." He shrugged. "Your body temperature drops as we speak, mine to dangerous levels considering your presence in both my dream and in the room."

I stood abruptly. "You could die!'

"Then I'd control myself if I were you." He tilted his head, his eyes twinkling with amusement. "Or if you'd rather kill me now I imagine all you'd need to do was think hard about freezing my human ass."

I smirked. "Human ass?"

"Humans have asses. Asses that freeze. Skin that falls off. Teeth that fall out. Wishes that never come true. Desires that are never acted on." His eyes rolled to the back of his head as he continued to speak, this time with his voice lowered. "Dark Ones are quite similar. More powerful, yes. But we are unable to save the very creation we are aligned with. How horrible, do you think it is to watch a part of yourself die every day knowing you can do nothing to stop it?"

His white eyes flashed blue.

I think he expected me to answer, but I didn't know what to say.

"You've seen it." Cassius leveled me with a cold stare as his black hair whipped around his face. "I've seen you staring at my skin, frowning as my cells call out to you for aid. You were doing it before I fell asleep, you'll be doing it for an eternity."

"Your cells… call out to me?" I gulped.

"All human cells call out to Dark Ones. They see Dark Ones as a way to fix what's been broken, it is in essence why a Dark One takes humans so easily as slaves, it is also why once a Dark One leaves a human he dies. The want is too great, the power is suddenly lost, the cells incinerate."

I almost choked. "And yet here you are."

"Here. I. Am." His curt use of the sentence had me believing it was the last place he ever wanted to be. With a sweeping gesture, he waved his hands over the flame. It rose higher and higher. "A Dark One is like this fire…" The flame cracked and whipped angrily into the inky darkness. "Humans are the wood that keeps the fire burning, but Dark Ones? We are the very air that surrounds the fire, we can cause the fire to heat, helping those who are cold, or use the fire for bad, allowing the air to set the entire forest alight with flames. As a Dark One you must always control the flame. Always."

"And if we can't?" I swallowed, throat dry.

Cassius's head snapped in my direction, his eyes sad. "Then you destroy all that you hold dear."

"I thought we held nothing dear."

"It is smarter not to feel."

I narrowed my eyes and glared at him, he'd completely ignored the question.

A heavy sigh slipped past his lips. "Better not to care. Then the pain doesn't slice all the way to the bone." He shrugged. "Surface cuts."

"Are more easily infected," I pointed out. "Sometimes deceiving in looks… they appear easily fixed, but scratches bring in more bacteria, causing a slow break down of the skin, of the organs in the body, killing you before you even knew you were sick."

"In rare cases." Cassius lowered the flame with his hand. "You are correct."

"So, control the fire." I stood, brushing the fur to the snowy ground. "I'm sensing a theme here, I need to control everything or lose control and kill."

"Killing is fun," Cassius said in a hollow voice. "At times it helps."

"At times?"

"In the moment," he corrected. "It helps."

"That's what I thought."

He hid his yawn behind his hand and stood.

"You aren't really getting much sleep right now," I said in a guilty voice.

"I shall sleep when I'm dead." He flashed me a grin, lifting his hands into the air. Snow started to fall, landing only on us, missing the fire completely.

"I like that trick," I whispered, holding my hands out to catch the snowflakes.

"I knew you would." Suddenly he was next to me, his hands holding mine in place as giant snowflakes kissed my skin. "You've loved snowflakes since you were born." I expected him to be smiling at the memory; instead his eyes were black soulless pits of despair as his breathing slowed.

"You saved my life as a child… and as an adult again."

"Saved the one who would later kill me." He nodded. "Poetic, isn't it?"

"Tragic." I caught a snowflake and pressed it against his palm. "I was thinking tragic."

Cassius wet his lips, his eyes focusing so intently on my mouth I had no choice but to lean in.

The flames sparked higher.

The snow fell harder.

We moved closer.

Our lips touched.

The fire roared to life.

"Control the fire," he whispered against my mouth. "Control the flame." He licked my lower lip, then kissed me harder as I greedily grasped for pieces of his hair tugging him against my body.

With a moan, he lifted me into his arms, his mouth making love to mine, kissing me so tenderly that I had to hold back tears.

He was kissing me with emotion.

Actual emotion.

Not lust.

But something else, something more important, more raw.

"Control the flame," he whispered again.

"What if I don't want to?" I pulled back just enough to gaze at his full lips and attack again.

"Then you'll destroy the forest."

"Burn it to the ground." I gasped as his hands moved to my hips, slowly lifting my shirt. My eyes blurred as the vision around us changed. Suddenly we were in a cabin, it felt warm, but maybe it was just the kissing.

Cassius tore at my shirt, dropping it to the ground. With a gasp I launched myself into his open arms as he muttered a curse.

I had no idea what I was doing—why he was letting me, or if it was a dream, reality. I had no sense of time.

Only him.

Cassius.

I breathed out his name as icicles formed in front of me only to disappear from the heat of his kiss.

Was I a completely selfish person? To want him so bad? In any way possible? That even if he was merely offering me a kiss, only to ignore me later, possibly fight me for his life—I would take it?

Ever since becoming what I was, the line between right and wrong had been blurred into lines that didn't quite go straight, they weren't completely left or right. And at times, when I felt like I was making the right choice, the line would simply right itself, going straight again.

Was that what life would always be like? A series of squiggly lines that made no sense until after my decision was made? And how was that fair?

"Humans..." Cassius kissed down my neck and then flipped over my arm as the blue veins made tiny little lines down my wrist to my fingertips. "The majority of humans are born with an innate knowledge of right and wrong. Angels aren't born, they are created. And created only with a duty. At least, that's what was believed. Until they became... jealous."

"Jealous?" I whispered as he continued drawing circles on my wrist. My shirt was gone, as was his. Every part of his stomach was thick with bulging muscle, his chest was the same. He might be human—but he still had the body of some mythological god. Maybe that was why people tried to falsely worship him and the rest of the immortals. They didn't know any better? To them beautiful was to be worshiped.

When a lot of times, beauty was to be feared.

At least in the immortal realm.

"I wish I could still hear your thoughts," Cassius whispered. "And I'm sorry for getting carried away, I simply..." He shrugged. "I wanted to taste."

"Was it worth nearly freezing to death?" I asked.

He chuckled darkly then kissed me again. "Yes."

Good answer.

He moved me toward the fire, grabbing a blanket in the process. Though I wasn't cold, I knew it was about chivalry, nothing else, he was covering me, though he stayed beautifully shirtless as he sat on the floor opposite me.

"Jealous," Cassius answered. "I won't go into details, but the issue now stands. Dark Ones have duty first, the curse of being both human and Angel second, and then lastly, they have... one of the worst of human emotions I should think."

"Sadness?"

"Loss. As if placed in a giant maze but never told the way out. We serve, we do our duty, we serve some more, and are never promised mates, never promised a life outside of the duty we are given. While our human counterparts live and are able to die, and the immortals we watch over, have mates, children. We watch. Always." Cassius cursed. "We watch."

"A Dark One has never mated? Never had a family?"

"No," he snapped. "To mate with a Dark One is choosing to take upon yourself thousands of years worth of pain… to know a Dark One is to know darkness. Why would I—or anyone else—want to wish that upon someone I care about? Besides, two Dark Ones could very well destroy one another and then where would we be?"

"War?" I guessed.

"Most likely with each other, yes." He stood, his body moving with a fluidity that I didn't realize I'd missed. "That's enough for this evening. I…" His cheeks flushed red. "I apologize for taking liberties. At first it was to get you to control the fire."

"So what happened?" I hid my smile behind my hand.

Cassius looked heavenward. "My humanity took complete control and decided it would be in both of our best interests to get naked."

I burst out laughing while Cassius smiled blindingly in my direction.

"You know…" I held out my hand as he helped me to my feet. "You aren't so bad at this human thing."

"Oh really?" His eyebrows shot up. "I'm cranky, constantly starving, nearly tried to kill your pet bird, and can hardly think of anything except your breasts when you bend over. And I'm doing good? I'd hate to see what I was like if I was doing horrible."

He thought about my breasts? Little tingles of excitement darted over me, creating an exquisite ache in those breasts.

I cupped his chin. "I like you like this."

"Like how?" He covered my hand with his, his mouth was so close again, just a few more inches and we'd be touching.

"This," I said again. "Just like this."

"I'm holding you."

"I know."

The flames near the fireplace went higher as I kissed him softly on the mouth. "If I told you I loved you, would you believe me?"

His eyes closed. "If I told you it was forbidden, would you stop?"

A frigid cold spread throughout my body slamming me into my chest as darkness descended between us like a thick blanket.

"To love a Dark One, is to invite certain death," a voice whispered just as I jolted awake in my bedroom.

Cassius

HER BODY WAS SPREAD across mine, chilling me to the bone, though I would never admit it out loud lest she move. And the last thing I wanted was for her to move her leg even a fraction to the left or right.

There.

Nearly on top of me, that's where I needed her, where I wanted her. Dark Ones didn't typically sleep, so I knew she must be simply relaxing while she let me sleep.

Though it didn't explain the way she was laying across me.

"Safe," she muttered. "It's ridiculous right? That I feel safer in your arms than any other, yet you wouldn't stand a chance against a man with a gun, let alone a Demon." Stephanie raised her head, her eyes swirling with specks of white as she reached for my hand.

I held it, my warmth and her ice meeting against our palms.

"How long did I sleep?" I changed the subject.

"Twelve hours," she whispered. "I got tired of waiting for you so I went downstairs to watch movies with Genesis since she hasn't been feeling very well…" She frowned. "If… if I see a future of someone, do I tell them?"

"Whose future are we talking about?"

Stephanie swallowed, her eyes darting away from mine. "Genesis. Her labor won't be easy, Cassius."

"For centuries, women have survived it all the same. Have a little faith."

Her head whipped back. "Faith?"

"Yes." I licked my lips. "Belief in something that has not yet come to pass, belief that regardless of the circumstances, we can still expect the best possible outcome in life."

"Is that the human side speaking? The one who never loses hope?"

I smiled as a comforting warmth spread through my chest. "Yes, I think it is."

"I like it."

"Sometimes… hope is all we have." I frowned as I said it. "And even if we had knowledge of the future, would we truly do anything differently? I should like to think so, but knowing humanity as I do, they would still squander each and every moment, unable to fully grasp the realization that each second that ticks by is another gift that they have been given, a gift given only because of great sacrifice by not only their ancestors, but ours."

"Twelve hours of sleep turned you into a philosopher, I think," Stephanie mused, brushing my dark hair away with the back of her hand. Her ice cold fingertips cooled my forehead. I kept them there and closed my eyes as her hand shook.

"Your dream…" she started, while I tried to keep my breathing even. "Did you mean it?"

"Which part?"

Her eyes searched mine. "If you were allowed to love me—would you?"

I opened my mouth just as the door burst open. Ethan made his way inside took in our comfortable state and shook his head.

"I don't have time to address whatever the hell this is." He pointed to us, "Because it seems like our little pet in the dungeon won't stop screeching until he sees you." Ethan sighed, his eyes flashing with irritation. "He's chained, he can't hurt you in your current state, it's probably best to see what you can get out of him."

"Come with me." I stood as dizziness took over and a growing hunger made its presence known. "Damn it, I need food first."

Ethan smirked. "I don't envy your human appetite."

"You eat blood," I fired back. "I don't envy yours!"

"Blood tastes like…" His eyes flashed green.

"Easy." Stephanie raised her hand. "No need to orgasm in the middle of the room."

Ethan scoffed. "Hardly."

Stephanie quickly put on a pair of boots and a sweatshirt and turned toward me. "Should you, er, put on clothes?"

"Clothes?" I frowned then looked down.

Completely naked. I'd stripped the human body bare of any stitch of clothing.

"Why the hell didn't anyone say anything?" I roared grabbing at my clothes with numb as hell hands and jerking them on.

Ethan held up his hands. "I thought you knew."

Stephanie burst out laughing. "I assumed you knew since you're the one who stripped yourself."

"I did?"

She nodded. "The minute you woke up from your dream you were burning up…"

Frowning, I felt my own forehead, not that it would do any good. In fact, I still felt hot. So damn hot.

Maybe the dizziness was coming from the heat?

Ethan was at my side in a flash, gripping my arm, still as a statue, within seconds he pulled back. "Your blood." He frowned. "It's hot."

"Are you saying…" I couldn't even utter it. "That I have a fever?"

"I'm saying you're sick." Ethan nodded. "Yes."

"Damn it!" I kicked my foot against the floor. "One body! What the hell do humans do all the day? Walk around in bubble wrap?"

"Hey he knows what bubble wrap is." Alex stepped into the room. "Progress?"

Zapping Alex with a sheet of ice had just jumped up to the first thing I'd do if my power was ever restored.

"Mason's waiting in the kitchen with Genesis, better hurry if you want any food big guy." I think I was the big guy he was referencing. "Genesis is eating for three."

Breakfast hadn't helped the dizziness, and by the time I made it down into the cold wet dungeon I felt like I'd been transported back to a dark time, a time I'd rather forget. A time where I used to help torture the worst sort of immortals and humans alike, the ones who'd tried to overthrow us through a deadly alliance that should have never been.

"How!" I roared slamming Timber into the castle wall, it crumbled around his lithe body as horns protruded from his head.

He stood on shaky legs. "Wouldn't you like to know?"

"You cannot simply give an immortal's essence, his blood to a human! You know what happens!"

"Oh, I know." His smile was arrogant as fangs pressed onto his bottom lip drawing black oil like blood. "And soon, you will too."

I barked out a laugh. "Do not test me, Demon. I will destroy everything you hold dear with my pinky finger. Push me and I'll make you wish for death."

As if I amused him, he smiled wider, harder. "Oh?"

To prove my point I slammed an icicle through the air impaling him against the castle wall.

He laughed.

I shot another.

And another.

"I'm sorry, does that tickle?"

"You don't even know, do you?" he spat. "You think you're the last. You think you're all powerful. I wonder what you will do," he whispered, "when you discover the truth."

"Enough!" Sariel appeared, slamming his feet against the ground. "Release him, Cassius."

"But—"

"He will be punished," Sariel finished. "Most of his followers were killed in the destruction of the city. And as you know, we cannot simply kill him for doing something he claims he didn't know was illegal."

"Every immortal knows the rules!" I yelled, raising my voice an octave.

Sariel lifted his large hand as a single black feather fell to the ground creating a hole at his feet. "And for his punishment, he will serve time underground without food, water, or light. A thousand years, should suffice."

Timbers eyes widened. "You cannot do this to me! Do you know who I am! I am the son of the—"

"Silence!" Sariel screamed, sending Timber into the hole. Then he closed it up with a flick of his wrist and turned. "Don't you have work to do, Cassius?"

The dungeon walls looked eerily like the ones I'd chained Timber to so long ago.

"You gonna make it?" Ethan asked under his breath. "If this is too difficult—"

"Ethan." I barked his name. "I mean this exactly how it sounds, shut the hell up before I find a stake and garlic."

"Hah!" He slapped me on the back. "I love your jokes."

"I'll impale you with wood, don't think I won't try."

"It would tickle."

"It would amuse me greatly, yes."

Once we reached the bottom of the stairs, the chains came into view, two attached to John's feet and two more attached to his arms.

"So," John said without lifting his head. "You've brought the immortal king. Finally."

Swallowing back my fear, I stood to my full height and nodded my head to Ethan. "Drain him."

John's head snapped as his hands jerked against the chains, already black putrid blood was crusting around his wrists. "You'll kill me before knowing the truth?"

"The truth?" I shrugged. "It's been thousands of years. Why should I care about the truth? You survived, someone made you a Demon, your body took the immortality—" I winced as his skin took on a green hue. "—semi-well, it appears. And you've used what I can only assume is more immortal Demon blood mixed with…"

Ethan sniffed the air and shrugged.

"Something else, to create." I paused and raised one eyebrow. "Am I missing anything?"

"Holy shit, are you truly that dense?" John cackled. "All of you! This has been going on for centuries. Do you truly think…." His eyes turned black. "…this is about you? There is a darkness coming." His fangs elongated. "A darkness that's been building… one you will not stop."

"Drain him," I ordered Ethan again as my body trembled with the truth of his words.

Eva had always warned me of the same thing.

Thousands of years ago.

Impossible that it was now coming to pass.

"We were the first experiment," John kept talking. "And look how well it went. Powerful beyond most of the Demon we serve! Able to create on our own."

Ethan took two steps toward John and pressed his arm against the wall slicing open his wrist with his teeth and moving to the next. John let out a animalistic scream as black blood dripped from the marks Ethan had made.

Vampires had the ability to make the bite burn like hell.

I had a suspicion Ethan hadn't held back.

John writhed in agony.

"There are more of us. You have no idea how many more."

Ethan rolled his eyes. "Hate to break it to you John, but even thousands of Demons against us wouldn't be a fair fight."

John laughed, his fangs digging into the bottom of his chin. I frowned and looked closer. Good Lord the immortality had made his fangs double the size. "Who said anything about Demon?"

I held up my hand to Ethan to keep him from taking more of John's blood. Already my strength was weakening. My head pounded from the exertion.

"What do you mean?"

Suddenly John's head whipped to the side and a blast of cool air hit me square in the chest as his eyes went completely white.

"Oh, hell." Ethan took a step back as the chains turned to ice then fell to the floor, John collapsed in a heap then stood as his body grew another six inches. "Impossible!"

My teeth chattered from the cold as I took a cautious step backward. "You aren't a Dark One."

"No." John smiled. "But I can call on his power."

"I'm the last one." He didn't need to know it was a lie.

"No," John said in a soft voice. "I think not."

Before he could utter another word, Ethan was on

John's back slicing across his neck decapitating him.

The head landed on the dungeon floor with a thud and a sick splat as the body crumpled next to it. With swift movements, Ethan pulled the feather from his pocket and slid it into the vertebrae. Seconds later, John was nothing but dust.

As a Demon it should be black.

Vampires and Sirens crystallized into small diamond like dust.

But Dark Ones… always went red, a signal of the human blood flowing through their veins.

The dust was both red and black.

Ethan cursed. "Cassius, I think we have a problem."

"The hell?" I leaned down and touched the dust. "It's… mixed." Angry, I shook my head. "Did Stephanie…" I hated to accuse her but it was the only explanation. "Did she give any of her blood to the Demons?"

"Maybe you should ask her yourself," Stephanie said from the stairway. "Would I betray those I love… twice?"

CHAPTER 24

Stephanie

I WAS WORRIED. Worried because Cassius had none of my blood left, and I didn't want him to face a crazed Demon.

Instead, the tables were turned back on me once I made my way down the stairs.

"Well?" Ethan crossed his arms.

"Great to know you guys really trust me," I said sarcastically while my chest tightened.

Cassius's face softened. "You're the only other Dark One we know of in existence."

"And what? You think I'd just give over my blood to a sick dirty little Demon? So he could use it?"

They both fell silent.

"Well." I crossed my arms. "You're more than welcome to let Alex invade my thoughts... but I'm telling the truth."

"Damn it," Cassius muttered. "It would be so much easier if you weren't."

"Pardon?" Now I was really confused. I glanced down at the dust at Cassius's feet and gasped. "Is that John?"

"John can't talk right now," Ethan said in a chipper

voice. "He was annoying the hell out of me, but his dust shouldn't be—"

"—red." I finished. "It should be black, mixed with flecks of gray depending on how old he was but… red means he was given the blood of a Dark One."

"Right." Cassius stood and then fell back to his knees. "Damn this weak human vessel!"

I pressed my lips together to keep from laughing, he sounded so medieval, looked it too with his long black hair hanging nearly to his shoulders, his aristocratic face was too pretty to exist in this modern era.

"Come on," I lifted him into my arms. "Bed."

"And my shame is complete," he muttered as I carried him upstairs. "A woman is carrying my weak body up the stairs as if I weigh nothing but a feather."

"Less than that, actually."

"Because that's ever so helpful to my pride."

"Sorry."

"Then why are you smiling?"

"You're cute when you pout."

"Cute is the word humans use to describe things with fluffy tails… hamsters… pet birds. Hell, I've turned into your pet! Release me immediately!"

Laughing, I carried him back into my room and set him on his feet. "You're not my pet, but you are weak."

"I tire of your compliments." He smirked. "My pride cannot handle any more—" He fell toward me.

Gripping his broad shoulders I slowly lowered him back to the bed. "You know, you only get one body, you better take care of it."

"I—" Cassius yawned. "Despise humanity."

"No, you don't," I answered quietly, bringing a blanket over his shoulders as tremors wracked his body. "You just need to rest."

"I cannot rest until the mystery is solved and I can't solve a mystery, train you, protect you, and love—"

"Love?"

"Er… food."

"You weren't going to say food."

"I'm sick, cease your arguing." He closed his eyes tight.

I kissed his forehead, only to have him pull me close.

"Stay," Cassius whispered, his bluster spent. "When you're with me…"

"What?"

"I feel… happy." He opened his eyes as if the concept had only just now occurred to him. "More than that, I… feel complete."

My heart soared as I answered back. "Me, too."

He pressed his hand to my neck, then pulled me in for a searing kiss, one that burned so hot against my lips I let out a gasp. "Damn, you taste good."

"Because you're hot."

"Attractive hot?" He pulled back, his eyes locking on mine with such heated intensity that it nearly took my breath away.

I brushed a kiss across his lips. "Still arrogant even when he has a fever. Good to know."

"My body is different…" Cassius's face fell. "But I find that my feelings… are very much the same." His head tilted as he cupped my face. "More confusing than ever."

"Cassius." I leaned in until our mouths nearly touched. "Why are you really here?"

"To train you."

The air twisted in front of me, it tasted bitter. With a smirk, I whispered, "Lie."

Cassius's mouth broke out into a blinding smile. "They taste different, don't they?"

"Bitter... wrong." I nodded.

"Because a lie spoken from your lips is a falsehood released into the universe, the atmosphere. A man's destiny is decided by what he speaks. And when he speaks a lie, creation cannot knit together the pieces correctly, the result is bitterness."

"So, why are you here?"

He was quiet and then, "I'm here for you."

No bitterness in the air this time.

"To train me?"

He was quiet again.

"Cassius?"

"To love you."

I expected the air to shift.

It didn't.

My heart was pounding so wildly that blood roared through my system at a rapid pace dropping the temperature in the room.

"And do you?" I was almost afraid to ask, but I had to know. "Do you love me?"

"Fear is never welcome. I can feel your trembling, Stephanie." He avoided the question. "Fear makes us weak."

"And love? What does love do?"

"It makes us both. Strong and weak, depending on which side you're on."

"Answer the question Cassius."

"I find I've suddenly developed some of that fear I'm always so easily dismissing."

"Afraid of what? My reaction? My response?"

"All of the above." His fingers threaded through my hair. "Everything about you terrifies this human body, to be sure. Words don't just create, they have the power to destroy, to level a city with one simple phrase, the words of a Dark One… even more so."

"Well then, one of us will have to be brave," I encouraged.

"Yes, one of us will." He smiled, his eyes crinkling at the sides, was he already getting wrinkles? And why was his body failing him so readily? So easily?

"I love you," I blurted. "I've loved you for as long as I can remember. And I'll continue loving, until time ceases to matter, to exist."

Cassius crushed his mouth against mine then pulled back. "I love you more than I should… I love you in ways I shouldn't. I desire you in ways that are hard to comprehend. And the love I feel for you is the scariest thing I've ever admitted out loud, to anyone. Because once those words are released, you can't take them back. You could try, but love, weaves a thread of its own and once you confess with your mouth, your soul has no choice but to follow."

My breathing slowed, nearly stopped altogether. "Who knew you were so romantic."

"More like, who knew, that as a human, I'd be so capable of telling the truth, rather than lying."

"You'd rather lie to me?"

"Absolutely. Lying is less scary. Honesty will always be terrifying. I've discovered I'm like a cat."

I pressed my lips together to keep from bursting out laughing. "How are you like a cat? Exactly?"

"The scaredy cats." He frowned. "Is that wrong?"

"Not at all." I covered his hands with mine, they were still burning up. "Tell me this feels good."

He leaned back against the pillows, his shirt inching up to show me an expansive area of lean abdominal muscles. "It feels more than good. I could lay in your cold forever."

"Funny, most people hate the cold."

His eyes flashed open. "Cold is life."

"What do you mean?"

"The earth." His eyebrows pinched together. "The source of life is not heat… nor is it cold, it is the perfect balance of both. Without one, the other ceases to exist. The cold you bring, reminds me of the way things work, the balance that must always be kept." His eyes closed again.

I wanted him.

Possessiveness washed over me.

Not in a way that I'd ever experienced before, but in a primal, surge of energy that I couldn't ignore as my heartbeat slowed in my chest, my eyes zeroed in on his neck.

Mine.

His humanity called to me, his… love, beckoned me.

There are two ways to mark a human… His words came to mind. *Force your will upon them.*

"Cassius?"

"Hmm?" He didn't open his eyes.

I leaned forward and cupped his neck with my right hand, my palm rested against his hot skin. "I'm sorry."

"For?"

"Doing something that's forbidden…." I closed my eyes and forced my will on him, but rather than forcing him into slavery, into a typical hero worship. I gave him my love.

I showed him my feelings.

Opened up my heart and soul to the man who'd stolen my heart as a immortal only to give it back as a human.

He was my everything.

And I refused to let another moment go by, without anyone knowing, without the world knowing, that we belonged together.

Even if it killed me.

With a cry of pain he screamed beneath my touch and shards of light spread throughout the room.

And then with a burst of white, Cassius's skin went from hot to frigid. His eyes rolled to the back of his head and then turned completely white. He reached for me just as I reached for him.

With one graze of his finger against the blanket, it evaporated into thin air, the clothes between us suddenly gone as if he'd willed them to disappear. Like slow motion the frigid air danced around us and then stopped.

Time.

Was.

Gone.

The world around us was black.

Nothingness.

Only Cassius and I existed.

Eyes still white, his body returned to its godlike state right before my eyes, as his hair went from black to red, and then black again. His skin was perfection itself, a dizzying myriad of tiny little crystals smooth, golden.

"Stephanie." His words came out with a godlike echo, shaking the foundation of my entire body as he reached for me and kissed me so hard that my lips hurt, but it was a hurt that craved more.

"Cassius." I sucked in the air between our mouths. It tasted like sugar. He wrapped an arm around me, reminding me again of my nakedness, then pressed me against a soft surface. Were we still in my bedroom?

I had no sense of minutes. Hours. It was as if the world had stopped, in order for us to have our moment together.

"I will love you." His voice shook. "Forever." Cassius pressed his lips to mine and then cupped my neck as a shot of pure ice went from his palm into my veins. "Mine."

Every thought he'd ever had was mine.

Every moment of darkness too.

I wanted to scream as I held Eva in my arms, as I watched her age, the sheer agony of that moment nearly destroyed my will to exist.

The scenes of people dying.

Screaming for justice.

The stench of death was all around.

The darkness was impossible to escape.

I wanted to run, but something wrapped around my feet, thick large black tentacles tightened around my ankles as a raspy voice whispered. "Watch."

Thousands of stars in the sky suddenly went dark.

And then the earth followed as an ominous darkness crept across the planet slowly inching its way into every single available space.

"No!" I cried. "No!"

And then, as if someone heard my call. A piercing

light broke through the dark cloud, feathers followed, so many purple feathers.

More blood was spilled as I tried to move, to join the fight.

Cassius led the armies against humans, against Darkness itself. Against the Demon who refused to be ruled by an immortal king.

Ethan was at his side, slicing his way through Demon after Demon.

Timber led the Demon forces.

I shouldn't have been surprised.

He was an ancient type of evil.

"Eva!" Cassius yelled. "Take cover!"

She sped out of the way then sliced the back of the Demon's knees, he fell to the ground as black blood spewed out of his mouth.

And just like that, I watched Cassius and Eva lead an army of five, including them.

Against ten thousand.

The darkness of the Demon constantly called to Cassius, and as the war raged on, clearly it was wearing on him, as light left his face. But every time it did, Eva pulled him back telling him how good he was, what he was capable of, and the shadows on his face would recede.

The Demon, all destroyed but a few hundred.

Sariel fell from the sky, landing on his feet so hard that an earthquake took out another hundred Demon. "Do you concede victory?"

They put down their swords, while Cassius clenched his. He wanted to kill the remaining.

"What good are they?" he spat, arguing with Sariel. "They are the very evil you wish us to exterminate. Yet, you let them live?"

"I do not allow anything." Sariel said softly. "It is not my call to make. In order for light to exist, we must also have dark, there will always be a need for balance."

With that he left.

And the darkness continued to assault Cassius.

With a roar he raised his hands and screamed. "Silence!"

The Demon cowered behind Timber.

"Cross me again," Cassius spat, "and I will tear you limb by limb, then remove every last drop of life from your pathetic body."

Timber laughed. "I'd like to see you try."

The Demon had lost that day.

Or had they?

Suddenly someone was grabbing my hand. I refused to look away as Timber made his way toward me. "Well, well, well, interesting… I did not think he would share such memories."

"You can see me?"

He nodded.

"But this is a memory."

"Of an event you are re-living through your dear Cassius, yes, I know." Timber sheathed his black jeweled sword. "In all the times he's relived this memory, he has never brought… you."

Timber clapped his hands while I felt like clobbering him in the face or turning him to ice.

"He's made it too easy. Exposing his cards so soon." Timber leaned forward and whispered in my ear. "Until next time… Angel."

Chapter 25

Cassius

Watching my life through her eyes was painful… almost as painful as her palm against my neck.

The woman had marked me!

And I was still alive.

No longer fully human.

But returned to my Dark One state. Was it truly that easy? That all she'd needed to do was love me back? And with that love, mark me? Would Sariel make it a riddle that had been in my power the entire time?

Stephanie's eyes returned to blue, she huddled against me, still naked as tremors wracked her body. "That was…"

"Completely irresponsible," I teased, feeling lighter than I had… in my entire existence. Because for the first time in my miserable life… I was sharing the weight of the darkness.

With someone who had never experienced it before.

Stephanie shuddered and pulled me closer. "A little warning next time."

I kissed her, I couldn't help it.

Our kiss shook the air in the room, as tiny little pieces of ice formed around my fingertips, encircling our fingers, linking our hands together. Her body moved beneath mine as her lips danced across my mouth.

I'd never taken my pleasure with another immortal.

Only with humans, who later died in agony at the loss of being near me. Several of them simply gave up.

The last one, a hundred years ago, had jumped off a bridge.

It was the last time I'd allowed my own carnal pleasures to destroy an innocent life.

Until Genesis, until I figured it was my duty to try to mate with a human to bring about the end of the curse.

Only to realize within days of knowing her—that she was never mine to have. Never would be.

And that, even a woman as beautiful as Genesis—could never fill the gaping hole Stephanie's absence had made in my life.

"Make love to me." Stephanie's body twisted underneath mine for dominance as she pushed against my chest then pinned me to the bed.

Chuckling, I drew the shape of a heart across her chest, my fingers etching an icy trail as they danced across her fair skin.

Stephanie's breath hitched as her eyes flashed white.

"Like that?" I asked.

She nodded. "But that's not what I meant."

"So you don't want me drawing hearts all over your delicious body until you beg me to stop?"

She hesitated.

I laughed.

"I've never seen you laugh this much." Her smile

was bright.

I sobered, kissing her again, tasting her. "I've never had reason until now."

With great care I lifted her into my arms, wrapping her legs around me as I kissed down her neck.

She gasped when my tongue slid between her breasts moving downward until the angle forced me to stop.

"This is…" She shook her head as the light above us shattered into a million tiny pieces blanketing us in darkness—our eyes glowed at one another. "Too much all at once."

"I wish I could tell you what to expect. But I've never been mated before," I answered, my body craving more of her kisses, more of her touch, just… more of everything.

"You're stuck with me now." She laughed against my mouth. "Basically married."

I nodded, then swirled my finger against her ring finger as a beautiful crystal diamond appeared wrapping itself in icy tendrils all the way up to her fingertip. "I shopped for hours."

Stephanie examined the ring. "Yes I can see that, great detail on the diamond and the rose petals around it."

"Eyes closed the whole time," I whispered.

"Keep them open." She cupped my face. "I missed you."

I frowned. "I've been here the whole time."

"You've been missing half of your true self," she answered. "And now… you're whole."

"Because of you."

"Because of my selfishness."

"That too, though it sounds less romantic that way, more needy."

She pinched me in the shoulder but it didn't hurt.

"Now that we've gotten all the technicalities out of the way." I motioned to her ring. "I'm going to make love to you."

"Okay." Her eyes brightened.

"And then..." I brushed a kiss across her lips. "I'm going to do it again."

Without giving her a chance to respond I molded my mouth to hers, my hands sliding down every inch of her body as if it was made for my touch, my every caress.

I never thought.

Never imagined I'd be allowed the privilege.

Of loving another woman.

Of mating with an equal.

My hands shook as they rested against her hips. Had my face not been frozen from emotion, I imagined tears would have found their place on my cheeks, proof of the undeniable love I felt for her—and gratefulness I had for the situation.

Stephanie rocked her hips against me as she tangled her hands in my hair. Each kiss was met with desperation, returned with aggression, and repeated. Our bodies slid against one another as I took my time exploring every part of her I dared not touch before our mating.

Mouth watering with the need to taste, I pressed her back onto the bed and began my wicked descent from her chin, down to her feet, stopping at each and every space in between, making my mark permanent as I bit and covered her skin with my mouth.

Stephanie's moans only encouraged me further.

The sound of ice breaking didn't even deter me from licking my way back up her body, careful to make sure I didn't miss any important spot or angle at which I could give her pleasure.

Her thoughts were my own as she screamed. "There." Only it was in her head, not aloud.

"Better?" I'd ask only to have her nod her encouragement.

I was able to pleasure her before she even asked.

With an eager lift, I had her on her stomach, realizing I had only pleasured her front, only made love to parts of her and left the other parts pressed against the damned mattress.

"Cassius what are you doing?"

"Touching." I answered simply. "Biting." Her pert ass jerked as I ran my hand down its curve. "Learning."

With a deep moan she relaxed against my hand as it pressed against her hip and slid between her legs.

"I don't think—"

"Good," I interrupted. "Don't think... It's extremely unhealthy to think in a Dark One's presence. Who knows..." Thoughts swirled around her head of me touching her, pleasuring her. "...what a Dark One may do with those thoughts?"

I fired back more thoughts of my own, my mouth covering every one of the spots she pointed out until she screamed so loud the room shook. "I guess he may do that." I moved my hand then flipped her over again. "Or he may do this." I sent her images of what I would do right before I did it, doubling her pleasure, making her slick with sweat only to have it evaporate within seconds. "But this," I whispered, envisioning my mouth on her core. "This I think you will like best."

She whimpered before each movement of my tongue only to cry out after.

And suddenly my vision turned to her pleasuring me. I could barely keep my composure.

"Two—" she panted. "—can play that game."

"I adore games," I fired back with a wicked laugh, in the vision I entered her hard and fast, only to go so slow that the air around us exploded. "Care to play one or two? I have time…"

"Cassius, I swear—"

"No swearing." I pulled her to her feet and pushed her against the wall, her back was to me as I pressed up behind her. "You can always end the game… concede to the winner."

"Never."

"Too bad," The vision shifted as I kissed around her neck, while I kept her pinned to the wall.

"Fine!" she yelled, "Just please… please Cassius."

With a growl I turned her around just as she jumped into my arms, we staggered back against the wall and then fell to the floor in a heap of arms and legs as she straddled my body then moved against me.

Our white eyes locked, and a knowing smirk crossed her face.

Oh yes, being human had been worth it.

For this? I would serve a sentence of a thousand years.

For one night with my true mate? Perhaps, a million.

"Yes." She hovered over me, slowly allowing me to enter her. Stephanie's slow movements nearly killed me as I lingered between ecstasy and greediness. I moved faster and faster, gripping her hips, holding her in place as the air between us cracked and sliced like lightning in the sky.

I moved tentatively, and she matched the movement, but the slowness was destroying me, so I imagined us against the wall, and there we were, against the wall. Using it to my advantage I pressed her back against it and moved her body in perfect cadence to my heartbeat—to hers, only to have her explode around me, tiny pieces of crystals exploded in front of my face as the air stilled.

Slowly, I dropped her to her feet.

We stared at one another, both exhausted.

The darkness surrounded us.

But we.

We were light.

Chapter 26

Stephanie

I SHOULD BE EXHAUSTED. Instead, it felt like someone had just zapped me with adrenaline. It was an odd sort of balance, to experience a beautiful moment with Cassius only to have it dampened by the darkness that being mated to him had unlocked.

It crept.

Like a slow choking blanket… it tempted, told me that if I'd just give in to the evil side of myself, I'd be complete.

And then, Cassius would smile in my direction and bring me back.

How long had he been trying to exist like this? Constantly battling the innermost darkest parts of himself? Alone?

"A very long time," he answered. "Eva helped."

"I would have liked her, I think." I led Cassius back to the bed, we both lay down and stared at one another.

"She was strong." Cassius touched his fingers to my face. "Like you."

I kissed his fingertips.

The door burst open.

Ethan stood there with Mason on one side Alex on the other and Genesis in the back trying to peek over their shoulders.

"The hell?" Ethan roared. "What did you guys do to my house?"

For the first time since we'd lain down, I glanced around the darkened room.

All of the lights were completely shattered. The walls were lined with ice, the window was completely frosted over, and the walls had cracks running up and down them as if an earthquake had occurred.

"We, um, had a…" I elbowed Cassius. "Fight."

"Is he dead?" Mason wondered aloud. "What I mean to say is, did he survive this… er, ordeal?"

"Yes, did the King last his first bout of lovemaking or shall I call the time of death?" Alex joked.

Cassius swore under his breath then in an instant rose to his scary full seven-foot height and glared down at them.

Ethan and Mason took a cautious step back while Alex stood there with a stupid grin on his face. "So, sex heals all, hmm?"

"I made myself a promise Alex, care to know what it was?"

"Sex before your old as hell anatomy falls off?" he guessed.

Cassius's grin widened. "I think I'll enjoy this." With a wave of his hand Alex's voice was gone.

"Frozen voice box… it may take a few hours to thaw, if it ever does."

Alex's eyes widened.

"But all Sirens have are their voices and good looks!" Genesis argued from her spot in the hall.

Cassius's eyes softened. "Perhaps he'll learn to choose his words more wisely in the future then."

Alex stomped out of the room, while Cassius faced everyone. "It seems that I am… restored."

"How?" Ethan's eyes narrowed. "Sariel took pity on your weakness?"

"More like—" Cassius glanced back at me. "—I accomplished what I was sent to do as a human, and he restored me."

"She's trained?" Ethan nodded seemingly impressed. "Fantastic."

"Yes," I lied, and the air immediately turned bitter, while Cassius laughed inside my head. "But it might be good to get a few more sessions in this evening, just in case."

"And by sessions you mean…" Ethan pointed between the two of us. "Never mind, don't tell me." He raised his hands above his head. "If you tell me the mental image will permanently ruin my existence."

Genesis sighed behind him. "That's so romantic though, don't you think? That they're finally together?"

A sudden wind whistled along the hall and swirled into the room.

"Sweet hell," Ethan muttered as Cassius tossed clothes in my direction. The air had shifted.

"What?" I glanced around the room. "What's wrong?"

"Angels," Mason spat. "Or just one in particular. Seems he's paying us a visit. Damn it, I only set the table for six. If he wants ham he's shit out of luck."

"Yes, because I'm sure that's what's on his mind," Cassius hissed. "Ham!"

"Says the one who tried to chase a blue jay with his pitchfork!"

"I had no pitch fork!"

"Yes, a lament I'm quite familiar with." Mason rolled his eyes. "If only I had a pitchfork, a bow and arrow, a gun, I could hunt my own meat. Thank God your appetite will disappear, I was afraid the goldfish was next."

Cassius shared a glance with me. "We have gold *fish*?"

"Goldfish." Genesis laughed. "Mason likes to see how long he can keep them alive."

"So they've died before?" Cassius asked.

"It's not like he revives them, just buys more." Genesis shrugged. "Now, you both need..." She glanced down and coughed. "Clothes."

Ethan was already stomping down the hall, most likely making Sariel aware that his sudden presence in his house wasn't welcome.

"Cassius?"

He turned, his muscles rippling beneath his simple black T-shirt. As a human it had fit him perfectly. As an immortal, it was almost like his muscles were straining to break free. Give him a cape and he'd be able to star in the next Avengers movie, no problem.

"It's about Alex. Look, I know he drives you crazy, he drives everyone crazy but... since Sariel is here, can you just... un-freeze him with your Dark Ones Mojo?"

Cassius tilted his head, a look of complete seriousness crossed his face. "Mojo?"

"You know." I lifted my hand in the air and twisted as power swirled to my fingertips. "When you do that."

"You have the power to do it, too."

"I do?" I twirled my hand again, my fingertips heavy as if something needed to release from them.

Cassius crossed his arms. "Will it."

I closed my eyes and flicked my wrist willing Alex to speak again.

"Son of a bitch!" Alex's voice erupted from downstairs.

"Think it worked?" I laughed.

Alex cursed so loudly I was surprised Sariel didn't silence him forever.

"A bit too well." Cassius held out his hand. "Now, let's go face Sariel."

I sighed. "You think he's going to be angry."

Cassius didn't answer right away. "I think that I often under estimate Sariel..."

"Is that good or bad?"

"I never know." Cassius led me down the stairs. "Until the exact moment it happens."

Chapter 27

Cassius

He was going to be angry.

I knew it in the way the tense air pumped around me, fanned, as if Sariel's feathers were flapping against the air—assaulting would be a more accurate word.

I clutched Stephanie's hand as we entered the kitchen.

Had Sariel's face not been void of any sort of happy emotion or amusement, it would have been funny, seeing an Angel seated at the kitchen table, tapping his rather large fingertips against the wood table only to get agitated and take a sip of coffee then shiver as if the taste not only repulsed him but offended every fiber of his being.

Purple and blue feathers shuddered, as if they, too, experienced the taste of the coffee and found it lacking.

Mason's jaw ticked as he braced himself against the counter, his muscles bulging with the need to fight and protect his family.

The only family the Wolf had.

What a sad, mismatched bunch. What a weird world, to live in a world where the Wolf's pack consisted of Sirens, Dark Ones, and Vamps.

Mason's eyes flashed to mine before his fingernails dug into the granite counter tops, leaving little marks of agitation before the oven made a loud ding. Sariel's eyes jerked to attention, locking with mine.

I smirked. "Staying for dinner?"

"It smells..." His nose curled up. "Like meat."

Mason let out a loud, aggressive snort. "It's ham."

"I don't care to eat animals."

Alex plopped down next to Sariel in an entirely too careless manner. "Hear that Mason? He's not going to eat you."

Another growl erupted from the kitchen as Mason started tossing around pots and pans, purposely slamming them against the granite so they made a loud noise.

His thoughts were just as loud.

But I chose to ignore them, shutting off what I knew wasn't my cross to bear. To listen in on Mason's thoughts was to experience raw pain over and over again. There was never a pause in his emotions, in the bleeding of his soul, the only balm in his otherwise dark life.

Was Genesis.

Proven yet again, when she quietly joined him in the kitchen, pressing her hand against his.

Light burst, pushing its way through his dark morose thoughts, calming the beast inside as they continued working in silence.

"Interesting." Sariel's eyes narrowed in on them.

Clearly he noticed the same exchange.

"Why are you here?" I pulled out a chair and all but shoved Stephanie into it then managed to push it away so that I was between her and Sariel, exactly where I needed to be.

"I think you know why." His voice held a raw destructive edge as his eyes flashed white. The blue and purple feathers shuddered red before returning back to the violet hues.

I made eye contact with Ethan as he moved himself between Genesis and Sariel and stood directly behind the Angel, ready to make a move if I needed him to, ready to commit an unfathomable crime in order to not only protect his mate, but mine.

I'd underestimated his friendship. Greatly.

To kill an Angel is inviting a soulless existence, death, nothingness.

But he'd do it.

For his family.

"I'm restored," I finally announced.

"Not that." he snapped. "Do I look like an idiot?"

Alex opened his mouth to speak but I sent him a seething glare of *shut the hell up* before he pouted and waited for more information.

"No," I answered for everyone. "But you're making Genesis nervous. You know it's impossible for a human to be in your presence too long without… heart problems."

"Genesis," Sariel said her name with reverence. "How are the twins?"

All talking and thinking ceased in that damn room.

"Healthy." She answered in a bold voice. "Thank you for asking."

Sariel's eyes went white. "It will be a hard birth."

"If it were easy men would do it."

Alex burst out laughing.

While Sariel's mouth curved into an amused smile.

"I think you've made your point."

Genesis bowed behind him while Mason started slamming plates again.

"We can talk about your mating at a later date. Right now, I have more pressing matters…. say, matters that deal with life and death, the death of a certain Demon, and the secrets he may or may not have spilled before his blood stained your hands." Sariel said the words with such indifference, my body trembled.

Did lives matter to him?

And why did they suddenly matter to me?

Why did I suddenly care about the Demon's blood downstairs? Or the lives that could be lost because of the secret he held?

Why did I care?

The answer?

Came to me as Stephanie lightly brushed the back of my neck with her fingertips.

Her.

It was because of her.

I cared because I loved her.

Her love made me feel.

All the things I'd pushed away.

The Darkness told me it was dangerous to feel.

The Darkness was right.

Because in feeling—I cared—I wanted fairness. I wanted equality. I wanted peace.

Hell, I wanted the impossible.

"So." Sariel stood, his feathers brushing from one edge of the room to the other, nearly pushing Mason to the floor as they spread wide in their vibrancy. "I simply came to ask what you've done. What all of you—" He turned only slightly since his wings blocked his ability to twist completely around. "—have done."

"We–" I stood to my full height, which matched Sariel's, though I had no wings; being a victim of the curse I was semi grounded. "—can ask the same question of you… can we not?"

Sariel's face twisted into a knowing smile. "I always wondered when this day would come. There were times I doubted it. Especially when Eva came along, throwing you off your purpose, your destiny." He shook his head. "And now look… still weakened by emotion. Will you never learn, my son? Emotions are frivolous, a curse upon the human race, one you bear because of your parentage. Give into that emotion, and you will only feel pain."

"I'd rather feel… something," I answered.

"Oh you will…" He glanced behind me at Stephanie. "Believe me, it will be the greatest pain of your existence. Now." He rubbed his hands together. "Direct me to the blood. If you would."

Mumbling out a curse, I clapped open my hands. "No need." The blood from downstairs spread between my fingertips, the different flecks of colored dust spread around the table. A possibility only because the blood was mixed with Angel blood.

Sariel stumbled backward.

"I think that means he didn't know," Alex whispered loudly.

"Don't Angels know everything?" Genesis mused out loud.

"Do I look all knowing?" Sariel fired back. "Believe me, life would be so much easier if I saw every angle. I see three and a half."

"Three and a half?" Genesis asked. "Three and a

half what?"

"Sides." Sariel picked up the dust between his forefinger and thumb, rubbing it together as the red parts of the blood stuck to his fingertip, clearly wanting to bond again with its true purpose. "I see every side, but half of a side is missing. It keeps me loyal."

Alex coughed wildly, and I shared an amused look with him while he shrugged his shoulders.

"The Demon…" Sariel sighed. "Are more trouble than they are worth."

"And we keep them around because… why?" Alex yawned. "Just say the word and I'll go all Siren on their asses."

"I think they'd enjoy that way too much," Ethan teased.

"No." Sariel dusted his hands together. "We do this the right way. There's no need to start a war, and there certainly isn't any need to exterminate an entire race just because they've been bad. Think of what would have happened with Dracula." All eyes turned to Ethan.

"Horrible example," Ethan grumbled.

"Cassius, since you've discovered the answer to your little riddle, your thirty days are now over." He snapped his fingers. "You are fully restored and are ordered to immediately investigate, with your mate's help, the sudden influx of Demon."

"And the Angel blood?" Mason asked. "Where the hell are they getting it?"

"Cease from cursing in my presence," Sariel snapped. "And if I knew I'd tell you."

A wry grin widened Alex's mouth. "That damned missing half side of things…"

Sariel shot him a withering glance, and the grin faded.

"So, it's only us then?" I braved the question. "Just me and Stephanie?"

Silence answered us, and then, "You have your orders. Keep me updated."

He moved away from the kitchen, as his wings disappeared, replaced by a leather jacket and dark-wash jeans.

"So he uses the front door now?" Alex asked.

My skin prickled with awareness. It was too easy.

The entire thing was too easy.

And if there was anything I'd learned in my time on earth, it was that things were never as easy as they seemed.

"Wait here," I whispered to Stephanie, following Sariel out the door.

His footsteps crunched against the gravel and then he stopped, lifting his eyes heavenward as stars shone down on both of us. Only I was still blanketed in darkness—the light couldn't shine on a Dark One.

We weren't given the honor.

Only Angels.

Pure bloods.

"There's something else, isn't there?" I asked.

Sariel pointed up to the sky. "How many do you think… look down on us… wish for more than their existence? None. I would venture none. Do you know why Cassius?"

More riddles. Just my luck. "No. No, I do not."

"Because their purpose is to shine, not to have an opinion or feelings. They rest in the occupation they have been given, and they excel at it."

"Yes." A few more stars twinkled down, casting a light glow across Sariel's face.

He turned to me, his eyes white. "Ask your question, son."

"A vision…" I nearly choked with the horribleness of it. "Stephanie saw the future, *a* future, she was killing me. You stood behind her."

Sariel didn't look surprised, if anything, his shoulders seemed to slump, his glow, defeated. "Yes."

"I die by her hand?"

"Futures… can change," he said in a chilling voice. "Though I've only seen it change once with an immortal."

"Once?"

His eyes went white again. "With you… your future changed the minute you saved the girl from death. Your future was certain, set in stone, until you chose."

"I've always had free will."

He posed a question. "But how often have you acted on it?" He held out his hand in front of him, closed it tightly then opened it as a small flower began to grow. "This flower does not choose to be planted, it simply is. What would happen, do you think, if the flower decided it wanted to be planted elsewhere, if it demanded of its creator to be given an entirely new occupation, a new existence, and this creator, in his divine love for this flower… allowed it."

"The flower…" I swallowed even though my mouth had gone dry. "Not knowing the dangers of life, could ask to be planted in the water, on a hill without sunshine, the flower could die, the chances are, the flower *will* die—if left to its own devices."

"Yet." Sariel held up his hand. "It's allowed… because one cannot truly love something yet keep it in a safe little box. That is not love. Love does not hold back, it allows us to fall, to break, and yes Cassius, sometimes, it even allows us to die."

"You're not making me feel better."

"I never was good at these sorts of talks." A foreign chuckle escaped between his lips and closed his hands. "I see many futures for you. I also am purposefully blinded from several outcomes. But I will tell you this. If she does not learn to control the Darkness, if you do not help her, she will kill you. And I will have no choice but to help her, or she will destroy herself in the process."

I sucked in a breath. "You'd help her kill me?"

"To save the girl you love? To save your mate? What would you have me do, let you both die?"

"No."

"Then you have your answer." He nodded curtly. "You've had centuries of practice. She's had a week, and if she's not careful, she'll get drunk on the power, she'll allow it to consume her, you realize how the Darkness calls… it never screams your name." He leaned in close his eyes turning black. "It whispers."

Chapter 28

Stephanie

Sleeping next to Cassius still felt forbidden, like someone was going to barge into our room and yell. Or like Alex was going to ground me, which was just ridiculous! I was a grown woman.

But still. I could see him trying it.

I only needed around six hours of sleep, and even then I could go days without rest, but Cassius, I'd learned, had turned into one of those over-protective boyfriend types.

When I told him I wanted to stay up and watch movies with Genesis, he picked me up, tossed me over his shoulder, and ran up the stairs with me. And when I tried to pull his shirt off, he lightly slapped my hands and told me to rest.

I didn't even realize I was tired until my eyes were too heavy to keep open, why was I suddenly exhausted? I knew Dark Ones rarely slept. Maybe it was just the day.

"Sleep," he'd kissed my forehead, and then lain down next to me.

I glanced at the clock.

Four in the morning.

Ethan would probably be up soon, Vampires liked to be up with the sun, and Mason had suddenly developed a horrible habit of baking first thing in the morning so that when Genesis woke up she was able to have a warm muffin to ease her morning sickness.

With a sigh, I tossed and turned, then finally got comfortable enough to close my eyes and nestle into Cassius's strong arms.

Sleep again overwhelmed me as the blackness of the room swirled around me in… warmth.

I didn't think I missed the warmth.

Until now.

"Cold?" a voice whispered.

I blinked open my eyes but all I saw was darkness. Was I dreaming? I felt the bed for Cassius. He was still next to me but I couldn't see him.

"I can make you warm." The voice chuckled. "Shall I start a fire? For both of us?"

"What?" I reached out in front of me, unable to even see my hand. "Who are you?"

"Darkness," it hissed.

I would have laughed if my body hadn't chilled in that very moment and then, nearly wept with the rightness of it. "Darkness, you say?"

"I am Darkness. Your other half. Hello."

Did it just say hello?

Frowning, I reached out this time, my fingers came into contact with something, the Darkness rippled in front of me, and then like a mirage, the Darkness turned into a face. The beautiful face of a man. He grinned. "Come a little closer."

I tried, but my feet felt like they were stuck to the ground.

"Mated." He shook his head. "That is unfortunate for you. If you were free to choose me, I'd make you warm. Now, you must stay cold. Grounded."

Black feathers surrounded his shoulders, attached in weird haphazard ways all around his muscled body. "Now, if he was gone… you would be mine."

The idea thrilled me, but I had no idea why.

"I'm extremely powerful…" His eyes became pensive. "All you have to do is embrace the power…" He shrugged. "The power in every Dark One…"

"Cassius, he has this power too?" I asked.

"For a while." The man shrugged. "He used it for a while, but his friends–" He spat the word. "–brought him back."

Confused, I tried to search for something familiar, but the room was still blanketed in black and the man in front of me was growing by the minute. "One day… one day you will call upon me in your time of need. Then, I'll prove my loyalty. And then, we'll be together."

The way he said it made it sound like a mating, but I already had Cassius. I didn't understand. Was I just having a nightmare? A weird dream?

"The power is always at your fingertips… imagine, you could save all you love, all you care about, by simply allowing the darkness to overcome the light. A Dark One is born with both, but it is your choice. Always your choice."

The idea that I had a choice was… life changing. Because my entire life, choices had been made for me. Even Cassius.

"Yes." The Darkness continued speaking. "Even your love chose for you, he chooses for you even now… Do you have a mind of your own? Or are you a puppet?"

"I'm not!" I shouted. "I'm powerful." Darkness swirled around my body.

"Yes." He nodded approvingly. "You are."

The Darkness suddenly warmed my body, singed me from the inside out, intoxicating in its warmth I allowed it to spread, when suddenly I was punched, or it felt like I was getting punched in the stomach.

"Wake up!" Cassius shouted.

I fell on to the floor and looked up at him. "What was that for?"

White eyes glared back at me as the smell of smoke filled the air. I scrunched up my nose as Cassius put out the fire on the bed spread. When I stood to look at the damage, I gasped. "What happened?"

The entire bedspread was singed.

The pillows, ash.

Cassius let out a loud curse and stood. "You." He swallowed, his eyes swirling with blues and whites. "It seems you've finally met Darkness."

"He, uh—"

"He?" Cassius chuckled. "I guess it would be a he for you, hm? More tempting that way. Darkness takes many forms."

"I don't understand."

"You wouldn't." Cassius pulled me into his arms. "Because Darkness… is you."

I was still reeling from my weird dream, or was it an introduction? The singed smell of burning sheets filled the entire upstairs. Ethan was irritated. Then again, ever since Genesis had become pregnant he'd turned into an over worried tyrant.

He'd already taken it upon himself to baby gate the stairway.

Mason was on board with that idea with so much enthusiasm he offered to install six of them.

Things were going downhill fast, and as much as I wanted to join in on the excitement…

There was… the whole darkness thing.

On top of trying to find whoever was making more immortal Demon.

Oh, and if life wasn't stressful enough.

In less than thirty days, I apparently was going to kill the man I loved.

Life sucked.

A plate slid in front of me, the pancake was fluffy, huge, and had been smothered in enough syrup and butter to kill a human.

Mason sat across from me, his plate filled with a spiky pinecone and a handful of raspberries. "You looked like you needed it."

I picked up my fork. "You remembered my favorite meal."

"How could I forget?" He grinned. "Every year on your birthday, once you joined the council, you wanted pancakes instead of actual cake. Apparently nobody taught you the difference as a child, so let's blame Alex."

"I heard my name." Alex limped into the room.

"What the hell happened to you?" Mason burst out

laughing as Alex found a chair and winced.

"Baby gates." Alex cursed. "A hell of a lot of baby gates. Who knew that would be my downfall?"

"I did," I said between bites. "You're a Siren, it's like your kryptonite. The fact that you could have sex and produce children... it's enough to make you abstinent."

Face blank, Alex outwardly trembled.

"Shhh..." Mason handed Alex a berry. "You're scaring him."

"It's like a mean bedtime story." Alex glared at me. "Also, a little bird told me you nearly burned down the house last night. Care to share any intimate details?"

"She met Darkness." This from Mason as he used his incisors to take a huge bite out of the pinecone.

"Ah, crazy right? Like meeting the worst part of yourself, while at the same time being seduced..." He pressed his lips together in a seductive pout. "I bet Darkness is hot."

"*He* is," I corrected.

Alex looked nonplussed, his expression didn't change. "You know I don't discriminate between the sexes, if he's good looking, good for him, good for all of us."

The sound of Mason chomping on the pinecone scraped over my nerves like nails on a chalkboard. I gave him a pointed look. Slumping, he dropped it back onto his plate and popped a berry into his mouth, his hand transforming into a claw so that he didn't need to use a fork to poke each berry.

"Circus freak," Alex muttered reaching for Mason's coffee.

"Why—" Ethan stormed into the room. "—didn't

you *warn* her?"

Cassius followed, close on his heels. "What the hell did you expect me to say? Oh by the way, in your dreams, you're going to get a visit from Darkness, have fun, be careful not to get to set the house on fire. Oh, and if you're hot and bothered, it's not me?"

"For the record," I interjected. "I wasn't hot and bothered, just warm."

They ignored me.

"If she can't control herself, she can't stay!" Ethan slammed his fist down onto the granite cracking it down the middle. "Genesis is pregnant! She needs protection from things like that." Pieces of granite flew into the air as Ethan pointed in my direction. I slumped low in my seat.

Mason let out a low curse. "I hate ordering new kitchen appliances. Home Depot employees are always so judgmental."

Alex winced as the crack in the granite extended farther. Then the counter slammed into the floor. "Just tell them you got carried away with your last stripper. I'd go with it. Then once we flash them nothing but cash lean in and whisper 'mafia'."

Mason poked another berry with his claw. "Maybe I'll just take you with me and tell them you're my lover. Last time we did that we got fifty percent off."

Alex sighed heavily. "Because she was totally into me, not you." He scrunched up his nose. "You smelled too funny for her tastes, which is why you hung out by appliances while I took her out back."

Ethan turned. "You did what? To a human?"

"Taught her how to saw." Mason interjected. "At the Depot of Homes."

I barely managed to keep my smile in as Cassius shared a confused look with Ethan.

"Lots of sharp edges." Alex nodded emphatically. "Very dangerous... but don't worry, none of your precious blood was spilled."

A low growl erupted from Mason. "One day you're going to get caught for tasting forbidden fruit." Another raspberry flew through the air and into his mouth. "And I'm going to laugh. What's going to happen when your tricks stop working on human women?"

Alex didn't look worried.

"They'll attack in mob-like fashion." Mason nodded. "Yes, what a fantastic day that will be."

Cassius frowned. "Do they... attack at the Depot of Homes?"

"It's Home Depot," I corrected. "And don't pay attention to them, they've been bickering all morning."

"Here." Alex tossed a pinecone into the air. "Have some tree."

"Technically, it's a seed," Mason grumbled, biting into his berries while Ethan slowly made his way over to the group. The tension in the room was extremely uncomfortable as his eyes blazed Vampire green.

Oh, good. He was pissed.

With a snarl, his fangs elongated. "Two days." He jammed a finger in my direction. "She gets her powers under control in two days and she can stay. If not, then you're on the streets."

"And when he says streets, he means you get to shack up with Cassius so you don't burn down Ethan's house with his precious human in it," Alex said.

"I thought we were beyond that?" Genesis breezed into the kitchen, immediately causing Ethan's eyes to go back to normal as he hissed and pulled away from us only long enough to tug Genesis into his arms and kiss her neck.

"No biting in public," Cassius mumbled under his breath. "That's against immortal rules, not that you listen to me anyway."

"I've been bitten," Alex announced as all heads turned in his direction. "I found it extremely erotic… then she tried to kill me."

"Surprised only one of your stories ends that way… I imagine if women were in their right minds while you seduced them they'd all want to kill you."

"An Elk followed me home once too. Thought itself in love with me." Alex yawned.

Disgusted, since I still thought of him as my brother, I stood and held out my hand to Cassius. "Should we get started?"

His face was void of emotion. I was almost afraid that we were going to go back to the way things were, him ignoring me, me ignoring the searing pain in my heart every time he refused to acknowledge that there was something between us.

"Outside." Cassis gripped my hand in his then raised it to his lips. "Lesson number one… Dark Ones know no fear."

I was about to respond when a cold blast of air slammed me against the wall. I tried to move but the air held me immobile. My breathing came in short gasps as air pushed against my mouth.

Cassius leaned in, his lips grazing my ear. "Afraid?"

"No," I wheezed.

The pressure increased.

Why was nobody helping me?

Because you can help yourself. Cassius's voice was a small whisper in my head.

I closed my eyes and then willed my hands to push out in front of me as I turned the wind on Cassius.

With a grunt, I had him slammed against the floor, the same wind pushing him down.

"Oh, no!" I covered my mouth with my hands and leaned over him. "Are you okay?"

His smile was bright.

Deadly.

A bit more erotic than I'd ever seen it.

"Oh, yes." He chuckled darkly. "More than okay, I think." He reached for my head tugging it down to press a hungry kiss against my mouth.

"Is that porn?" Mason whispered.

Alex let out a groan. "No, Wolf..."

"But they are engaging in front of others? Is that not what Porn is? Why Genesis said no to the other store we walked by with the bright lights and—"

"Where the hell are you taking him at night?" Alex yelled. "Geez, Genesis, he's like an innocent. You can't just prostitute the pinecones out of him!"

Genesis let out a loud laugh. "Don't worry about it. What's between me and Mason is between me and Mason."

Another loud crunch of a pinecone.

Cassius pulled away from me. "Outside?"

"Yeah, let's take this outside."

"Big boy."

Cassius's warm laughter made my entire morning.

CHAPTER 29

Stephanie

"TEACHING YOU," HE EXPLAINED once we were outside. "Isn't the same as showing you… therefore… we're just going to get into it."

"Into it?" I asked.

Cassius grabbed my arm, the cold stung like icy needles running up and down my arm.

When my eyes were able to focus again, I wished I was stuck with temporary blindness, everywhere I looked, Demon were sleeping. Somehow we'd gone from standing outside Ethan's house to somewhere else completely, all within the span of seconds.

"This," Cassius whispered, "is the fun part."

A loud whooshing sound crashed in the middle of the warehouse and then it started to pour rain.

Demon scattered to the farthest edges of darkness. That was, until Cassius held up his hand, and like a light was being turned on, every single shred of darkness was removed from the room.

They shrieked and bellowed, and then finally, one stepped forward. I didn't know his name, didn't recognize him at all.

"You know why we're here." Cassius's voice

boomed, like it often did when he was exuding an enormous amount of power. He reminded me of the Disney cartoon Hercules. When he'd turned into a god, his voice had developed an echo to it while his body was light itself.

That's what Cassius looked like.

Only better looking.

Real flesh and blood.

A man.

Not a cartoon.

"Y-yes." The Demon covered his eyes. "Could you at least dim the lights, Cassius?"

With a slow nod the lights lowered to a mere glow while the Demon paced in front of Cassius.

"Well?" Cassius asked. "We don't have all day."

"It's Angel blood." The Demon tilted his head in my direction his eyes moving to the back of his head. "It smells like her. Like you."

"Dark Ones possess elements of Angelic blood, you know this." Cassius said in a bored tone.

"The spice…" The Demon took a cautious step toward me and sniffed. "It isn't as sweet as her scent or yours… almost like the Dark One was born out of…" He shuddered. "Fear."

Confused, I figured I could just ask later, but Cassius must have thought I needed to know right away.

"Most Dark Ones are born out of one of the seven sins, lust, greed, envy…" He sniffed the air in front of him. "But from what you're saying… this mating… that took place was—"

"—rape," the Demon finished. "Which is impossible, a human raping an Angel? Or Vice versa? They'd be killed on the spot for even thinking it."

"Unless it was no human."

"Unless the human wasn't fully human… immortal, maybe?" Cassius wondered aloud. "Can you track it?"

"Whatever you wish. You know my friends and family are innocent, you've tasted the truth in the air the minute you arrived."

The air was clear with honestly with nothing but truth, and yes, a bit of fear. Funny, I'd never recognized fear before, always thought of it to be this weird fleeting emotion that paralyzed humans.

But fear was small.

If I closed my eyes tight enough I could see it in my mind's eye, it was like a child or toddler, and then, all of a sudden, it was given food, growing before my very eyes until it was a giant, until it eclipsed everything in its presence.

"Fear is born small," the Demon whispered. "We are the ones who make it big."

Pity rushed through me; the Demon were cursed just like the Dark Ones, cursed to live out the rest of their existence knowing that in the end, they would be judged just like the humans, just like everyone else.

It was also why they weren't allowed to create.

Creating more Demon was creating more curses.

While creating a Vampire or a Siren, wasn't as frowned upon, they actually possessed their souls.

Demon. Did not.

Though they did still have feelings.

And that was the saddest part of all. They could feel, they could hope all they wanted… it was always in vain.

"But we still try." The Demon locked eyes with me.

"We will try every day until our penance is over. We will try to stay in the good graces of Angels and Dark Ones alike."

"Thank you," Cassius mumbled. The rain stopped, and the darkness returned. "Track the blood."

"The Darkness…" The Demon whispered as Cassius grabbed my arm. "It has her, Cassius. I can feel it."

Chapter 30

Cassius

I blocked my thoughts from her. The last thing she needed was to be aware of my concern. Bringing her to the Demon was twofold. I needed information, and next to the wolves they were the best trackers we had, besides, there was no loyalty within their ranks.

Someone would talk.

Because they were constantly fighting for dominance, control. And when that person did talk, I hoped it would be loud enough for me to hear.

I also wanted to see if the Demon could sense the dark swirling within her, I was too close to the situation. Funny, I suddenly cared too much about our joint futures, our destinies that I was also blinded from hers.

The minute we mated.

Her future was lost to me.

Every time I touched her, I heard Darkness whispering.

She wasn't even aware that Darkness was speaking, but like a slow storm it was building, brewing, and I could do nothing but hope that in the end, I would be strong enough to bring her away from the temptation that every immortal being who possessed Angel blood was given—to be like a god.

It was a lie.

Darkness twisted its lies in such a way, that the air didn't taste bitter, but clear for the first time, because not every lie spoken, was done outright, yet woven with tiny bits and pieces of truth.

I shuddered and returned my thoughts to the Demons.

My money was on Timber, but I refused to visit him until Stephanie had more control of her powers.

She might be stronger.

But Timber was evil, and the Darkness in her would recognize his evil, and want to unite with it. Regardless of who was standing next to her, regardless of who I was to her, she'd be tempted, because we're always tempted when we don't understand things.

I had never told her the road would be easy.

I wished it were.

"What does he mean?" Stephanie asked once we were in the parking lot near the water at Pike Place Market. So normal, to walk with her hand in hand as we maneuvered our way through fish throwing and people selling flowers.

The flowers leaned toward us as we walked by, sensing the lifeblood flowing through our veins.

The wind picked up as insects paused whatever they were doing and watched. Curiously waiting to see if we would bring about the destruction we were so known for—or if we truly were just walking by the flowers.

Nature held its breath.

And I held Stephanie's hand.

Her fingertips pressed against mine. It was really

all I needed, but like a sick reminder of the direction of her thoughts, I sensed the Darkness in her, wrapping its black tendrils around her neck, choking her.

Whispering to her.

Give in, give in, give in.

It had taken me years to recognize that the voice was like the devil that sat on my shoulder. Most of the time it was right.

Most of the time it told me to destroy every human I saw.

It told me to drink their blood.

To snap their necks.

It told me I was a god.

It told me I should be worshipped.

And most days, I didn't believe it.

But at my weakest—I did want those things. I wanted to destroy life… because life didn't respect life.

Life was a fantasy, and the road to paradise was ridden with people who didn't deserve to be traveling it in the first place. It would be my given right, to exterminate them.

And then, the light inside me, reminded me, you are just like them. Undeserving, at times very weak, and cursed. Yet, you are allowed to live.

Why not them?

People passed in front of us. I stopped Stephanie and pointed at the couple as the man fell to his knee and proposed to his girlfriend.

"What do you see?" I asked.

She sighed happily, squeezing my hand tightly. "Love."

"Look closer," I instructed.

Frowning, she stared harder. "I don't know what

you want me to see."

"Call the Darkness, but do not touch."

"How do I call it?"

"It's you." I nodded, allowing my eyes to go black as I stared at the couple again, through what I knew would be my own shades of darkness. The couple that looked so happy, that appeared so perfect.

Was far from it.

The woman was worried for her safety. But he was so happy, the man proposing, that this was it, she thought, he was going to stop beating her. He was going to stop, because he loved her.

The man smiled brightly, his thoughts were of killing her… finally, he breathed a sigh of relief… *she'll be mine and nobody else's, I'll kill her before I let her touch anyone else. Mine. Mine. Mine.*

As they embraced, bruises spread across her arms, her teeth fell out, blood spewed from her mouth, and the man began strangling her, and then, wrapped something around her neck, only to shoot himself in the head after.

With a startled gasp, Stephanie clung to me.

I pushed the darkness away, ignoring the tug to look further, and hugged her tighter instead.

"It's getting worse!" She looked around at the people walking by, bumping into us, with each bump she was given a vision of the horror of their lives, of what they were capable of. "Stop! It needs to stop!"

"Shhh." I held her as tight as I could and linked my thoughts to hers, pressing the darkness away. But it pressed back. Stronger than I'd realized. I tried again only to have it laugh in my face. "Cling to the happy… the light."

"There is no happy," she sobbed. "Everything is dark."

"I'm light," I whispered in her ear. "Look at me."

She opened her eyes and then slowly, the black slid away from her irises, returning them to a milky white and then bright blue. "What just happened?"

"That..." I led her away from the crowd. "Is Darkness. It's why it's so tempting. Why let that couple live... when their certain future is doom?"

Cassius

"It's my job to keep the peace." Stephanie shuddered in my arms then jerked away from me as black spread throughout her white eyes. "We should destroy them all."

"And then what?" I asked. "To what end?"

"Peace." Her voice took on a gravelly edge that I recognized.

Was it so long ago that I'd lost Eva? That I'd allowed Darkness to consume me? That I'd wanted nothing more than to jump into the black hole and allow it to embrace every part of my soul I still possessed? For a few minutes, it had felt right. But Ethan, Mason, and Alex had not allowed it.

Luckily, Ethan's words had made sense at the time, enough sense that I used my strength to push away from Darkness and allow myself to mourn.

Mourn the life I felt like I should have had.

The life Darkness said I deserved.

But Darkness, didn't just call for the death of humanity, it also called for the death of Angels and immortals alike.

Darkness was within everyone.

It lays dormant, until it sees the perfect opportunity to offer a better suggestion to your circumstances.

Darkness is in humans.

It's in immortals.

It's in the very air we breathe.

But the worst type of darkness is the kind we keep in our hearts… we treasure it, hold it dear, allow it to help us justify our actions, and when it's too late, we blame it for everything while it points its finger back at us and laughs.

Sighing, I reached out and pressed my fingers against her lip allowing the frost of my fingertips to cool her hot body down.

With a gasp she sucked in one finger, then two, then jerked my body against hers our mouths fused in a battle of dominance as I spread my cold around her.

Darkness was always hot.

Comforting, to a Dark One, until it burned that Dark One alive.

"Come back," I whispered, my lips pressed against hers as I called to her light…"Come back to me."

Stephanie slumped against my body her breathing erratic as her fingers dug into the muscles in my back.

"I think I want to be done training for the day." Her voice was scratchy, like she'd just spent the last few minutes screaming at the top of her lungs, and who knew? Maybe she had. Maybe she was yelling at Darkness, maybe that's what it took to pull away.

"It will get easier," I promised. "It just takes time." Still trembling, I held her as tight as I could, swearing to myself I'd die before I let anything happen to her, and in a thought of true irony—to save her from the darkness, from herself, I'd allow her to kill me.

If that's what it took.

I'd accept my fate.

Gladly.

"You know how Ethan gave Genesis lessons about immortals and our history?" Stephanie asked, changing the subject as we walked hand in hand down the sidewalk.

"Yes."

She stopped. "I think it's my turn."

"Hell." I released her hand. "I'm not sure that's the best idea."

"You don't even know what I'm asking!"

"Yes, I do." My laugh was completely without humor. "You want to know what the darkness really is, you want to know Dark Ones history 101."

She nodded.

"Hell."

"You said that already."

"Steph..."

"Please?" She reached for my hand, gripping it. "If I just understood it, I could fight it."

I wrapped my arms around her waist and whispered. "Lie."

"Huh?"

"You lied to yourself."

"We can do that?"

"We're half human, we can do anything they can."

"Can Angels lie?"

"They could," I said slowly, then rolled my eyes. "Damn it, you're going to get it out of me one way or another aren't you?"

"My next offer was some sort of mind blowing sexual experience... with snow."

I chuckled despite myself and the tense topic. "Snow, huh?"

"Lots of snow. You like snow."

"Who told you that?"

"Genesis." Stephanie shrugged. "I may have let it slip that I could dream walk and she said in your guys dreams you always had snow surrounding you. You said it was comforting."

"Home." Emotion clogged my throat. "Always brings comfort."

"Home?" Stephanie repeated. "What do you mean home?"

"Where I was born. It always brings comfort. Snow… represents where I was born."

Stephanie leaned in, sniffing the air. "Truth. So, Cassius…" She patted my stomach, I'd seen human couples do that before in teasing and never understood the need for such trivial flirting with one's hands… until her hands were on me, until I was part of the couple, and every single glance and caress my way was like breathing for the first time, after being without air for an eternity. "Where were you born? Siberia?"

"Da." I confirmed in Russian and then pressed my fingertips to her wrist.

Chapter 32

Stephanie

"Where are we?" I gasped, rubbing my arms, they weren't necessarily chilled, but they felt colder than ever before. The sun was just starting to set, casting a beautiful orange glow across a small city.

It reminded me of Christmas.

And the movie Frozen. The one that Genesis had forced Mason to watch only to ask him later if he could morph into a reindeer instead of a wolf for Halloween.

He'd said he'd attempt it. Ethan and Alex still made fun of him for his promise, but that was Mason. He lived to make others happy—maybe it was because he wasn't capable of happiness himself.

"Mason," Cassius said, interrupting my thoughts, "has a bright future."

"And Alex?" I couldn't help but ask.

"Once you can control your power you'll be able to comb through futures at ease," Cassius explained. "And Alex has… an intriguing few months ahead of him."

"Hmm." I liked the sound of that.

The wind picked up just as the sun made its final descent behind the snow covered mountains blanketing everything but the few street lights in darkness.

"I forgot how quiet it was here." Cassius mused, grabbing my hand in his. We were both still in our street clothes. Jeans and T-shirts.

He quickly tugged me into the first store on the main street and pulled out a fur coat, hat, and pants that looked two sizes too big for my legs. Boots were tossed in my direction, and then he was at the counter speaking in a harsh language I'd never heard him speak before.

Could it be that Cassius really *was*… Russian?

The man at the desk laughed loudly then pulled out a shot glass and a bottle of vodka. He poured one for himself, took it, then poured one for Cassius.

Without breaking his laugh, Cassius tossed the alcohol back and slammed the shot glass back onto the table.

They shook hands.

While I stood there open-mouthed like I'd just seen a miracle occur. Cassius, almost appeared normal. Almost.

And then he smiled, and I was reminded all over again why he was so beautiful, so effortlessly gorgeous that it hurt to look at his face for too long of a stretch. His beauty was like a constantly changing painting, I always noticed something different about his face, his bright blue eyes, how dark his lashes were ,the angle of his jaw, the shape of his sculpted lips—there was always something interesting something unique, different, and I was immortal, I was used to seeing pretty things.

I self-consciously tugged at my dark hair. Had my appearance altered much since the glamour wore off?

Humans didn't seem to stare at me any differently, maybe longer, but they were born with a natural fear of things they didn't understand—and immortality was something they would never be able to comprehend, meaning, they usually gave us a wide berth, even if they were interested.

Sensual lips pressed together in a wicked smirk as Cassius held out his hand. "Do you like the boots?"

"I'm wearing Mason." I stared down at the furry boots and laughed. "I think he'd be pissed if he saw these."

"They don't hunt those types of wolves up here," Cassius promised. "Even Mason's kind stay away from the bitter cold of Oymyakon."

"Siberia…" I shivered again even though the cold was normal for my typically frigid body. "So you *were* serious."

Cassius smiled even wider, maybe being home was good for him.

"So…" I spread my free arm out as we walked down the abandoned icy streets. "This is where young Cassius grew up."

Cassius's face darkened for a brief moment before he grabbed my hand and started whistling.

The tune wasn't familiar, but its haunting melody had me shivering as he continued to whistle and the wind picked up. I wrapped my jacket tighter around myself and ducked into his body.

I'd always hated the wind. When I was little it had reminded me of anger, of cold, and now that I was a Dark One and didn't really get cold in the same way, I still hated it because it was still angry.

Wind was nature's temper tantrum.

At least it had always felt that way.

"Wind..." Cassius stopped whistling. "...is a warning of things to come."

I frowned. "In nature or in life?"

The wind dipped and roared down the street as we made our way toward a small dark house.

"Both." Cassius began whistling again, and the wind howled right along with him. By the time we made it to the house it had started to snow, the wind causing near white out conditions.

"Be afraid," Cassius whispered. "Of the beauty of the heavens."

"What?"

"Humans are afraid of what they do not understand, but the minute they come into contact with the very thing that brings them fear, and aren't burned or harmed in any way, bravery takes over... they touch." He winced. "They explore." His body trembled. "And they fall."

It seemed liked he was talking in riddles.

He pushed the door open.

A fire was lit in the hearth taking the chill away from my body immediately.

Stepping into the house was like stepping back in time.

A woman rocked back and forth in an old rackety chair, facing the fire, her small hands knit furiously at what looked like a child's sweater. "I knew you would eventually come."

Cassius hung his head, then pressed his hand to my back, pushing me toward the woman.

With a sigh, the woman stood, the fur blanket fell from her shoulders and she faced me.

"What..." I shook my blurry confused head. "What are you?"

I didn't sense that she was human... but there was something about her blood as I sniffed the air.

She smelled human.

She looked immortal.

With pitch black hair and bow-shaped red lips, she was like a princess, her eyelashes had pieces of snow in them as if she'd just been outside dancing and twirling underneath the moon.

"Mother." Cassius's greeting made me gasp. "Meet—"

"—your destiny." The woman held out her hand. "I see a great darkness in you, Stephanie."

I pulled my hand back and grabbed Cassius's arm.

"Something we all possess, Mother," Cassius said in a low voice. "Darkness is not new to you."

"No." She sat back down. "I guess it is not."

I watched their exchange in silence. Still unable to understand how that woman could be Cassius's mother.

How was she even alive?

"Sit," his mother instructed me. "And I'll tell you a story."

In silence, I sank onto a tired-looking wooden chair, a bit surprised at how sturdy it turned out to be.

"I was told the beauty was unparalleled, like walking through paradise." The woman sighed in contentment. "The problem with humanity has always been its need for more knowledge and power, never satisfied, never content." Shivering, she wrapped the blanket tighter around her as Cassius moved to her side and tucked the edges around her small body. "Immortal beings have always... been." Her eyes lost focus for a brief second as she stared into the fire. "They were created right along with the Angels, have always co-existed in perfect harmony. Like two worlds that paralleled one another. The immortal plane existed, and the human plane existed. But there have always been situations where humans have learned of immortals or been forced to work with them. That is where your stories of lore come from." She rocked back and forth in her chair, back and forth, so far she wasn't telling me anything I didn't already know. "There was only one rule." She sighed. "Do not fall in love." Her eyes locked on mine. "But I did."

The fire crackled as she spread her hands wide, her palms facing down. "My father was trusted with the immortal secret, with the knowledge of another world. He helped bring them humans in the beginning, he was the one who helped start the calling of numbers once immortals realized that humanity would need more help reigning itself in. The immortals were a type of police, and they didn't have the numbers for it. So my father helped start the calling of breeders. They discovered that if an immortal Vampire for instance, mated with a human, the human not only gained immortality but she was able to birth children. It was the perfect plan."

"But not all immortals are created equal," Cassius mumbled and then pressed a kiss to his mother's hand. "Why don't you sleep? You look tired, I can tell her the rest of the story."

"Yes." His mother nodded, tears pooling in her eyes. "Yes, I'll do that."

She stood and walked off, softly shutting the door

behind her.

"How is she alive?"

"A gift." Cassius answered. "From my father."

"Sariel?"

Cassius nodded. "You said you wanted to know what Dark Ones really were and how it happened, so I'm going to take you back to the beginning."

"The beginning of the Dark Ones."

His eyes flashed. "To the first one ever created." He sighed as if he bore the weight of the world on his shoulders. "Me."

Cassius

THE PAST WAS A painful reminder of my uncertain future, and exposing her to that, unsettled me completely, but if she wanted the truth.

I could not.

Would not, keep it from her.

"Watch," I whispered, lying down with her near the fire, as her body relaxed against mine, I waited for her to fall into a deep sleep and prayed that she wouldn't hate herself for what she was.

Because Dark Ones… were not the heroes.

But the villains.

I kissed her forehead and began my story as I walked into her dream, grasping her hand tightly. "Look, look at the ones who watch."

Two hundred men stood on the edge of the mountain, each of them well over seven feet tall, their faces were perfectly shaped as if the person who had created them had special knowledge of just how far away eyes should be from the nose, and the nose from the lips.

To stare at them was to experience the fullest of contentment.

To be in their presence was absolute adoration.

A battle brewed in front of them, yet they were immobile.

"They were called the ones who do not sleep." I pointed at the line of men as their gold armor glistened against the sun, a sword and shield was placed in each hand. They continued to stand, their hair tangled in the wind, a mixture of reds and black tendrils escaped out of their gold helmets.

One of the two hundred flinched as a man was decapitated.

He lowered his head for a fraction of a second, while one of the men next to him grunted.

And still, they stood.

"Why aren't they helping?" Stephanie asked. "Humans are dying! Getting slaughtered by one another. Why don't they intervene?"

"Because it's not their job," I answered. "Their job is to watch, their job is to never close their eyes. For when you close your eyes, even for a brief moment, you lose sight of what's in front of you, and at times, you can lose sight of what's inside."

"That makes no sense." Stephanie pointed back down at the humans. "Blood's everywhere, it would take two of the men on the mountain to stop this."

"One," I corrected her. "It would only take one."

The scene changed and suddenly the village in front of them was getting swallowed up in flames.

And again.

They watched.

Stephanie screamed at them. And yet they watched. "Cassius! Do something, there's women…" She choked out a sob. "Children are dying!"

"Children die every day." I spoke in a soft whisper.

"They see it every day, they've been watching for hundreds of years, what makes this day different?"

Stephanie covered her eyes as a child was tossed into the fire—alive.

Screaming she tried to run toward the men watching, but I held her back. It shattered my heart, to see her reaction, to know that the men could have done something—but that they couldn't.

"Stephanie." I licked my lips. "To act is to go against every cell in their body, every reason they were created. You have to understand, they were not made to feel, they were made to act."

"Then why don't they act!"

"Because they have not been told to… yet."

More children screamed.

And then suddenly a light shone down on the two hundred men, flickering against their gold shields. Each shield held the design of a tree, but every tree was different, as if its origin came from a differing country or region.

The shields swiftly moved to the front of the men, and with a roar the two hundred descended upon the crowd of humans getting slaughtered.

It was over in thirty seconds.

Less than that.

The humans thanked the men, the same men who had watched them suffer for days, weeks, years, not knowing that this wasn't some army marching through as they had claimed, but actual beings, created to watch over humanity.

My mother stumbled out of her hut, then fell to her knees in loud choking sobs.

The man, the same one who had flinched while

watching, stopped in front of her then knelt down. "Woman, why do you cry?"

His voice was so hollow, as if he didn't understand emotion.

"My son." She choked out a long horrendous sob. "He was thrown in the fire..." Even through tears stained cheeks, blood caked to her fingers, and her hair matted, she was beautiful. The man sucked in a sharp breath, admiring her for the first time. "He was only a year, sir."

"A year," he repeated. "To be so new..." He shook his head. "I cannot comprehend such a short amount of time."

"It wasn't enough." My mother hung her head. "I'll mourn him forever."

As an angelic being, the man could feel the woman's sadness as if it was his own. He pulled off his helmet, set down his armor, and helped her to her feet.

It was his first mistake.

For without his armor.

He'd forgotten his purpose.

And when he touched her.

He closed his eyes. For the first time in his existence.

And when he opened them—her.

Only her.

And nothing else existed.

How, he wondered, had he gone so long watching, but not truly seeing?

As his men walked back up the mountain, to regain their rightful place, to stay awake, to watch.

He hesitated.

He never hesitated.

He wasn't aware of the meaning of it.

Until that moment.

So beautiful.

I.

Want.

His breath came out in a whoosh.

Want.

Want.

Want.

Heartbeat slowing, he pressed her hand to his cheek as his blood roared for something more—than watching.

Watching was no longer enough.

He closed his eyes again.

And again.

And again as she continued to touch his face.

"Why are you crying?" the woman asked.

"Name?" he whispered. "What do they call you?"

"Nephal," she answered. "It means—"

"—fallen." He jerked away, took one step, then two. As if his very life depended on it, he put distance between him and Nephal.

"And yours?" she asked.

Want.

Want.

Want.

He knew he shouldn't tell her, something cried out inside of him, that it was wrong, the entire exchange, something told him it would not end well, but he only wanted seconds, minutes, hours, maybe he wanted days, and was it wrong to want time? When he was given so much of it? After all, he was still watching, he was just watching. Her.

"Sariel." The minute his name was released into the

atmosphere, the wind picked up, a warning, from nature, from the very earth that he'd sworn to protect.

Do not do this. The mountains trembled.

Do not do this. The wind hissed.

Do not do this. The ground shook.

"I will not do this." Sariel repeated out loud as the wind died down.

The woman hung her head. "Thank you… for all you've done."

She turned her back.

He didn't want her to.

He wanted.

Want.

Want.

Want.

"Sariel!" One of his men barked out his name. "We return to the mountain."

"To watch," Sariel said, his tone bitter.

Azeel looked stricken. "Brother, of course we watch. It is our purpose."

And for the first time, Sariel… wanted more.

The earth shifted that day, without his brother's knowledge, for when he watched, he watched Nephal.

When he watched, he dreamed of her.

And when his brothers were doing their duty.

He was closing his eyes and remembering her hand on his face.

It was years before he would see her again.

And the opportunity arose as the village was yet again attacked. The men, disbursed from the mountain.

They went in all directions.

But Sariel went to Nephal.

Once he reached her hut, he knocked on the door then burst through when she did not answer. "Nephal? Are you hurt?"

"No." She frowned, rising up from her bed, the fur fell from her naked body. Sariel had never seen anything so beautiful in all his life.

Already he could sense that the battle was nearly over, his brothers, returning back to the mountain.

"I missed you." Tears filled her eyes. "I do not know who you are… but I miss you. Why do I miss you?"

He didn't know why.

He just knew he felt the same way.

"Why do you only come when we are in trouble?"

"I cannot answer that."

"Why do I feel strongly for you? A man? A stranger I do not know?"

"I cannot answer that either."

She nodded, covering herself with the fur and laid down.

Sariel was immobile, and then he found himself peeling his armor off, layer by layer.

He lay by her, pulling the woman in his arms as his body whispered *mine*.

But his heart.

His heart was in the most danger of all.

For when she sighed against him, it was as if time, did not slow, but picked up, reminding him, that it would run out. And his precious woman, would die.

Sariel returned to his men, to his spot on the mountain a different being that day.

And his brothers knew.

"What have you done, brother?" Ezaju whispered under his breath, rarely did he ever speak. "You smell of humanity," He turned his head, taking his eyes off the village. "You stink of earth."

Sariel looked down, in shame. "I love her."

His brothers, all one hundred ninety-nine of them, seemed to gasp in unison, and then began talking all at once.

"Do you want to send us to hell?" One spoke above the rest. "Do you realize what will happen if one of us falls? All of us fall!"

Sariel sighed. "You think I don't know that? You think I'm unaware of repercussions. I cannot help how I feel."

"Try!" Ezaju yelled. "You must try. For the sake of all of us!"

Sariel nodded. "I will… try."

"We watch," Bannik replied. "We do not sleep. We do not close our eyes." The brothers all returned to watching in one loud clap of thunder and repeated. "We are the ones who keep our eyes open. We are the awake."

But Sariel… did not repeat it.

For his vow was long ago broken, the minute he closed his eyes and wanted.

Stephanie hid her face in my chest. "I'm not sure I want to see anymore."

"The story ends soon."

"But does it end well?" she asked.

"It ends the only way it can." I licked my lips as the vision disintegrated in front of us.

Sariel was again at the village.

And Nephal was already waiting for him.

He knew his brothers were watching, but he kept thinking, if only they saw the joy, if only they saw what they could have.

He slept with her.

Not once.

Nor twice.

Many, many times, and each time he grew more and more attached to the woman who held his heart. The woman he would bind himself to forever.

She was lying across his naked body when she whispered, "I am with child."

"Impossible." Sariel shook his head. "We are not human."

Already he'd told her too much, about the heavens, about the stars, about his race.

"It is possible. It must be." She touched her belly. "Already I feel his movement."

"And how do you know it is a boy?"

"Is it?" She smiled brightly and Sariel caught on to the excitement, pressing his hand against her stomach in joy until the destiny of the child played out in horrific visions of the future.

With a gasp, Sariel pulled his hand back. "He must… not be born."

Nephal jerked away from Sariel. "How could you say that? This child was conceived in love?"

"This child." Sariel shook his head. "Will be hated… scorned, constantly surrounded by darkness."

"Darkness?"

"He will never experience true joy or contentment, constantly pulled between two planes, between immortals and mortals alike. He will know division and darkness, the darkness and cruelty of the human race will be his lover, his companion. I cannot allow him to be born. My love for him, for you, is what guides this."

"Never!" She shouted, tears streaming down her face. "If you touch me I'll kill you!"

"Nephal—"

"Go away!"

Sighing, Sariel did as she asked.

And didn't return until the babe was born.

That night, with Bannik at his side, he entered the tent, ready to destroy the abomination, when his eyes locked on the child's.

Bannik tensed next to him and then uttered, "I cannot kill our flesh."

"He is..." Sariel swallowed down his emotions. "He is part of us."

He joined Nephal on the bed as Bannik looked on.

And then a great thunder sounded.

Bannik sighed, his eyes heavy, his heart heavier. "They're here."

And as if the sun had descended to earth, a legion of Angels landed in the camp, shining bright with gold and silver armor. The Archangels joined the first part of the ranks, while the rest of the soldiers fanned out around the tent.

And one hundred and ninety-nine of his brothers, marched down the mountain, for the last time.

To their death.

Sariel wrapped Nephal in one arm protectively while hovering over the child.

"Cassius," he whispered. "We will name him Cassius."

Nephal nodded, tears streaming down her face.

The tent door was opened.

"Creation is forbidden," the Angel said in a booming voice. "What, brother, have you done?"

Bannik stood next to Sariel's side, hand on his sword.

The Angel held out his hand. "We did not come to fight. We refuse to fight our own blood. We came to pass judgment, but what are we to do with a young child? Innocent in ways of the world? Innocent in ways of humanity and immortals alike?"

Sariel stood to his full height. "I could not…" He lost his voice and tried again. "This is my sin, but I cannot punish him for it. I could not."

"Nor would it be asked of you," the Angel fired back, his eyes blazing like fire. "Children will always be protected…" He sighed. "But this child or any born in this way, will forever be cursed." The Angel's eyes went black. "He will carry a darkness, and every day it will try to consume him. If he gives in, he will be killed. We will have no choice, for he has the knowledge of the heavens and the power to command at will. If he gives in to the darkness, there will be no saving him from himself, for he will be pure evil."

Cassius, the child, cried.

Sariel nodded. "I will train him."

"Your punishment." The Angel spoke low in his throat. "Your curse… is that you will always carry the weight of his decisions. Sariel, we leave you twelve brothers, to help you keep the immortals and humans in balance. Now that you have mixed the blood, we are no longer at peace." The wind swirled, nasty and angry. "But, brother, a lifetime of war. Between the races. Between each other, for you have created, and that is beyond our realm. It is forbidden."

Lightning flashed as Sariel made his way out of the tent.

Two thousand Angels stood, ready to fight as fire struck down from the sky, destroying the mountain where the brothers had watched.

A deep sadness ripped through Sariel as most of his brothers, the ones who were awake, were commanded to sleep, and fell to the ground.

"They will slumber," the Angel commanded, "until their penance is paid. As for the rest of you." He pointed at the twelve remaining brothers and spread his hands wide. "Do not fail again."

In another loud clap, the Angels returned to heaven.

All but one.

He was small.

Like a child.

Slowly, he took a step forward and held out his hands to Sariel.

"We give second chances." He nodded. "To our creation."

The child smiled brightly like that of a star shining in the sky, sucking the breath from the very air Sariel breathed.

And then wings grew out of Sariel's back. "Your brothers will not slumber forever. And you will need the strength and knowledge of the heavens for the darkness that is coming." He spread his hands again. "Remember, where there is darkness..." His voice lowered to a whisper. "There is also great light."

The dream ended.

Stephanie woke up sobbing against Cassius, he held her while his mother returned from her own sleep.

In one final gift, Sariel's human was given immortality.

So he would never see her age.
But they were to never lie together again.
Or he'd be cursed to roam the earth for an eternity.

Cassius

We said goodbye to my mother. I knew I'd see her soon, I did always try to visit at least once a month. She always claimed she wasn't lonely, that she had plenty going on in their small town to keep her company.

But, I knew the truth.

The day I was born, her world had changed forever.

As had mine.

As had Sariel's.

Stephanie held my hand tightly, darkness still blanketed the snow-covered hills as we quietly walked back through town, through the way we had come, our feet crunching against the snow.

"That's why Darkness is so dangerous," Stephanie finally whispered, I'd been worried that the story had been too traumatic for her, hearing it is one thing, experiencing it through a dream, quite another.

"What do you mean?" I asked, the rhythm of her heart picked up as she leaned her lithe body against mine. "Why do you think it's so dangerous?"

"It makes promises," Stephanie finally answered, her voice somehow, sounded broken, altered. "It promises contentment. It promises peace."

"To touch Darkness..." I stopped walking and faced her. "Is to experience war, it is untouchable, do you understand? The minute you grasp it, you're already lost. Damn it Stephanie, if you have one flicker, one nanosecond of hesitation, it will wrap so tightly around you that all you'll know is war."

"One thing I don't understand." She brushed off my lecture. "Why was Sariel punished for falling in love? Isn't love good?"

"You don't understand the story clearly." I kissed her gloved hand then pulled it off, one by one, kissing each finger. "He was punished for going against why he was created."

Stephanie frowned. "That makes no sense."

I wrapped my arms around her and turned her toward the mountain, it wasn't as high as it used to be, rumors of the village stated that in the beginning of time, the ancestors experienced earthquakes along with a shot of bright light, when the light died down, all that was left was rubble. Half the mountain was gone.

The glorious mountain that used to protect the village from the cold, for it stopped storm systems before they were able to make it over the mountain.

Was suddenly defenseless.

And cursed with an eternal winter.

"Siberia," I whispered, "Was never meant to be cold." I wrapped my arms tighter around her, as tightly as I could. Unapologetic about the feelings I had for her, the fierce desire I had to protect her from the darkness inside. "The reason Dark Ones are cold, using ice particles and water with a simple flick of our wrist. It is cold because of us, we are the cold, we are the curse that surrounds us." Tiny pieces of ice flew into the air. "You miss the point of the story, my love."

Stephanie stilled in my arms then melted all at once. "Did you just call me your love?"

I purposely ignored her question and pointed to the mountain. "What was their job? Their purpose?"

She swallowed, her hands digging into my forearms as she swayed in my arms. "To be awake. To watch."

"And what did Sariel do?"

"He fell in love."

"Before that."

Sheets of ice froze in front of our faces as we stared at the mountain.

"He closed his eyes."

I sighed heavily. "Yes. He closed his eyes. He was not punished for his love, but for going against what he was created for. He was not meant to close his eyes, not made for it, possibly for the very reason that once we close our eyes, we look inward, we lose focus of what is right in front of us. The scariest things do not always lie outside..." I kissed her cold cheek. "...but within."

"Ick." Alex took a step back from us. "You're both frigid and I mean that in a completely nonsexual way." He winked at me and then scrunched up his nose as if we smelled. "Reindeer?"

"Close." Stephanie shoved past him. "We were in Siberia."

Alex shared a look with me, one I knew well, his thoughts were along the lines of, *Why the hell would you take her there only to scare the ever loving shit out of her?* Always so eloquent, Sirens.

I ignored his yelling in my head and continued walking through the house. With every step I took more and more ice released itself from my body, melting into a puddle on the floor.

Stephanie seemed agitated, a quick learner, her thoughts were getting harder and harder for me to read, as if she'd put up a block.

A block of something hazy.

Gray.

I couldn't see through it.

And at times, I wondered if she even knew it was there, if she realized that even now, she flirted with things she had no knowledge of.

"Living room," Alex called after me. "They're watching Beauty and the Beast."

I rolled my eyes. "Of course they are."

Bickering was what I was greeted with as Stephanie took a seat as far away from me as possible, her eyes trained in on the fireplace, watching the flames lick and hiss.

"All I'm saying," Ethan said as he stood, spreading his hands wide. "Is why can't they make movies about Vampires? I mean a beast? It's ugly as hell! What if—"

He held up his pointer finger. "—the beast was really a Vampire prince, held under a spell, and the rose was her blood—"

"You'd ruin the entire story"! Mason roared. "Besides..." He sniffed the air. "I am beast."

"You were the reindeer yesterday," Ethan pointed out. "From Frozen, you can't be every character that's an animal just because you're the only one with claws."

"Man has a point." Alex came in behind me and slapped me on the back. Mason, as if suddenly realizing my presence looked at me then at Stephanie, and then, unfortunately at her feet. "In three, two, on—"

"What have you done!" he roared. "My favorite wolf friend was white!"

Stephanie's eyes widened and then she looked down. "Oh, um, Cassius convinced me it wasn't your type of wolf."

"All wolf is my type." Mason gnashed his teeth.

"Be still, Wolf, before I throw a pinecone at your ass," I hissed, sending a shock wave of icy cold air directly at his face.

He tumbled backward cursing then mumbled, "Didn't hurt." As he shot to his feet and took his place back on the couch. "And I'd appreciate if you'd kindly remove my people's fur from your feet!"

Slowly, Stephanie peeled off the boots.

Genesis bit down on her lip and held out her hands. "Those look really warm."

"Ethan's warm," Mason barked. "Use him as a blanket, not these."

He snatched the boots and hugged them close to his chest.

"Ten bucks he sleeps with them tonight." Alex

chuckled.

"Where were you guys?" Genesis stretched her arms above her head and yawned. I smiled at the gesture. She was so sweet, so… pure.

Ethan shot a glare in my direction. Good to know he still didn't trust me even after finding my own mate.

A mate whose destiny was now threaded with mine.

Heaviness weighed all around me, inside, outside, settling on my shoulders like a boulder.

"Do Dark Ones drink?" I wondered aloud.

Alex clapped his hands. "Let's find out, I'm bored and the last girl I took wasn't to my liking, too much…" He shuddered. "Talking."

"You are supposed to talk when you mate," Mason said under his breath while all eyes shot in his direction. He looked up. "I mean, that is our… way."

Alex sat down at Mason's feet. "Ooh, a bed time story. Continue when you're ready… don't leave any sexy parts out, those are my favorite." His eyes glowed for a few brief moments as his essence nearly choked the life out of the room, causing even the potted plant to strain toward him in adoration.

"Alex." Stephanie made a face. "Learn how to turn off the charm."

"Since when do you care?"

"Since now!" She clenched her fists, her eyes going completely white, while Alex stood, he never could help himself when there was a chance to bicker or fight.

"Cease," I whispered as the air in front of his face crystallized, the world spun in slow motion as I made my way over to Stephanie just as she lifted her hands into the air to blast him with what would be a painful blow of icicles."

I caught the icicles mid air, one of them missed my hand hitting me in the side. With a wince, I fell to my knees as time began again, and the ice crashed against the ground.

"Cassius!" Stephanie was immediately at my side. "I'm so sorry, I don't know what came over me, I just... he was making me angry and—"

"Learn how to control it," Ethan snapped, his eyes green with rage. "Council member or not, I would not hesitate to remove your head from your body if you harm Genesis." Fangs elongated out of his mouth as he let out a loud growl. Mason protectively covered Genesis with his body, while Alex paled, his thoughts nothing but confusion and hurt.

"It's not you," I said.

"She's getting worse," came his answer back to me. "Fix it."

"I can't."

Silence.

Admitting that this was a battle she could only fight on her own, one that she had no training for, one that I could not win for her.

"Stephanie." I held out my hand. "Upstairs."

She placed her hand in mine, offering an apologetic glance at everyone as we slowly put more distance between the council members and her.

"I'm dangerous," she said once I closed the door to her bedroom.

"Yes."

"I could have killed him."

"Harmed... not killed. Big difference."

"That doesn't make me feel better."

"That wasn't me trying to make you feel better." I cupped her cheek and kissed her mouth softly. "This is."

Tears welled in her eyes. "I've loved you for a lifetime."

"And I you."

"I'm afraid."

"Don't feed the fear with irrational thoughts. They have no place in our lives, and the more you think upon them, the bigger Darkness gets. Insecurity will always be a part of you, just like emotions, jealousy, anger, it's all there, but as a Dark One, you can harness the power, push them away, long enough to regain control of yourself. You must, otherwise…"

"That's the scary part…" She muttered. "The otherwise. The but. The if."

"Think upon this," I kissed her again and again, showering her face with kisses, spreading the love I felt for her as far and as wide as was possible, kissing every inch of her face, until I thought I'd go insane with dizzying desire to take her. "Think on us."

Stephanie

I IMAGINED THAT YEARS from now, centuries even, I'd still think his kiss was paradise, the greatest touch, the press of his fingertips against my skin. To love Cassius was to be wrapped up in rightness.

But that was now.

When he was near.

When I was touching him—the fear was gone. Everything ceased to exist but him. Clarity filled my head and I realized yet again how right he was, about everything.

If anyone had reasons to be upset about his life, parentage, or even the curse he'd been given, it should be Cassius.

And he was comforting me.

An outcast from birth.

The first of his race.

With two powerful races up in arms—over his tiny existence.

His being born, caused centuries of continual unrest between immortals and humans—it caused a giant tear in the balance of life, of exiting.

One that has never been fixed.

One life.

One life did that.

One choice did that.

"Your thoughts are heavy," Cassius whispered, his mouth was warm, the complete opposite of the way our cold bodies pressed against one another. His tongue grazed mine and in an effort to keep him close, I grabbed onto his hair, pulling his body onto mine.

"You're heavy," I fired back.

His full lips spread into a grin. "You could lift me with one hand."

"Maybe two." I nodded. "For sure two."

He ran his fingers through my hair, bringing it to his nose only to close his eyes and exhale as his eyes turned white, his lips the same color. "I wish to look upon you for an eternity. I would watch… if it were my job to watch you." He kissed my lips softly. "I would never close my eyes."

My heart swelled. "Who knew Dark Ones could be so romantic?"

"Romance," he answered quickly, "is inherent in everyone—like a treasure that is opened only when you find the one worthy of its words, sonnets, its adoration."

His hands slinked down my body, bracing my hips grazing my bare skin near my stomach as he raised my shirt and brought his lips to my belly button. "Let me kiss you…"

"Please." I whimpered. "Please kiss me."

"Only because you begged," he teased, assaulting me with his mouth, with his lips, making me yearn for more of him as my body twisted and arched in every direction, needing him, only him.

My mate.

Eyes a blazing white, I felt him, not just physically but mentally, pushing me, almost like there was this invisible wall he was trying to break.

I pushed back.

His eyes blazed whiter. "Let me through."

"No." Where had that response come from? It didn't sound like my voice. I wasn't even thinking of saying no, it just came out through my lips, guttural, evil.

"Stephanie," Cassius tried again, rocking his body into mine. "I need all of you, not just a piece. Give me everything… I need your trust. I need the essence of who you are."

I shook my head and slammed my hands against his chest, sending him flying in the air, he barely stopped himself from hitting the wall. With a snarl he stood to his full height and started stripping.

"What?" I shook my head as my vision clouded. "What are you doing?"

His smile was lethal—beautiful. "Distracting you."

"What?" My eyes honed in on his perfectly sculpted body, its thickness as muscles flexed and strained as if they were ready to break through his skin. In a flash of light he was in front of me, pulling at my clothes. "What are you doing?"

"Making love," he said simply, his hands worshiping my body while something inside of me said it would be a bad idea to let him in, then he'd see. He'd see all the horrible thoughts I'd been having about him, humans, all the darkness.

He'd see the darkness.

If we were together again, he'd have access to everything.

He'd see my shame.

"No." Darkness seeped out of my voice, as a trail of soot left my palm and imprinted against his bare skin.

Hissing, he pulled back, his skin blistering where I'd touched it.

"So that's how this is going to be?" he asked, his eyes cheerful as if I didn't just burn him, as If I wasn't hiding everything from him.

"Y-yes."

"Well." He stretched his arms above his head. "I guess I'd better ready myself for a battle. I was never good at winning wars, but battles? Excellent speed, aggression, timing." He kissed me harder and harder as my body weakened against him, wanting him so desperately while my mind screamed that it would ruin everything.

But what? What would it ruin?

My thoughts were a confused jumbled mess.

Let him in, and he'll see you for what you really are. Evil.

"No." I shook my head.

"My voice." Cassius held my head, our eyes locked. "Focus on my voice, my body, the feeling of us joining, focus on nothing else. And Stephanie?"

I swallowed.

"Whatever you do, do not close your eyes."

It was what I needed to hear as Cassius pressed a searing kiss against my mouth, his eyes never wavering, never leaving mine, as if his job, his duty, the only reason he had been created.

Was to watch.

To watch me.

I was afraid to blink, afraid I'd miss the planes and

angles of his perfect face as he moved his head left, then right, kissing me in every different direction, only to increase his speed, taking his time tasting my mouth, while at the same time leaving remnants of his own flavor, the richness of his blood called to me. He was under my skin, every inch of my body was aware of Cassius in such a real, almost unnatural way, that I had no choice but to kiss him back, match him touch for touch.

His large hands cupped my breasts, staring down at my body in reverence before a guttural groan escaped between his lips, as his head again descended, pleasuring me with his mouth, causing me to whisper his name, until whispering wasn't possible anymore.

The room trembled.

While my body shook.

Time again seemed to bend and alter right before my very eyes as the air around us stilled, moisture froze midair into tiny pieces of floating ice as Cassius's head lifted, his eyes white, his mouth swollen from kisses.

"You will never have her." His voice was loud, dominating, as his body moved against me, slowly… and then faster. "She will never be yours."

I knew who he was talking to.

I could feel the anger reverberating inside, the maniacal laughter of Darkness as it tried to break free.

"Look at me," Cassius instructed, his breath like smoke as it froze in front of my mouth. "Watch me. Love you."

When we joined, it wasn't out of hurried passion.

Or even pleasure.

But love.

His eyes flashed with swirling white as his hungry

kisses made demands of my mouth and his body commanded my pleasure, taking me beyond the mortal realm, into something so beautiful that I ached.

"This," Cassius said softly as every ounce of darkness drained from the room. "Is what we have together…"

I cried out against his chest as he moved one last time, triggering every pleasure point in my body simultaneously.

Limbs weak, I sagged against him. "I love you."

"I love you, too," he whispered, rocking me in his arms, back and forth, back and forth, our legs still tangled, our bodies with frozen beads of sweat.

It was then, that I forgot his words.

And closed my eyes.

CHAPTER 36

Cassius

As IF THE LIGHT was getting sucked into a black hole, the brightness diminished within the room leaving us blanketed in the soft glow of the moon and the slithering darkness of night.

"Stephanie?" I pulled back to look into her eyes. Anger swirled beneath the surface of her heart shaped face, like I was seeing her but not truly seeing her. Black specks of darkness spotted her white eyes as she blinked up at me again and again as if trying to clear away the mess of cobwebs.

She shook her head again.

"Fight it," I urged. "Learn how to fight it, learn how to focus on the good, the bright, the joy. Feel the cold, let it become a part of you."

"He's warm." Her voice was hollow. "He's so warm."

"Do not allow the temptation of something so fleeting as warmth cause you to lose your footing on reality." I spoke quietly taking her face between my hands. "All Dark Ones are born with this choice… stay between the mortal planes of humanity and immortals alike, or give in to the darkness."

She gritted her teeth together and slammed her hands against my chest with a scream.

White hot flames teased my skin as I flew through the air toward the window, I held up a block of ice just in time to keep myself from damaging Ethan's home further, while Stephanie fell backward off the bed.

The room smelled like burnt skin, but already my body was healing, knitting cells back together while I maneuvered around the bedroom to see if Stephanie was okay.

I froze as she stood to her feet, still naked, wobbly. The palms of her hands were black with soot and near her left cheek was a strip of red hair.

The sign of fire.

The sign of Darkness taking hold.

"I'm sorry." She ran toward me. "Are you hurt? I just, I was trying to push *him* away, not you."

"No." I grabbed her wrists, carefully examining her hands. "It's fine. I'm fine."

Nodding, she tugged her hands free and wrapped her arms around me. "I think… I need to go for a walk."

"I'll go with you."

"No." She shook her head violently. "I need to go by myself… It's not you, it's…" She shrugged as her words trailed off into the empty atmosphere of the room.

They held no physical power, words, but being dismissed felt like being punched without warning.

I wasn't sure how to respond.

How to react to the fact that my mate, the one I'd just loved, joined with, promised my life to—was shutting me out, this time purposefully, right before my very eyes.

"Stephanie." I reached for her hand but she jerked back. "You don't need to hide from me."

"I know," she said quickly.

The lie hung in the air between us like a giant visible rift of separation. She might as well be on another planet. "Then take all the time you need."

She didn't just walk out of the room.

She fled.

"Sariel…" Weakness consumed me. "Help where I cannot."

I waited in anticipation for his answer.

But instead of words, it was the sound of feathers blowing in the wind, ruffling up all at once and taking flight.

And finally. "I will try."

"It is all I ask."

"No." Sariel's voice carried inside my head. "You ask a great deal more, son, more than I am allowed to give."

I hung my head then slowly, robotically, put my clothes back on and made my way downstairs.

The kitchen was empty.

Mason wasn't hidden behind some pot cooking and ordering people around, and Alex wasn't sitting back on the table, smug look in place as he looked down on everything that dared not be enraptured by his presence.

And Ethan.

His scent was near, but that was all.

"Cassius?"

Genesis's voice was so unexpected that I startled, nearly running into the door frame in an effort to turn around. Her scent was different now that she was mated with the Vampire, I had forgotten its lingering sweetness, the way the mixture of human and Vampire blood hummed through the air like an electrical current, pulling and tugging.

Her bright green eyes glistened. "Did I? A mere human? Frighten you, oh, great one?"

I held back my laugh—just barely—as a smile spread across my face. "I believe you did."

"And to think, Dark Ones…" She made a face. "So terrifying."

I rolled my eyes.

"Did you just roll your eyes?"

I paused and then released the pent-up laugh. "First time for everything. I blame Alex."

"It's just easier that way," she agreed holding out her hand.

I hesitated at first, old habits died hard. There had once been a time when I would have done anything to touch her, to mate with her, to break the curse that Ethan and I had started when his mate betrayed him.

Touching humans wasn't a normal occurrence. With a sigh, I pressed my palm against hers and then linked my fingers, enjoying the softness of her hand, the warmth that was so foreign to my own skin as it simmered.

"You're eyes are white again," she whispered.

"I like your warmth," I said honestly. Not in a way that meant I wanted her. "You comfort me. Imagine that?"

She squeezed my hand lightly and led me into the adjoining living room. Next to the fireplace she had a mug of something sweet, hot chocolate perhaps? And a blanket. I scooted a chair next to her and sat, our hands still touching, still grasping, feeling one another.

It was the most calm I'd felt all evening.

Sitting with a human, by the fire.

Sitting with a Vampire's mate.

Sitting.

Watching.

Maybe I inherited that from my father? The keen ability to be able to stay awake and watch, in hopes that by keeping my eyes open I'd, what? Save the world from itself? Save the woman I loved?

"You look sad," Genesis said.

"I find that I'd rather allow the human side of me to mourn what has transpired between me and Stephanie than push it away. Sometimes it's better to feel, no?"

Genesis ducked her head as she took a sip of hot chocolate. Her dark wavy hair fell across her soft skin as her green eyes glowed over the rim of the cup. "Feeling is almost always painful, but with pain, is always beauty… pleasure." She glanced at the fireplace. "You aren't truly living if you are choosing to ignore the most vibrant parts of yourself, including, emotions."

"Pesky little things, emotions," I joked.

Her laugh was soft. "They do tend to get in the way."

"I want to save her," I admitted.

Genesis's eyes saddened. "You can't."

"I keep telling myself if I wouldn't have—"

Genesis' eyebrows arched. "Go on, wouldn't have what?"

"Bargained," I blurted out. "I made a bargain with Sariel. Allow me thirty days to pursue her, to love her, he made me human while restoring her immortality as a gift. At the end of thirty days, if I had not succeeded,

I would die. But, of course, Sariel failed to mention that if we mated, I'd be restored."

Genesis frowned. "It doesn't seem like Sariel to leave something like that out. Are you sure you are restored?"

I frowned. "I have all of my powers, look at me." I spread my arms wide, releasing her hand in the process.

"But do you have your immortality?" She wondered aloud.

I paused as the room itself tensed, and then like a warning, the lights flickered. Because if I could die, if it was possible to die without the draining of my immortality, that meant… the future had not truly changed.

Because in the end.

Stephanie could still kill me.

Stab me in the heart.

And I would perish.

Chapter 37

Stephanie

TEARS BLURRED MY LINE of vision as gravel crunched beneath Mason's old boots. They'd been by the door, and I'd been desperate. Maniacal laughter bubbled up inside of me. What was happening? No matter how hard I tried, the temptation to give in to something so dark and forbidden, was like inviting warmth into the icy parts of my soul.

The air around me stilled, but I continued walking down the street toward the small wooded area where I used to go running—before my life had changed, before I'd discovered that I was an abomination.

Shoving my hands into the pockets of my sweatshirt, I picked up my pace, only to slam directly into an invisible wall.

Confused I took a step back.

There was nothing in front of me.

But air.

The wind teased my hair as it whipped against my cheeks and then the smell of cinder burned my nostrils.

"Angel," a deep voice whispered behind me.

Slowly, I turned on my heel.

Timber leaned casually against a tree, his muscular

body tensed up like he was ready to fight.

"I could level you by simply thinking it," I threatened.

"You could." He nodded, then shoved off the tree and started walking forward. "But you won't."

My eyebrows shot up in surprise. He really didn't want to piss me off, not after everything that had gone down with Cassius. "You have no idea what I will or will not do."

"And I would never try to guess a woman's thoughts for fear that I'd be on the wrong side of her affection for a century." He smirked. "At least."

"Possibly longer," I added.

His dimpled grin grew, perfect white teeth snapped together in a crushing smile as he finally stopped in front of me. We were matched for height, but he was older, a lot older, and ever since seeing the battle Cassius led against him, something a lot like fear told me that to fight him would be more trouble than it was worth.

"Clearly you wanted to talk about something since you went to so much trouble," I said.

Timber continued to stare through me. "It's growing."

"Your ego?"

His smile dimmed. "I think that ship sailed long ago, I'm afraid. After all, I can only allow so much arrogance before it blinds me."

"Good point."

"And now…" His dark hair fell in waves across his forehead; he was beautiful. And wasn't that the point with Demon? Beautiful was trustworthy. Beautiful meant safe.

Or did it?

To humans, beauty always meant security.

To immortals, it almost always meant you were courting death.

"Now?" I prompted.

Timber inhaled greedily, sucking in air so deep through his mouth that it looked awkward, his eyes rolled in the back of his head. "I sense—"

"—the darkness." I tried to sound casual. "Got it, I know. It's like I'm in Star Wars and everyone can sense the force but me, thanks, but no thanks, don't need your help or anything else from you. Unless you plan on telling me how the Demon are creating more numbers, we have nothing to discuss."

"But of course." He shrugged. "I would love to show you my pet project, but what would your mate say? You'll have to touch me," he held out his hand. "You'll have to taste my blood to see through my eyes. And what's worse, you may enjoy what you see."

I laughed. "I highly doubt that."

"Do you ever think about the battle Cassius fought? The wars raged between the immortals? Why would Darkness call to him when he is half Angel? Why would it tempt him so? Is it because humans are so dark? But no," Timber tapped his chin. "That would not make sense would it? For a human's blood to be stronger than the Angel blood within…" He paced in front of me. "So many puzzle pieces, spread around your feet, yet you keep picking up the wrong pieces. Darkness, is just a small clue as to what you are my dear, what Cassius is. It's sad really, possibly pathetic, how he's allowed himself to be used all these years without really understanding that he's been in chains the entire time."

"Chains?" Dread filled my entire body, making me heavy because even though the words made no sense, at the same time, they did. Why did we fight Darkness so much? Why was it an issue? Why were we cursed?

"Bingo." Timber whispered into the crisp night air. "What are you?"

"A Dark One," I said confidently.

"Oh no, my dear…" He threw his head back and laughed. "That's a simple label for something far worse. Think more…" He flipped his hand over and waved it through the air. "Along the lines of a nightmare, a scary story perhaps, one you were told when you were little. Careful not to venture into the forest too late at night, or look under your bed, or how about this one, don't play with magic beyond your understanding…."

My head started to pound. I pressed my fingertips against the sides in order to alleviate the ache.

Timber grinned wolfishly. "Cassius leads the immortals, he keeps the peace between the humans, because of Sariel joining with his human. The Darkness, the curse, the pull… toward Demon. Why is it, do you think, that darkness represents…" He leaned in and pressed a searing kiss to my cheek his lips scalding my skin. "…heat?" he finished in a whisper against my skin.

With a gasp, I touched my cheek just as he stuttered back and burst out in mocking laughter. "I see your mind working." A sudden chill filled the air, his eyes dilated before he let out a low hiss. "Until next time, Angel."

He disappeared into the shadows just as Sariel appeared to my right, his feathers sticking straight up as if offended by the scent of a Demon, the mere fact that he still lingered in the air.

"You're late." I sighed. "He's already gone."

"Not late," Sariel answered. "I was here the whole time."

"Well, you weren't very helpful."

"Did you need my help?" he countered, his white eyes growing wide with light.

I swallowed and looked down, crossing my arms. "No."

"He knows too much."

"And yet you let him live." I tilted my head. "Riddle me this, Sariel. Why, all those years go, didn't you destroy the Demon? We're on the brink of war, we have Demon creating more Demon, using who knows what to do it, and this all could have been prevented."

"Light and dark cannot exist without one another." That was the same thing he'd said to Cassius, but this time, it was in the present, and I was standing there, not worn out from fighting, or being pulled toward the darkness, so I tasted it.

A faint bitterness floated by my mouth.

With a gasp I took a step backward. "You just lied!"

Sariel's body stiffened. "I did not lie. I simply did not tell you the whole truth."

"Omission is still lying."

"Is it?"

"Stop asking questions to my questions! Why do you let them live?" I charged toward him, allowing the anger and confusion to spread out my arms and slamming my hands against his rock hard chest. Of course, he didn't move, but that wasn't the point, the point was I was angry, so angry that he was ignoring a simple solution.

With a haggard sigh, Sariel grabbed me by the wrists and thrust me back, I flew ten feet into the air and landed on my hands and knees.

My head jerked up as he held out his hand and pulled me back to my feet. "Never." His voice was low, filled with anger. "Touch me. Again."

"Sorry." I shrank back while he dusted off his pristine black leather jacket and designer jeans.

"You want the truth."

"Yes."

Sariel looked up toward the night sky, then closed his eyes as a flicker of light shone down on him. "I refuse to watch more death than is necessary. I know Cassius showed you. My job was to stay awake, to watch. My job…" He turned his head to the side, his features twisted in utter agony. "…is still to roam this realm, to watch." He swallowed and closed his eyes again, this time keeping them closed as he pressed his hands to his face then spoke. "Don't you see? I cannot watch it again. I refuse to watch those I love suffer. I refuse to watch them die."

"People die every day."

"Yes."

"Immortals don't."

Sariel nodded. "But they can."

"I don't understand."

"Then let me speak plainly." A muscle twitched in his jaw. "If I kill the Demon. You and Cassius will both die. I wipe out their race, and you will cease to exist, dust to dust. Is that plain enough for you?"

My eyes widened, "But, the war—"

"To keep their numbers down, for they're a gossiping sort. They horde together, make plans, but up until now they have been silent. They've been silent for a thousand years. And now, they are at it again, and it will be your job to squelch the uprising before it is too late."

My mind finally caught up with what he was saying.

"Why would we die… if the Demon race was annihilated?"

Sariel's eyes were sad, but he said nothing.

Instead, he reached out and touched my face with his fingertips.

And disappeared.

Was it seconds? Minutes? Or hours? I had no idea how much time I spent staring off into space, wondering what my next course of action should be. All I knew was that I had a suspicion Cassius was in the dark just as much as I was, and that maybe, maybe it was time for someone to do something.

Cassius's self-deprecating thoughts had always affected me, made me afraid of what I had inside, afraid of the darkness, afraid of what would happen if I lost control. It was a juxtaposition, being told not to be afraid yet seeing what we were capable of if we did fall off that cliff.

How was I supposed to stay strong when every fiber of my being told me I should be leery? When I saw thousands of years of war, when I witnessed firsthand the way he was conceived into this world.

Air brushed past my cheek.

Had my relationship to Cassius come to this? Me keeping secrets while he watched and waited for me to snap?

Waited for me to kill him?

The vision of the knife in his chest while he fell to the ground seared through my memory.

Why would I do that?

Why would I hurt him purposely?

The answer came swifter than I thought.

Because as strong as I was—Cassius would always be stronger. He would eventually hunt me, track me, find me. I couldn't keep my walls up forever.

But injured?

I shivered.

And knew, as the wind picked up and swirled like madness around me, what I had to do.

Oddly, as I took those first steps toward the house it wasn't Darkness rejoicing, it wasn't warmth I felt, but a deep sense of cold, and that was the most comforting thought at all, as I grabbed the knife I knew Ethan kept in the hall closet right along with a few guns—not that he'd ever used them.

I thumbed the blade.

Not the twist I thought our fairy tale would take.

Not at all.

Chapter 38

Cassius

The thought that I didn't still have my immortality never crossed my mind, and frankly, I didn't want to take any chances. I would call upon Sariel once Stephanie returned.

If she returned.

She would return.

The last few hours had been a painful reminder of the way she'd blocked me from her consciousness, her thoughts, her feelings, everything. All I saw was a shield every time I tried to communicate with her.

The front door opened and closed.

Her scent hit me first.

Another door opened.

Curious, I waited, it was closed faster, more abrupt, as if she had thought about slamming it but decided against it.

Footsteps followed.

And then Stephanie was standing in front of me. Slowly, I lifted my head, unsure of what I'd find. Would her eyes be black? Was Darkness finally having the last laugh? Or was it truly a simple walk?

Genesis had gone to bed hours ago.

Leaving me by the fire.

Though it did nothing to aid the cold seeping throughout my body.

"I saw Timber," Stephanie whispered. Her eyes were a clear blue. "He said some… things."

"Timber likes to talk." My eyes narrowed. "What the hell would he want with you?"

Stephanie crossed her arms in front of her chest, taking a protective stance against me, not only was I dealing with mental walls but physical too. "He hinted at something… and then Sariel…"

"Sariel." I said his name. "Was he helpful?"

"He said—" She bit down on her lower lip, opened her mouth, then shut it. "You know what? I'm tired… why don't we go to bed?"

The air filled with bitterness.

A chasm opened up between us, separating me from her, her heart from mine. My soul screamed in outrage.

Lies were like little walls shoved between someone you loved, eventually, you'd have so much separation, so much mistrust, that you'd become strangers.

Why push me away?

When all I wanted was to hold her close?

Was her connection to me different? I could hardly go five seconds without wanting to kiss her, make love to her, simply hold her in my arms and calm her racing heart.

"I love you." Stephanie's eyes filled with tears. "You know that right?"

I stood and pulled her into my arms. "I love you too."

"So you also know that…" She sniffled. "Sometimes, when you love someone, you make sacrifices."

I didn't like the direction she was going.

I pulled back from her, just in time for a knife to slide between my ribs and stick.

With a gasp, I stumbled backward as a mixture of red and silver blood leaked out of the gaping wound. "Why?"

"I needed time." She quickly pushed past me. "To figure things out before you followed me, and I figured, you can't chase me if you're bleeding. It will at least give me a few minutes."

A few minutes where I couldn't trace her.

"Stephanie." I jerked the knife out of my ribs and held my hand to the wound as blood continued to seep between my fingers in a runny-sticky mess. "Don't do this. Let me help you."

"Ever think that maybe, what I'm doing, is helping you?" she countered. Then she ran out of the house while I fell to my knees and screamed her name.

Stephanie

"TIMBER." I WHISPERED HIS name into the air. I'd never summoned a Demon before. And wasn't sure how exactly it worked, yet I had no choice but to try.

I continued running down the street, my feet taking me faster now that I was part Angel.

A half mile in, and a black Mercedes pulled up on the road, the back door opened.

Timber's voice barked from the darkness. "Get in."

His eyes slit vertically as they went from their normal clear blue color to a yellow. I wanted to shrink back. I was alone. With a very old Demon, one who hated my mate, hated me for some reason.

Hated his existence?

"Not too far off, Angel." He smiled then tipped back a thick red liquid, the smell of earth filled the air. "Human blood, my pet."

"I thought only Vampires drank blood."

"It's an acquired taste, also a necessity if we want to keep human form. Do they teach you nothing these days?" He laughed. "But of course they don't, the council is perfectly happy keeping their innocent little female in the dark, just like Cassius."

"That's why I'm here." I cleared my throat. "What are—"

"No," Timber rasped. "Not in the car, and definitely—" He shivered and glanced outside as the trees filled with watchful eyes of the Werewolves, the ones who protected Ethan's house. "—not around those who have perfect hearing."

We drove in silence to downtown Seattle.

Once we were in front of yet another one of the bars Timber owned, the car door opened and another Demon helped me out.

The club was dark, humans danced in mindless abandon. They laughed, took shots of whiskey and tequila, danced around poles.

While Demon sat in the darkest corners.

And watched.

One crooked his finger at a human female. She giggled and walked over to him, straddled his lap and started kissing his neck.

I shivered. "Your kind disgusts me."

"Hah." Timber slid his hand down my back. "It shouldn't."

Being in their little den of sin was so not where I wanted to be spending the evening, but I needed answers, and I was tired of Cassius being the pawn.

It was time for someone else to take the brunt.

And although I sensed the darkness, I was too focused on my mission to pay attention it.

Maybe that's what Cassius meant? Why Eva had helped him so much? As long as you had something else anchoring you—you could ignore the darkness.

We stepped through a large hallway. A red door was positioned at the end. When we reached it, Timber knocked twice, and then opened the door, shutting it quietly behind us.

The office had no windows.

The walls were black.

Facing the door was a desk finished in rich mahogany red. Nice black leather couches lined the perimeter of the room. Each couch had purple velvet pillows. The entire room was gaudy, as if it belonged in another time period.

Not to the present.

The chair behind the desk was turned.

Someone was sitting in it, I could see the top of his or her head, but the color of the hair was unusual. Red and dark brown?

"So, she comes on her own." The voice sounded so familiar, masculine, warm. The chair spun slowly.

With a gasp, I covered my mouth with my hands.

He smiled. "How nice… to meet you in person."

"But…" I shook my head. "You're Darkness…"

"I prefer the name Bannik."

My world crumbled around my feet. Because Bannik had been Sariel's brother, Bannik was there in the beginning.

He was also in my mind, though a dark black haze had always been in front of him, transforming his features.

But they were the same.

I felt it.

I knew it.

Terrified, I took a step back.

But Timber shoved me forward. I turned to punch him but he was already exiting the room, leaving me alone with—

I whipped my head around. "What are you?"

His black and red hair shimmered within the heat of the room as my body felt heavy.

"I believe the question that's been plaguing your mind is… what… my dear…. are you?"

"I'm a Dark—"

"If you say Dark One I'll simply laugh." Bannik's smile was cruel. "Did you know, I was never meant to be in the US? It wasn't my territory. Twelve of us were sent to the ends of the earth to watch. Only this time, we knew human emotion. Imagine the difficulty in watching, helping humans keep the peace…. and knowing nothing but fighting and war? My brother was never good at following the rules, and I learned soon after, when he refused to see me because of his shame, that I was tired of following them as well." He shrugged. "It seems that warmth… agrees with me."

"You're like Sariel," I said dumbly.

"I'm exactly like Sariel." He shifted in his seat. "*If* Sariel hadn't repented." He paused. "And so are you."

"What?"

"Ever wonder why the darkness calls?" His smug laughter was grating on my nerves, along with the way he spoke down to me like I was stupid. "It calls because it is in your nature. But by all means, sugarcoat your true identity and call yourself a Dark One… yet you are still the same as I."

I licked my dry lips. "An Angel?"

"Hah!" He clapped his hands. "You amuse me." He spun his large body around in the chair before slamming his hands down on the desk. "You. Are. Evil." His teeth snapped and popped as his jaw clenched together. "Humans and Angels do create half breeds, beings so powerful that they are condemned to the earth. But the half breeds must even make a choice, serve their angelic fathers... or follow after the ones that are fallen. You call yourself a Dark One, but really? You're half of a Fallen Angel... just waiting to turn into a Demon."

I let out a little gasp of disbelief. "But, Demon are a race. They're in the immortal book as a race that was created—"

"Goody," he said dryly while blocking a yawn with his large hand. "Please continue, don't let me interrupt."

My head was spinning out of control.

I opened my mouth, but he silenced me by holding his hand in the air. "Keeping you in the dark has always been the plan. After all, what do you think would happen if the rest of the immortals discovered that most Demon had angelic powers?"

I shook my head. "Most Demon I've met are weak creatures who prey on humans."

Bannik stood, towering over his desk as claws seeped out of fingernails. "Oh?"

Swallowing, I took a healthy step back.

"You sense it even now." His eyes closed for a few seconds, and when they opened, they were black, soulless. "When Angels give up, break the rules, or decide not to say sorry..." His laughter was deep, empty. "They are suddenly unwanted, sent to the earth for the rest of their miserable existence, most of them were under the impression that they were like humans, without any sort of abilities. Until Sariel."

"Sariel's good," I whispered.

"Sariel said sorry, but he was still punished, like the rest of us. Because of his mistake I will never again taste the air of heaven, or feel the warmth of the sun as it rises over the horizon. The earth no longer speaks to me. The mountains no longer sing in my presence, and when the moon makes its appearance it turns its face away in shame." He lifted his hand into the air. "The tides pull away when I walk near the ocean, but I think," His black eyes glistened, "The worst has to be the songs."

I kept moving backward as he spoke, trying desperately to find the door knob.

"The melody of the earth as it tilts on its axis, the planets as they sing in their specific languages all joining together in the chorus of the universe." He glared at me his black eyes locking in on mine, like a tractor beam pulling my feet toward him. "I can no longer hear the song of creation."

"If it makes you feel better, I can't hear it either."

"Silly immortal, you hear it every day. Your human side is simply too busy ignoring it to pay attention, so busy with inconsistent emotional thoughts that, in the end, truly don't matter. The worst part—" He laughed again. "—is walking by a human who by all means should hear the music, who hears it on a daily basis, and doesn't appreciate its beauty. I've killed humans for less. I'll continue to kill them in their ignorance."

"And me?" I asked, "What about me?"

He grinned. "I no longer have any use for you."

"So you're going to kill me?"

"No." He shrugged. "It seems I won't need to, since you've cheerfully done the deed yourself. Killing your own mate, why, it seems the darkness truly has taken hold."

"No!" I screamed, lunging for him. "I just slowed

him down."

"Oh, you slowed him down all right." He cackled. "Even now his heart slows to the rhythm of death. What did you think? Immortality is a fickle thing, my dear. He's your mate, your lives are interconnected in a very special way that I'm sure Sariel… omitted."

"Tell me," I said through clenched teeth.

"I wonder if this is how Samson felt… after his hair was cut." Bannik tapped his chin. "After all, you've done the same thing without realizing it… when you mate, it is possible, that one or the other person may give all of his angelic powers to the other, say, if he is worried about her safety, or about her leaving him—"

"—human." I gasped, throwing my arms out to the sides as shreds of ice slammed against the walls.

Bannik ducked. "Before you leave…."

I stared him down then closed my eyes, forcing my will on him, trying to remember what Cassius had explained in training, only to have my eyes open and see that nothing had happened.

"This…" He smiled wickedly. "Is my favorite part."

The wall behind him moved to the side.

I counted ten.

Ten men.

Huge.

All with red and black hair.

Chained to the walls.

With blood being drained from them.

"It seems…" Bannik shrugged. "That I've been very bad."

The men's mouths were covered—but their eyes conveyed fear, anger, hostility and shame. I didn't need to stare long to know who they were.

Sariel's brothers.

The ones who had been punished.

And sent to different corners of the earth.

"Sariel won't let you get away with this."

"Hah!" Bannik clapped his hands. "And what will dear brother do? Not only am I creating an army—but I'm harnessing their power for my own. I'm untouchable. And now." He dismissed me with his hand. "I'm bored."

The door behind me opened.

Timber grabbed my arms and jerked me out.

"He's insane," I said through clenched teeth. "Do you truly think you can trust someone? Like that!" I pointed at the door.

"And my other choice?" Timber asked in a calm voice. "Rot until an immortal finally kills me then take my place in hell." He shoved me down the hall. "I'll take my chances."

"Sariel—"

"Yes, let's talk about the good angel." He laughed, an evil sound that slid over me like warm butter. "Tell him, a war is coming. One he cannot win. Oh, and do say hello to the immortal king for me as he takes his last breath. We had a good run, a really good run."

With that I was tossed into the street.

"Home," I breathed, hoping it would work, that I would be able to imagine myself in a place and end up there.

After two seconds of nothing, desperation finally kicked in. I pushed all of my emotions into willing myself home with Cassius.

And opened my eyes just in time to see Ethan yell. "He's coding!"

Cassius

The wound hurt—but what hurt more, was the physical pain of my heart as it demanded I run after her. So with all the strength I possessed, I closed my eyes and willed it. I willed my strength to her, every ounce I had—and hoped it would be enough to keep her alive, even if it meant my death.

What have you done?

Sariel's whisper was as always… so helpful.

I fell to my knees with a grunt, confused as to why my wound wasn't healing; it typically took mere seconds for my skin to knit back together, leaving me without any sort of scar.

But now? It was as if.

I'd truly been injured.

I was about to yell for Ethan when he appeared by my side, his hands shoving mine away as he examined my chest. Eyes grave, he pulled back. "You aren't healing."

"No shit." I huffed. It was getting more difficult to breathe by the second, as if a heaviness had taken hold of my chest and squeezed, the pressure building up into my lungs.

"Alex! Mason!"

They ran in, Genesis was close on their heels.

"Run into something sharp?" Alex teased.

"He's not self-healing." Ethan hissed. "And I can't stop the bleeding."

Immediately Alex sobered, shoving Ethan away so he could take a look, but what good was a Siren?

"I'm slowing your heart." Ethan pressed a hand to my neck. "Try to calm down."

"Sure." I nodded. "I'll do that, I'll just tell myself to calm down while I—"

A Dark One could always calm down, always compartmentalize. "Genesis, what color are my eyes?"

Face pale, she answered in a tiny voice. "Blue. They're blue."

Mason let out a little howl as he knelt by my side and took my hand in his, apparently my emotions were causing him to change as claws replaced hands.

"It's fine," I lied, unable to taste it in the air. "There is no better way to die, then in the presence of friends."

Brave words for someone who didn't feel so brave, because regardless of my human state—I would die as a Dark One.

I would be nothing.

Feel nothing.

Know nothing.

To die as a Dark One is to have never existed.

And for the first time in my existence, I wanted the pain that memory brought, because it meant that I had lived, that I'd suffered, that I had loved and come out on the other side better for it.

Genesis squeezed my hand just as Ethan shouted. "He's coding!"

Suddenly Stephanie was at my side, shoving everyone out of the way. Was she glowing?

Why the hell was I seeing a light?

She slid her wrists along Ethan's teeth so quickly Ethan didn't have time to protest, and then knelt next to my head pressing her wrist against my mouth.

"It won't be enough." Ethan said sadly.

"It has to be." Stephanie said through soft sobs. "It has to be. I love him. It has to work!"

I smiled. "Love—" Exhaustion took over. "You." I reached up to caress her face one last time and failed as my hand slumped to the floor, right along with my body.

I stood near the edge of the building where darkness met light. It was the perfect spot for me to be standing, all things considered.

That *was* my life.

The perfect rapture of darkness—light flirted on the outskirts, trying to seep through, but I knew better than anyone its chances of succeeding were slim. I held out my hand, and my fingertips kissed the sunlight peeking through the clouds. I twirled my hand around and let out a defeated sigh.

"Cassius." Sariel, my father and one of the head Archangels—the same angels that hadn't appeared to the immortals for over three hundred years—spoke my name with such authority and finality that it was impossible not to feel the effects of the words as he released them into the universe. They slammed against my chest, stealing every ounce of oxygen I'd just greedily sucked in. "You have failed."

"Yes." I swallowed the lie, felt it burn all the way down my throat into my lungs. My cold, rotten heart picked up speed, maybe I really was dead inside like she said, maybe it was hopeless, all of it.

"I taste the lie on your lips, half breed."

"So taste," I fired back, as my eyes strained to focus on the light. The yearning to *be* light, to fully allow it to consume me, was like a fire burning in my soul. "I have nothing more to say to you."

"You realize what this means?" The once purple feathers surrounding his bulky body illuminated red. My heartbeat slowed to a gentle rhythm as droplets of blood cascaded from his feathers in perfect cadence with my breathing.

"I do."

"Yet you do not fight?"

Finally, I lifted my gaze to his. His strong jaw ticked as his black hair blew in the wind. I knew I was the only one who could see him, compliments of my ancestors… my angelic blood.

"When one has lost everything worth fighting for…" I swallowed. "Tell me, what is the point?"

"You've never given up before," he said quietly, his voice filled with disbelief.

"I've never been in love before!" I yelled, slamming my hand against the brick wall. If anyone passed by they'd simply think I'd gone insane, and maybe, maybe I had.

Because of her.

Everything was because of her.

"It's best that I die. Best that I leave her."

Sariel's face broke out into a bright smile. The blood from his feathers pooled at his feet forming the shape of a heart. "Very well."

I prepared myself for the pain, for the sheer agony of ceasing to exist. I knew from stories that when a Dark One died, it was horrific, terrifying, for we never knew if we would rejoin the light or the darkness.

I assumed I would go dark.

I assumed I would be consumed with evil.

I assumed wrong.

Because the minute Sariel touched my skin.

I felt nothing but empty.

"A gift," Sariel whispered into the air. "For my only remaining son."

His fingertips pressed against my skin, they burned, they seared everywhere they pressed.

"What are you doing?"

He didn't answer.

When he stepped away, light flashed in front of my eyes, and I was back in Russia, back where it had all begun.

Tears filled my line of vision as I imagined the pain and suffering of the mountain.

So it was over then.

Sariel's lips twitched into what looked like a smile though I couldn't tell, maybe I was hallucinating?

Maybe this was death.

A lonely existence of living in the past, while still being able to remember the touch of the present.

"Watch," Sariel instructed, crossing his arms in front of the golden armor placed around his body. His helmet had been restored along with his shield and spear.

A large tree with heavy branches twisted around the shield and then suddenly started to grow from the shield as roots grew into the snowy ground. I took a step back as the tree spread its branches from East to West, its trunk doubling in size, only to stop growing once it reached at least thirty feet into the air.

"The tree of life." Sariel spoke reverently. "We watched. But we didn't just watch… we watched over something very specific. My gift was life. I was to watch over life." He hung his head. "So when I helped create it, it was not just an abomination that was created, but something that was never supposed to be." He motioned to the tree. "Humans were supposed to born with limited knowledge of the unexplainable. When you were created you were born with both. Humanly, your brain cannot morally comprehend your angelic side, and as an angel, the human side not only fascinates you, but disgusts you, goes directly against everything you've ever fought for. So how, do the two co-exist? It will always be a battle. To kill you…" He sighed. "To kill a life that the Angel of life has created—would not only kill an entire race of Demon—or fallen." He shared a look with me. "But humans as well."

The heaviness of his words stunned me.

"But to tell you of your own importance… of how

you, Cassius, keep the balance of good and evil within the world right along with your mate—what risk would I be taking? To give you knowledge that part of your soul will never understand? Part of your body may reject? It was not my place, nor did I see this far into the future to know that had I possibly told you sooner—war could have been avoided."

The tree dissipated in front of me as twelve thrones grew up from the ground. They were made of pure gold. And like Sariel's shield, each throne had a different tree.

"Bannik watched over death and destruction," Sariel whispered. "And because of me—it consumed him." He turned his head in my direction. "Even angels are given a choice. Do we give in to the darkness? The comfort of knowing that we can selfishly do whatever we want using the powers we've been gifted with? Or do we follow? I'm sad to say, because of me, Bannik was bitter, bitter enough to allow the darkness to turn him into a completely fallen angel, a powerful Demon who has abilities that far surpass anything you've ever seen." He licked his lips. "So, son, today, today will not be the day that I take your life from this world. Today I gift you with more than you could possibly imagine—in hopes that you will do what I could not."

"I don't understand."

Sariel's eyes filled with tears. "A sacrifice, must always be made, my son. Blood, must always spill. It is the way of the earth. The way of the heavens."

"Father!" I reached for him. "What are you saying?"

Sariel closed his eyes as a silver tear ran down his strong face. "All I wanted…" His white filled eyes blinked up at me. "Was to be worthy of that word, just once." He smiled. "And today... I hope, that you remember the way you effortlessly released the most beautiful of words into the air, giving me a peace I've been waiting for, for millennia." He smiled. "The test of your humanity was twofold. Yes, you needed her love, but you needed to also see that without all of this..." He spread his arms wide. "You still had something to offer."

The thrones disappeared into the ground as the earth started to tremble around my feet.

"Save my brothers, my son. Finish the work." He nodded his head at me and walked toward the middle of the valley just as five thousand angelic beings descended out of a silvery mist onto the ground.

They were in full gold armor.

Hands placed on their swords.

Facing every direction of the earth. North, South, East, and West.

They parted down the middle.

And a little boy, made his way slowly toward Sariel.

Sariel nodded at him and then swiftly passed him and took his place in the middle of the cavalry.

But the little boy approached me.

The same one from Sariel's visions.

He stopped a few feet away.

"Rules have never been easy for you to follow, Dark One."

I hung my head. "Yes. I'm aware."

He smiled brightly. "It seems to be hereditary."

"Apparently."

"Where there is Dark, there will always be Light..." he whispered. "And where there is light... power exists, for things that have been hidden will be visible. And there is so much power within your sight." He stepped away. "I will take good care of him."

"I won't see him again." The thought stunned me, made me want to chase after the father I'd always despised but the only family I'd ever known other than my mother. "Will I?"

"We all have our time. This is yours. His was ending. And a life must always take place of a life. He is simply sacrificing his—so that you will have yours."

"But—"

"I love you," Sariel whispered in my head, as his normally light-infused body turned strangely human.

The little boy lifted his hand and pressed it to my chest. "Use his power well. Love fiercely. End this war." His eyes turned an eerie silver. "I see many futures for the immortals."

Power surged through me as I fell to my knees.

The little boy tipped my chin toward him. "Be the light in the darkness, Cassius."

Chapter 41

Stephanie

I HUNCHED OVER HIS lifeless body. The house started to shake as lights flickered around us.

Ethan held up his hand for us to be quiet as the shaking continued. Lamps fell off of the tables, pictures dropped to the floor.

And then… everything suddenly froze.

As if time was stopped.

The atmosphere was a mixture of complete silence and an eerie ringing in my ears.

A huge gasp emitted from Cassius as he opened his eyes and locked onto me. They were a silvery white, different yet the same.

"It worked!" I kissed his mouth then wrapped my arms around his neck, unable to help myself. I'd almost lost him. Tears streamed down my face.

"Um, Stephanie." Ethan coughed.

I kept choking the life out of Cassius as I hugged him.

"Stephanie." Ethan said my name again, this time more urgent, as his strong hand landed on my shoulder in an effort to jerk me away.

"What?"

His eyes widened as he nodded toward Cassius. I pulled back just enough to see a purple feather greet me, followed by a few hundred more. Stumbling back onto my butt, I let out a gasp of surprise as purple wings spread twelve feet across Cassius's back, poking into the couch and kissing the fireplace.

Cassius's chest heaved with an over exaggerated inhalation as he fluidly rose to his feet.

The atmosphere remained timeless, serene, as he glanced around the room then into each and every one of our faces and whispered, "Sariel has passed on."

"No shit, did you eat him?" Alex grumbled earning an elbow from Mason.

Cassius hung his head as his body trembled. Purple feathers shuddered in unison with him as if mourning the loss of the soul they'd once been united with, and then all at once the feathers released a purple mist.

"Even the feathers weep of his absence," Ethan said in a grave voice sliding his hand behind Genesis back and quietly escorting her out of the room. Alex and Mason followed, maybe they too sensed the stillness in the air, the absolute paralysis of the cells around us as if they too were confused on what course of action to take. After all, what was the protocol when a Dark One suddenly sprouted wings out of his back? And not black, ripped up wings, but true wings, the ones of his father, an archangel.

I stayed glued to the floor as Cassius hovered near me. Was it possible for him to be more beautiful than before? It must be, because he was, his strong jaw was smooth, cut perfectly across a flawless face. Sensual lips curved downward into a scowl as his wings slowly retracted back toward his body then disappeared altogether.

"What happened?" I asked, slowly rising to my feet and making my way toward his shivering body. He might look gorgeous but he also carried an air that he'd just undergone the most traumatic experience of his life.

"Everything," Cassius whispered. "And yet, nothing I shouldn't have seen." His eyes flashed. "I should have seen it. I should have seen all of it, but he was always so vague." Cassius's shoulders rose and fell with each laborious breath he took. "It was a future that was too closely tied to mine."

I pressed my hand to his shoulder, he reached out and caressed my fingertips, his skin was smoother than before, as if it was brand new, barely created a second ago and placed on his body.

"A life for a life," he said in a low tone.

"And the life taken?"

"Offered. He offered his life, and everything, all of his power and his job, fell to me."

"More heaviness," I guessed as Cassius shared a look with me and in that look I saw everything, Sariel offering himself up, the child I'd recognized in the dream, trees, the thrones, and all of the angels.

"When you stabbed me, I didn't know what I was doing, just tried to give you as much power as I could, I knew you were running into danger. I had no idea that by doing that, I was condemning myself to death."

"I wanted to help," I said in a small voice. "It's my fault he's dead, if I hadn't run off—"

"There were several futures, Stephanie." He cupped my face with his hand. "Believe me when I say, this was the best one, the one—now that I know Sariel's thoughts— that he very much hoped for."

"And the others?"

"Altered, only slightly."

"I haven't told the others about Bannik, about what I saw."

"Well." Cassius pulled me in for a hug, pressing my body tight against his. "I think it is time they know what we are up against, not just a race of unruly Demon, but a fallen angel hell bent on destroying both humans and immortals alike."

"He doesn't want everyone dead." I squeezed my arms around Cassius. "He wants them enslaved."

"Death is better."

"It is."

"If it comes to a choice." Cassius tensed up again. "I will kill myself, destroying both humans and immortals at the same time. I will kill us all before I let him make slaves out of us."

"Is that your choice to make?"

Cassius paused, his voice grave. "It is now."

Cassius

To be a Dark One was to know perfection, but be unable to reach it. Now that I had Sariel's blood flowing somehow miraculously through my veins, I could touch it, smell it, bond with it. But my humanity, or whatever was left of it, rejected the notion completely. Logic shook its head in denial, and so I appeared different, but I was very much the same.

Split completely down the middle between two races.

The answer as well as the end.

In a cruel twist of fate, the angel of life and death had created both—me. I had no idea if I possessed enough power to fight off Bannik on my own, but what I did know was that the battle between dark and light was just starting to get interesting.

Mason was hovering over the stove flipping a steak as he so often did when he was upset about something. I had to wonder if he had some Italian or Greek running through some of those wolfish veins. The blood of Sariel called to me to use it—no longer would I have to guess about anything—but my humanity pressed the fleeting thought away, what fun was life when you knew all the answers already?

I'd learned that as a human.

I'd keep living that way as a Dark One.

Alex sipped a cup of coffee and pretended to be reading but he rarely turned the page, just stared it down, lost in his dark thoughts, the same ones he so often tried to play off when really, it was quite possible he had the hardest future of us all.

And Genesis, lovely, beautiful, pregnant Genesis sat on Ethan's lap while he drank from her neck.

If you blinked, you could almost miss the small cut near her ear where he kissed and sucked.

"Gross." Alex said in a bored voice. "At least have the decency to do it in private."

"You eat at a table," Ethan pointed out. "Why can't I?"

"Hah!" Mason flipped the steak in the air again. "Vampire has a point."

Alex scrunched up his nose while I sat between the two of them, Stephanie still gripped my hand, offering her support, her love, it floated off of her in perfumed waves, stabilizing me, altering me so completely that I knew had I been in Sariel's place—I would have made the exact same choice.

Because when I closed my eyes.

I saw her.

And only her.

"Sariel has given his life for mine." My voice didn't shake, it was smooth, in command, something I didn't feel, but everyone knows just because you have a feeling doesn't mean you are that feeling. I felt unsure; that didn't mean I needed to actually follow through with it and become unsure when it came to my decisions, because they effected every being around me, mortal and immortal, I had to focus on my knowledge, on my heart, on the love surrounding me, not the flimsy feeling that told me to be afraid.

After all.

Fear.

It is not welcome here.

Alex spoke it for me, his eyes locking onto mine as he leaned forward in anticipation.

"Bannik, one of Sariel's brothers, has fallen. He's captured the ten remaining archangels of the realm. Each was to be guarding a different part of the human plane. They are all missing."

Genesis's mouth dropped open while Mason stopped cooking and turned around eyes wide with shock.

"How the hell did we miss that?" Ethan raged through clenched teeth. "It's our job to keep the peace and some archangel's been luring others into his keep? And creating Demon? Where have we been?"

"We can't blame ourselves," I said. "Even Sariel did not see it coming until it was too late. Bannik has been planning this ever since Pompeii, ever since his first taste of human blood. At the time I blamed Timber for giving out immortal blood, and now I suspect it was Bannik pulling the strings the entire time."

"Well damn." Ethan sighed running his hands through his long dark hair. "That's been a few… years."

Alex's lips twitched. "Try a few hundred, but sure yeah just saying few sounds so much better, like we blinked and oh, look, they invented cars!"

"You—" I jabbed a finger at Alex. "—will need to visit some old family."

Alex's nostrils flared. "Watch me curb my enthusiasm."

"And Mason," I nodded toward him. "You'll need to notify all the wolves in the district. Let them know we will need to fight… we've been living in peace for too long, we've gone soft while they've grown strong. We will need to teach our people once again how to draw up their swords."

Alex raised his hands. "Don't you mean draw up their semi-automatic weapons?"

Ethan scowled. "Bullets don't behead."

"If you're a good shot they do." Alex smirked.

"Not the point." I sighed and tried again. "They need to know how to protect themselves." I stood, "And we need to keep our secret from the humans at all costs."

"It's always such a joy." Alex yawned. "Protecting the weak while they continue to kill off one another without any realization they're still alive and breathing because we choose to protect them."

I smiled as more visions of Alex's future laid themselves out before my eyes. Maybe I would get my payback a lot sooner than I originally thought.

"One more thing," I added, waiting until every set of eyes was on me. "You are your strongest when you're mated."

The room fell silent.

"I'm calling numbers for you both. You will have a human by sunset next week or so help me I'll kill you myself."

Mason let out a guttural howl as he fell to his knees, then got up and ran out of the room.

All eyes fell to Alex.

He was pale.

So very pale.

"Is that going to be a problem, Alex?"

"No." He swallowed. "No, my King. It is not."

His thoughts screamed at me.

His words and actions said otherwise—because Alex, might be a lot of things, but he was loyal. He would obey me in this.

And it would eventually be for his own good.

Eventually.

"And what about you?" Ethan asked.

"Me." I grinned for the first time since I'd woken up. "I have Stephanie."

"But you have wings." Genesis blurted out. "Isn't that... forbidden?"

"Red Bull..." Alex laughed. "...also has wings, but I touch my lips to that can like it's my job—"

Stephanie shoved him out of the chair, he fell to the floor with a giant thump while Ethan laughed.

"We were mated before all of this and regardless, I'm still a Dark One, I just have actual wings... believe me, you cannot redeem the damned."

Ethan stood. "Seems to me your wrong... what did you say happened to Sariel again? He went dark? Lost his mind? Ceased to exist?"

"He was taken," Stephanie blurted out before I got the chance. "With over five thousand angels as an escort."

The room was silent and then Ethan added, "Seems to me, you can very well redeem the damned... doesn't it?"

He was right.

Because Sariel had been cursed.

Yet, something told me, he was still—present. Not in the same way as before.

But… aware.

Stephanie slid her hand into mine. "Can we go talk?"

"No," I grumbled pulling her hard against my chest. "I want to kiss. I want to make love. I want to forget the fact that you stabbed me in the chest and ran away. That we can do anything else is off the table."

"He gonna throw her on the table right here then?" Alex asked from his semi comfortable position on the floor, even leaning back against the counter he looked like a sexual deviant, just waiting for a lady in a short skirt to walk by so he could steal a peek while she peeled her clothes off in ecstasy.

"Upstairs." Stephanie smiled pulling me in for a searing kiss. I was already carrying her as fast as I could through the house when I heard Ethan yell.

"Please don't burn down the room! Keep your feathers under control, Cassius!"

Stephanie

"I LOVE YOU." I pressed another kiss against his mouth as he ripped the rest of my clothes from my body, his hands sliding down my waist. Then he lifted me by the hips and tossed me roughly onto the bed.

I was a tangled mess in the sheets as I tried to pull myself up and give him my best glare. Instead, all I could do was openly gape at his naked body.

Nothing about Cassius was imperfect.

And it was so amazingly difficult not to stare at every plane of his body. His muscles bulged with every breath he took.

And like a knight from the fairy tales I'd read so long ago, his dark black hair cascaded over his shoulders in a magnificent fashion, he looked both wicked and heroic.

"I desire you." His eyes fluttered closed. "More than you will ever know. And my love for you," A silver tear ran down his cheek. "Would move mountains."

Tears blurred my vision.

"His job was to watch life," Cassius whispered pulling me into his lap. "And I plan on watching yours very, very carefully." He kissed my lips hard. "Slowly." His hands gripped my sides. "Thoroughly."

Our bodies joined, there was no warning, nothing but him moving within me, watching me.

Loving me.

The moment was so beautiful, so perfect, I could have wept. Instead, I placed my cold hands on his body.

And felt warmth.

Gasping, I jerked back. "Why aren't you cold?"

"A gift," Cassius whispered across my lips as he moved languidly against me. "So that when you are tempted to fall to the darkness—you see light instead." Our mouths tangled then broke free. "You'll see me."

Instead of closing my eyes, I watched, I watched him, I locked onto his light and held on for dear life as he embraced me, rocked into me, loved me with his words, with a language I didn't understand as he pressed gentle kisses to my face.

And as my body released, the darkness dissipated as if it had never been there in the first place.

I had no strength to ask.

But Cassius must have known it was there because his next words were. "Where there is darkness there will always be light."

Body still trembling I whispered, "What are you?"

"The same." He hesitated for a brief second then added. "Fallen, evil, a curse, abomination. I'm all of those things."

"But—"

He silenced me with a kiss. "I'm just more angel than human now."

"So seventy-thirty?"

He shook his head.

"Eighty-twenty?"

Another shake.

I opened my mouth again.

"Stop!" He laughed, the sound did funny things to me, making me want to kiss him and never stop. "More like ninety-nine to one."

"Oh." I felt my eyes go big.

"Still fallen."

"By one percent."

"Numbers." He shrugged and raised one eyebrow. "What are they anyways?"

"Important?" I teased, licking his lower lip while a small growl erupted between his teeth. "I take that as a no."

"I'm the same…" He smiled gently and captured my gaze. "I still hunger for you."

"And the bird outside my window?"

With a burst of sunny laughter, Cassius threw me back onto the mattress and braced himself over me. "I won't eat your blue jay."

"Now," I said.

"I love you." He sobered. "Completely."

"Stay with me forever?"

We linked hands, palm to palm, as our fingers clenched together.

"I can do that." He brushed a soft warm kiss across my forehead. "I can do that."

Alex

I SENSED THE SEX.

Or *love*.

A female would scrunch up her nose or possibly be aroused by my use of the word, after all when you were with your mate, it was love and sex, a beautiful heady mixture of sugars, spices, alluring scents that would drive any sane person—just the opposite I supposed.

With a scowl I tossed the tennis ball hard against the wall over and over again, the rhythmic beat was the only thing calming my racing heart, well that and the distinct impression that if I asked Ethan to slow it, he'd probably kill me and say "oops" afterwards.

Mated.

I rolled the word around in my head.

I wasn't the type.

At all.

To love one person went against every cell in my body, every fiber of my being. I was a Siren. I did not love one. I loved all.

And I loved them well.

All sizes.

All shapes.

Every sex.

Every plant.

Animal.

Creation.

I loved everything.

I spread myself around as all good Sirens did, and I was damned good at it. The very thought that I'd be tied to a measly human for eternity had me tempted to write a suicide note and steal Genesis's little purple feather, draining my own immortality mid-orgasm.

The sound of my door opening and closing softly interrupted my bitter thoughts, and then the scent of cedar and dirt joined me on the floor.

Mason slumped next to me.

Silent.

And then, grabbed the other tennis ball.

And started slamming it against the wall opposite me.

We stayed there for hours.

Neither of us talking.

Until finally, the Wolf opened his mouth. "I can't do this."

I knew how it would work, one of us would go first, we'd call one number, the ceremony would take place, we'd be given time and then the next number would be called.

It never happened all at once.

Maybe I was feeling suicidal, because the first words out of my mouth were. "I'll go first."

WANT MORE DARK ONES?
BE LOOKING FOR ALEX'S STORY FALL 2016!
DARKEST SEDUCTION!

Rachel Van Dyken is the *New York Times, Wall Street Journal,* and *USA Today* bestselling author of regency and contemporary romances. When she's not writing you can find her drinking coffee at Starbucks and plotting her next book while watching "The Bachelor".

She keeps her home in Idaho with her husband, adorable son, and two snoring boxers. She loves to hear from readers.

You can connect with her on Facebook at facebook.com/rachelvandyken or join her fan group *Rachel's New Rockin Readers*. Her website is www.rachelvandykenauthor.com.

Eagle Elite

Elite
Elect
Entice
Elicit
Bang Bang
Enchant
Enforce
Ember
Elude

The Bet Series

The Bet
The Wager
The Dare

Seaside Series

Tear
Pull
Shatter
Forever
Fall
Strung
Eternal

Seaside Pictures

Capture

Wallflower Trilogy

Waltzing with the Wallflower

Beguiling Bridget

Taming Wilde

Renwick House

The Ugly Duckling Debutante

The Seduction of Sebastian St. James

The Redemption of Lord Rawlings

An Unlikely Alliance

The Devil Duke Takes a Bride

London Fairy Tales

Upon a Midnight Dream

Whispered Music

The Wolf's Pursuit

When Ash Falls

Ruin Series

Ruin

Toxic

Fearless

Shame

The Consequence Series

The Consequence of Loving Colton

The Consequence of Revenge

The Dark Ones Series

The Dark Ones

Untouchable Darkness

Other Titles

The Parting Gift

Compromising Kessen

Savage Winter

Divine Uprising

Every Girl Does It

RIP

www.rachelvandykenauthor.com

Manufactured by Amazon.ca
Bolton, ON